Ruthless Crimes

ALSO BY MICHAEL HAMBLING

THE SOPHIE ALLEN BOOKS

Book 1: Dark Crimes
Book 2: Deadly Crimes
Book 3: Secret Crimes
Book 4: Buried Crimes
Book 5: Twisted Crimes
Book 6: Evil Crimes
Book 7: Shadow Crimes
Book 8: Silent Crimes
Book 9: Ruthless Crimes
Book 10: Brutal Crimes
Book 11: Hidden Crimes
Book 12: Vicious Crimes

Michael Hambling

RUTHLESS CRIMES

Detective Sophie Allen Book 9

JOFFE BOOKS

Revised edition 2024
Joffe Books, London
www.joffebooks.com

First published in Great Britain in 2020

Cover art by Nick Castle

ISBN: 978-1-83526-896-4

FOREWORD

This is a work of fiction, and none of the characters and situations described bear any resemblance to real persons or events. Many of the locations, however, do exist and provide some first-rate walking breaks. Dorset's Golden Cap estate, situated between Lyme Regis and Bridport, is owned by the National Trust and forms the centre point of an extensive network of footpaths and tracks.

A glossary appears at the end of this book.

CHARACTER LIST

Dorset Police Violent Crime Unit (VCU):
Detective Superintendent Sophie Allen
Detective Inspector Barry Marsh
Detective Sergeant Rae Gregson
Detective Constable Tommy Carter

At Dorset Police Headquarters:
Chief Superintendent Matt Silver
Assistant Chief Constable Jim Metcalfe
Inspector Karen Brody (Special Branch; security)

Dorset Police Uniformed Officers:
Sergeant Rose Simons
Constable George Warrander

Other Dorset Personnel:
Detective Sergeant Stu Blackman (Weymouth CID)
Dave Nash (County Forensic Chief)

Hampshire Police CID:
Detective Chief Inspector Jack Dunning
Detective Sergeant Gwen Davies

Metropolitan Police Officers, based at New Scotland Yard:
Assistant Commissioner Paul Baker
Detective Chief Inspector Steve Lamb

Home Office Politicians:
Ken Burke (Immigration Minister)
Yauvani Anand (PPS to the Minister)

Home Office Special Unit:
Corinne Lanston
Peter Zelinski (Field Operative)
Angus Catchcart (Part-time advisor)

This book is dedicated to all the medics and care staff in this country and across the world who have worked selflessly during this coronavirus pandemic, and in particular those in my own family. My brother, Rob, a GP in Cheshire and his wife, Nicola, a nurse who has come out of retirement in order to track and trace. My niece, Jennifer, a GP in Edinburgh, my nephew, Matthew, a doctor in Livingstone, my nephew, Cameron, a doctor in Croydon. My daughter-in-law's brother, Tom, a doctor working in Slough Hospital and his wife, Henrietta, a doctor in Oxford. The same daughter-in-law's father, Tony, a doctor still doing work in X-ray analysis in Hull despite being retired for some years, and her sister, Jo, an asthma nurse in Harrogate. Finally, my nieces, Karen and Alison, both working as medical therapists in Paisley.

I also need to mention my friend Heather. She lived on the Isle of Portland but has recently moved to Weymouth, where she works providing day services for adults with learning disabilities. During the Covid-19 lockdown, she has been caring for elderly dementia patients in their homes. She and her fellow care workers have done a fantastic job during this killer pandemic. This country needs to get its priorities right and lift their earnings from the mediocre minimum wage that many of them receive. I would urge you to remember this next time there's an election and vote accordingly.

PROLOGUE

The station tannoy hissed and crackled before it settled into its usual monotone listing of destinations. Jason Lamb stamped his feet and blew on his chilly hands. It was only early October, for God's sake. Was it usual for frosts to arrive this early in the autumn? He stood back and yawned as the train doors slid open and the guard waved the handful of passengers onto the first morning train from Weymouth to London. Jason couldn't understand why the doors were only unlocked five minutes before departure. The train had remained stationary all night, having been the last train to arrive the previous evening. And given that it was so cold, why couldn't the train be ready and waiting, warm and comfortable, for when the passengers arrived? For a start, it would give him an extra few minutes snoozing on a soft seat. Not that he was travelling very far. He just needed to get to work in Poole, about forty minutes away, by seven o'clock. He was an apprentice boatbuilder, normally based at a yard near his home in Weymouth, but currently in the middle of a two-month-long attachment that took him to a specialist yard in Poole every Saturday, and the early morning start was getting him down. Having to get up at five in the morning was just too much. Even getting this first train barely gave him enough time to get to the quay by his allocated start time, and only if he hurried. It was madness. And it ruined the best night out of the weekend, leaving him feeling so worn-out that he just wanted to curl up and sleep while all his pals were out enjoying themselves. Thank God the placement would be over in a couple of weeks and he'd be back at the Weymouth yard full time and on 'painting duties.' He smiled to himself as he remembered where that odd phrase had come from. He'd spent a week on a lovely oceangoing yacht, painting its slightly tired, grubby white hull and superstructure a sleek, shiny, navy blue. And tracing out its name, *Lady Charmaine*, in a tastefully soft cream colour.

He made his way to his usual seat at the very back of the train. Not that he ever had any competition for a seat, not at this god-awful time in the morning. He was often the only person in the carriage. But he'd always opted for a front or rear seat, ever since his grandparents had taken him on train trips as a young boy. Habits died hard with Jason.

He reached the first set of seats and stopped dead. His hand slid to his mouth. There was a body on the floor in front of him, curled into a ball, up against the seats. A large ominous stain had spread across the floor, dark and viscous. Jason turned and ran for the door, yelling for help. He stood outside on the platform, shaking and gasping, causing the few travellers in the other carriages to poke their heads out of the open doors.

CHAPTER 1: CRIME SCENE

Saturday morning

Detective Constable Rae Gregson steered her car into the second available parking slot, leaving the most convenient one free for her boss. She'd only had a short twenty-minute drive from Wool to Weymouth, whereas he'd the much longer journey west from Ringwood. He wouldn't be a happy bunny. She clambered out, flashed her card at the uniformed officer standing nearby and suggested he ensured the better slot was kept free for the DI. She made her way through the packed crowds milling around the station concourse and onto the near-silent platform. She spotted the bulky form of DS Stu Blackman already there.

She never knew quite what to make of Stu. He'd recently been transferred to Weymouth CID from Dorchester following the shake-up of the unit in the resort town. Maybe it was all part of his rehabilitation programme. Several years earlier he'd come close to being disciplined for laziness and incompetence but now appeared to be a reformed character. Rae wasn't convinced. He had a way of looking at her that made her flesh crawl. Was she imagining it? She'd never mentioned it to anyone on high because it might look vindictive. Anyway, she was a member of the county's specialist Violent Crime Unit and that carried kudos. Even though Stu was more senior, he would know the limits of his influence. In practice, she had more. Even so, she always ensured that she referred to him as *sir* at the start of any encounter. Only once, mind. Then she'd do her best to remind him of her position in the elite unit, just to rub it in.

She wouldn't be his junior for very much longer, though. She'd learned just a few days earlier that she'd passed her sergeants' exam with flying colours. She was due to celebrate her success later in the month — a meal out with her boss, Barry Marsh, and both their partners. Her biggest concern in recent months had been her place in the VCU following Barry's promotion to detective inspector rank. This had left a gap in the unit structure and she'd worried that someone would suddenly appear, slotted neatly into the sergeant role, and her own position would be diminished or put at risk. But both Barry and Superintendent Sophie Allen, the latter still nominally the head of the VCU, had reassured her that her future was secure. Not that she'd seen very much of the 'big boss,' as she referred to Sophie Allen, in recent weeks. She and Barry had dealt successfully with all the recent cases. Most of them had been straightforward assaults and related crimes, open and shut cases, really. That had to end sometime soon, though. Was this to be the case that brought Sophie back on board in a big way? The initial report certainly gave Rae that feeling.

She dodged under the ribbon of crime-scene tape and reached the cluster of uniformed officers at the front of the train. She nodded to Blackman.

'Morning, sir. Any details for me?'

'Dead body in a pool of blood, right at the back of the carriage. Looks like a stab wound to the chest. Forensics should be arriving any minute. The young bloke who stumbled on it is in the station manager's office, having a coffee. Name of Jason Lamb. The only other person to go in was PC

Warrander here. He was first on the scene and checked for signs of life.'

Rae turned to the youngest member of the uniformed group. 'Hi, George. I take it there weren't any? Signs of life, I mean.'

Warrander shook his head. 'Looked like the victim had been dead for hours. Male, maybe mid-thirties. Lying on the floor, tucked in front of the last row of seats. You can't see the body through the window or from the aisle. But it looks just the position someone would be in if they curled up to avoid being seen. From the amount of blood my guess is that he's been stabbed. There are stains trailing down from the carriage door and out here on the platform. It looks as though he was bleeding before he got on.'

She was puzzled. 'How could that happen? I mean, if he's been there all night?'

'This was the last train to arrive last night. All the passengers would have got off, but the doors might have been left open for a few minutes while the guard or whoever checked that all the carriages were empty. If they started with that carriage, which is logical because the guard's booth is there, the victim could have crawled on during the few minutes it took for the guard to check further on before closing the doors. Jason Lamb, the man who found him, was one of the first to arrive on the platform this morning. As soon as the train was unlocked and the doors opened, he went inside. It checks out with what two other witnesses who arrived at the same time have said.'

'Are they still around?' Rae said.

George nodded. 'Yeah. In a separate office.'

Rae smiled at him. 'Good work, George. That looks like the first forensic unit arriving now, and DI Marsh will be here any minute. The super isn't around today, I'm not sure where she is. Barry will know.'

George spoke quietly so that Blackman couldn't overhear. 'She's off to Oxford. Jade starts university today, so both her parents are going with her.'

Rae looked at him with raised eyebrows. 'Does that mean the rumour's true, then? You're, umm, "seeing" Jade?'

George looked as though he wished the ground would open and swallow him. 'Oh, God. Has it leaked out then? We've been so careful.'

Rae laughed. 'Small place, Dorset. No secrets are safe here. Barry spotted the two of you a few weeks ago. But don't worry, it hasn't gone any further. And the boss hasn't said anything herself. She does know, doesn't she?'

'Yeah. I've been round their house a few times. She seems happy enough with it. But it kinda worries me. You know, going out with the boss's daughter.'

Rae gave another chuckle. 'My heart bleeds for you.'

She had a few words with Dave Nash, Dorset's forensic chief, then walked across the platform to the six-foot fence that separated the station complex from the car park outside, following the trail of dark spots on the hard surface. She looked around to orientate herself with the layout of the station, then went out through the station entrance, in order to approach the same fence from the outside. A railway works van was parked up against the fence. Spots of blood could just be seen on the grubby blue paint. Had the victim clambered onto the top of the van and found a way into the station that way? But why would a badly injured man do that? And how? Had he been trying to get away from someone? Rae wondered if all the climbing had sealed the victim's fate. Just imagine trying to clamber over a six-foot fence and down the other side with a deep stab wound in your torso. It must have opened the wound up further and worsened the bleeding.

She saw the DI's car pulling into an empty parking slot, so she walked across to greet him. This already had the look of a puzzling case.

* * *

Jason Lamb, the man who'd discovered the body in the train, was clutching an empty coffee cup and staring into space. He was short and thin, with curly brown hair and sparse stubble on his chin. He wore denims, a blue T-shirt and an unbuttoned grey windcheater jacket. He looked up when the two detectives entered the room. Barry Marsh gestured for the uniformed constable to leave and took the seat opposite Jason.

'DI Barry Marsh. DC Rae Gregson,' he said, waving his hand vaguely. 'Tell me everything that happened. You can start with why you were on this train so early in the morning. Take your time.'

Jason told him of his apprenticeship and his Saturday morning stint at a Poole boatyard, followed by his usual travel arrangements. He finished with the moment that he'd run out onto the platform, gasping in fright.

'You did well, Jason. I've no complaints about how you reacted. And the station staff did everything by the book.'

'I kept thinking that whoever did it was still on the train. I mean, I saw the guard operate the door lock. All the doors opened so I went in. And I saw the body. How could that happen? It meant that whoever done it was still on the train. Or that's what I thought. That's why I got out quick. I still feel a bit faint at the thought of it. He was stabbed, right? That's what it looked like to me. Then I guessed he'd probably been there all night.'

'The pathologist's doing a quick examination right now but we're pretty certain he's been there for hours,' Barry said.

'It is a he, then? It's not a woman?'

'It's a man,' Rae said. 'But that's all we can tell you at present. Did you spot anyone you wouldn't normally see on the platform this morning?'

Jason shook his head. 'Can't be sure. I only get this train on Saturdays. I recognise two of the others but the couple with the suitcases, I haven't noticed them before.'

Barry frowned. Neither he nor Rae had been told about a couple. The only other people waiting to be seen by them were in the adjoining office, just two as far as they knew. Had the facts become confused?

'I'll go,' Rae said.

She poked her head around the neighbouring door. Sure enough there were only two people inside, other than a uniformed constable. They were sitting on a bench seat looking bored.

'We'll be with you in a minute,' she said, and hurried away to find Stu Blackman.

He was munching on a pasty, watching the forensic team working.

'Stu, the guy who found the body said there was a couple with suitcases on the platform, waiting at the same time as him. Where are they?'

He shrugged. 'Don't know anything about that. They weren't here when I arrived. Just the three in those offices. Is he sure?'

'Yes, he is. So, does that mean they slipped away after the body was found? We'll need to speak to the staff. Someone else must have seen them, surely? Can we work our way through the station staff together? Take half each? It'll be quicker that way.'

'Sure.' Stu swallowed the rest of the pasty, brushed the crumbs from his clothes and belched. 'Pardon me,' he said, grinning slyly.

With some difficulty, Rae restrained her anger at this inept detective. If they were to work together there was no point in causing unnecessary friction. 'We're looking for a man and a woman, probably middle-aged or thereabouts, each with a small wheelie suitcase. I'll get a couple of the uniformed guys to search the station and surrounding area. Maybe you could start talking to all the station staff who were on duty at the time? I'll move onto the ticket office staff. That okay with you?'

'Sure thing,' he replied.

Was he really so lacking in gumption? He was the supposedly experienced sergeant, for goodness sake, and here she was, taking the lead. Of course, he'd spent years partnering the odious Phil McCluskey, who'd totally dominated him, despite Stu's more senior rank. Stu had recently told Barry that he was a reformed character, willing to work hard to improve his poor reputation in the force. Evidently that ambition had been pretty short-lived, judging by his lacklustre attitude this morning. The adage about leopards and spots came to mind. Rae turned away and hurried across to a group of uniformed officers, giving them a description of the missing couple. They scattered across the station, looking for them, so she made her way to the ticket office.

Fifteen minutes later she was reporting her findings to Barry. Several staff members had seen the couple in the few minutes before the discovery of the body. They hadn't bought tickets, either from the desk or at any of the machines. They hadn't been found anywhere on the station or in the vicinity. They must have left quickly because soon after the first police squad car had arrived, all travellers were asked to remain on site until they'd given the police a short statement and their contact details. They weren't on that list.

'Do you think there's anything in it, boss?' Rae asked.

Barry grimaced and ran his fingers through his ginger hair, a sure sign that he was worried. 'It could be relevant. But they could have been innocent travellers in a hurry who realised they'd be delayed for some time if they hung around here and went to find another means of travel. We need much more detailed descriptions if we're going to try and track their movements. Let's get busy.'

* * *

By the time the early afternoon came around and they were back in the station incident room, the three detectives had largely pieced together a coherent account of the chain of events, although the couple seen on the station concourse that morning had still not been traced. The forensic sweep of the area outside the station had yielded one important conclusion: the victim, local resident Robert Bunting, had been stabbed in a corner of the station car park. The bloodstains there left little doubt. The knife wound had been intended to kill him, early indications from the pathologist indicated that the blade had only missed the heart by a millimetre or two. Somehow, Robert had survived the initial attack and managed to make his way towards the station buildings but had then veered away from the main entrance towards the van parked against the wall. He'd managed to climb across and into the train but had succumbed to blood loss once inside.

'It doesn't make sense,' Rae said. 'Why didn't he just go inside the entrance lobby? There were still staff about. Wouldn't he have been safer there? They'd have phoned for an ambulance. There's a chance he might have survived.'

'He could have been trying to escape from his killers,' Barry said. 'Some witness reports from the last train to arrive last night suggest that there were two or three people scanning the car park as if they were looking for someone.'

Barry's phone rang. He listened, and then looked at Rae. 'There's a bike still chained to a rack, close to where the stabbing took place. It's been there since yesterday morning. It could be his, so I've asked for forensics on it.'

Rae frowned, thinking. 'So, do you think he came in on that train? Came out of the station on his way to his bike, was stabbed and then escaped somehow? If there were two or three of them, they'd try to cut him off when he went to get help. Maybe he made for that fence and back into the station to get away from them. His fall onto the platform the other side would have opened up his wound and he started to lose blood fast. He crawled onto the train and blacked out. How does that all sound?'

'Sounds good to me,' Barry said. 'We need to get some statements from people who came in on that train last night, to confirm that he was on it and see if anyone spotted anything suspicious going on.'

'And the missing couple from this morning?' Rae prompted.

'Them too. They could only have been on that platform for five minutes, by all accounts.'

'How did they get onto the platform without a ticket, boss? You need one to pass through the barrier.'

'Well, that's the interesting bit. The barriers recorded five entries this morning — Jason Lamb, our two other witnesses and two other unknowns. That train was London bound. So, who were they and where were they going?'

'And how did they get off the platform?' Rae asked.

'What?'

'You can't just walk out, can you? The barrier works both ways — it won't let you in or out without a ticket. They couldn't have vaulted the barrier with a wheelie case each, surely? The thing is though, there were only two staff on duty that early, and according to them they both went onto the platform to see what the fuss was about. So, maybe the missing two did clamber across somehow. It might be worth checking to see if a car left the car park at about that time.'

'I can do that,' Stu Blackman suggested.

'Okay,' Barry said. 'Rae and I can pay a visit to the victim's home now we have the address. By the way, the knife hasn't turned up yet, despite a fingertip search of the station area. Can you organise a search of the town centre, Stu? Start with the main roads that radiate out from the station, then the side roads. You know the drill. Litter bins, skips, waste ground. There's something about all this that's making me uneasy, but I can't put my finger on it.'

CHAPTER 2: BICYCLE

Saturday afternoon

Robert Bunting's home was a two-up two-down house in the middle of a town centre terrace. The front door opened directly to the street but there was also rear access from an alley that ran along the back of the row of houses. Each property had a gate leading into a garden or yard. Some had well-tended flower or vegetable beds, others were left in a semi-derelict state of weed-infested gravel. Robert's was somewhere in between, showing neither great care nor total disregard. Characterless — that was the feeling Barry had about both the garden and the house. Of course, Robert may have rented the property and was reluctant to invest time or money in it, leaving the place as it was when he moved in: tidy and plain.

Barry looked out from the rear upstairs window. His feeling of unease hadn't dissipated. Even in the house, something didn't seem quite right. It was comfortably furnished but revealed nothing of his personal life, not even the random untidiness often seen in the homes of single men. Was he a single man? He clearly lived in this house alone, but that meant very little. Maybe he had a partner or family elsewhere? Maybe the neighbours would know. Rae was speaking to them now, while he probed the cupboards, shelves and drawers inside. There had been very little to find. Now he thought about it, the place had all the hallmarks of a convenient short-term let. Maybe Robert hadn't even owned the furnishings and fittings. That would explain its lack of character. It was almost as if the house had been fitted out from a mail order catalogue, and a cheap one at that. There were few magazines and even fewer books. The bedroom wardrobe was largely empty, and the clothes drawers didn't have much in them.

The detective team was also finding it hard to flesh out the details of Robert's life. They'd found no clue about his work or any idea as to why he'd been singled out to be killed in such a brutal way. Barry couldn't shake off the notion that their victim had chosen to keep a low profile and that finding anything about his life would prove to be a difficult task. He hoped that Rae was making better progress with the neighbours. He hadn't even found a passport. Did that mean Robert had never been abroad, or was it held elsewhere? If so, why?

Barry went downstairs and had another look around. This time he went around each room in turn, just standing and looking. Was he missing something? He heard the front door open and turned to see Rae coming into the hallway. She shook her head at him.

'Sorry, boss. Not much to report. According to three sets of neighbours, he kept himself to himself. He's only been living here for two months and it was clear he wanted a quiet life. All of them said they offered their help when he first moved in, but he didn't respond. He wasn't an unpleasant man, but they all came to the same conclusion, that he was a bit of a recluse. Apparently, he rented the place as a ready furnished let but no one could tell me who the letting agent is. I've got nowhere. Anything inside?'

Barry shook his head. 'Nothing. It's a Teflon house. Nothing of him has stuck.'

Rae shrugged. 'Maybe he wanted it that way.'

He shook his head. 'There was a flat I went into, years ago, on my first job with the boss. She was suspicious right away. She said it had no personality, it had picked up nothing from the occupant. She predicted we'd find another home, somewhere else. And we did. The dead woman was a call girl, and it was her work flat. In some ways, this place reminds me of it.'

'What, you think he was a rent boy or something?' Rae was laughing.

Barry felt offended. 'Of course not. But it makes me wonder if this was just some kind of temporary place. We'll need to trace the landlord and find out more. Let's do one more walk through and then go. You take downstairs, I'll go up.'

He didn't really know the purpose behind this final look. Maybe he still felt that the small house had a clue concealed somewhere, some tiny thing that they'd overlooked. It was a false hope, though. Nothing new declared itself to his careful gaze. He took one last glance out of the rear window. He could see across the top of the fence into the narrow alley that ran along the backs of the houses. A dark blue bicycle was leaning against the fence on the other side of the alley. It looked relatively new and expensive. Moreover, it didn't look as though it was secured in any way. Barry moved to the side of the window where he was partly hidden by a curtain and looked more carefully. Had it been there earlier? He couldn't be sure one way or the other. He recognised the make and model of the bicycle. His partner Gwen's younger brother, Tom, was a keen off-road cyclist and had suggested that Barry should take it up. Wasn't that bike the very model Tom had recommended? He could remember his reaction upon hearing the price — a combination of a snort and a gasp. Three thousand pounds. For a bike. If this was the same machine, what was it doing casually leaning against a fence, unlocked? Unless, of course, the owner was nearby.

Barry looked more closely at the right-hand corner of the garden, where a shrub overhung the corner fencepost.

Someone was standing there, watching the house, hidden behind the greenery. It was difficult to make out any features through the thin foliage. Barry backed away from the window and rejoined Rae on the ground floor.

'The place is being watched at the back,' he said, leading her to the front door. 'Stay here but watch the street. I'm taking a closer look.'

It was some fifteen yards to the street corner and then he turned up the side street to the alley entrance. It was wider than it had looked from the upstairs window, broad enough for a vehicle to get along it. He guessed this was probably for coal deliveries in years gone by. There was the bicycle ahead of him, and a dark-clad youth standing against the fence. A look of fear appeared on his face as he spotted Barry's approach, he grabbed the bike and made off in the opposite direction. Barry considered giving chase but gave up after a couple of steps. It was a waste of time, given the speed with which the fast-receding figure was progressing towards the far exit some forty yards away. Barry stopped by the bush and looked around. Cigarette butts, sweet wrappers, marks in a patch of dirt. A forensic examination might yield something useful. He turned and made his way back to the house.

'Anything, boss?' Rae asked.

'We might have something to go on.'

'One of the neighbours has just passed by, someone who was out when I called earlier. Said he's seen a car hanging around in the last few days. A black BMW with someone in it reading a newspaper. He's seen it twice.'

'I don't suppose they took the number?'

Rae grinned. 'You must be joking. What are you looking for? Miracles?'

* * *

It was mid-afternoon by the time the two detectives made it back to the local police station, where the county headquarters support team was busy setting up an incident room. It was the same room they'd used the previous winter when they'd been involved in a frantic, but ultimately unsuccessful, hunt for a missing CID officer, Andrea Ford. She'd been found dead several days later. Once the computer systems were ready to use, Rae got busy with some basic fact-finding. They needed to flesh out the rather sparse details they had on the victim. She didn't find it easy. The man seemed to have no online presence.

Robert Bunting's neighbour had told Rae that, as far as she knew, he'd once worked on the fishing boats. Another had said that he might have tried his hand at lorry driving. The company name Rae had been given failed to show up on any searches. Rae wondered if she'd been given the wrong name, so she phoned the neighbour to check, but she stuck doggedly to the original information. That's what Bunting had told her. She was adamant about it. Rae then did what she could to trace other haulage concerns, but none seemed to employ anyone by the name of Robert Bunting, although a Saturday afternoon was not the best time to be contacting businesses with a query of this type. Maybe if she tried on Monday morning, she would get more productive results.

Rae tried the voters roll and other council-based systems. The name Robert Bunting failed to appear on any of them. How strange was that? Maybe he hadn't yet registered his address with the council, although if his previous residence had been in Dorset, something should have shown up. The surname Bunting wasn't a common one, after all. This was getting weird. Time for the last resort. She tapped the name Robert Bunting into several other databases open only to the police. None of the identified individuals in the short list that was generated seemed to be their victim.

How could someone live so far below the radar? It was as if the victim didn't exist. A niggling thought lodged itself in a dark recess of her mind.

* * *

Sophie Allen and Barry Marsh were standing by the window, looking out. The yellowing early evening light illuminated the nearby buildings, and gulls squawked noisily, their keening cries echoing among Weymouth's rooftops. Sophie had just arrived after dropping her husband at home following the drive south from Oxford. Both detectives were holding mugs of coffee. Sophie, now in her late forties, was the commander of the Violent Crime Unit, though the wider responsibilities that had come with her recent promotion to detective superintendent meant that she was less hands-on than in previous years. In practice, Barry was now in day-to-day control. They were talking about the urgent need for another junior detective to join them, now that Rae's promotion to detective sergeant was imminent.

'Things never work out quite as I hope. The trouble is, I always expect situations to develop in a neat linear way and they rarely do. Every time, I underestimate the ways that people can botch up my best-laid plans. The world is just too complicated for a simple soul like me.' Sophie sighed and took a sip of her drink.

Barry said nothing. He had a vague idea of what she might be talking about but he'd discovered a long time ago that when she started on one of these formless ramblings, it was better to let her get to the point in her own good time. He took a sip of coffee and murmured something unintelligible, meant to signify agreement.

'I mean, how was I to know my daughter would get in the bloody way and cock things up?'

Barry was beginning to see where this was going. 'Right,' he said, non-committally. He took another sip from his mug and waited.

'I had George earmarked to do his detective training and join us as a DC. It was all so perfect, but it's all gone to pot now, hasn't it?' Sophie scowled melodramatically.

'To be realistic, ma'am, did George know about these plans of yours? And isn't it an unwritten rule that newly qualified detectives need to learn the ropes in routine CID work before they're allowed to join a specialist unit like ours?'

'Mere details, Barry. It might have worked on a fair day with a following wind. But it's all come to nothing now, hasn't it? How could I ever get away with appointing Jade's boyfriend to be the new member of this unit? Really, how would it look to the powers that be?' Another dark scowl.

Barry frowned. He didn't feel in a particularly indulgent mood at the moment. It had been a long day, and he was tired and irritable. He and Rae had been up working on this perplexing new case since the crack of dawn, while the boss had been spending a comparatively relaxed day delivering Jade to Oxford and attending a parents' lunch at her new college. Added to which, she was talking complete claptrap.

'Easily,' he snapped. 'If he's the best person for the job, just do it. Mind you, that assumes he wants the job. And that he's done the basic training and completed a suitable CID placement. Along with coming through that with really good recommendations and top appraisal ratings. Maybe another year or two? The fact that he's Jade's boyfriend is irrelevant. With respect, ma'am, he can't solve our present problem. We need someone straight away. We could always try borrowing Jimmy again, but Kevin McGreedie won't be best pleased. He's got the whole Bournemouth team involved in a complex investigation into a series of violent break-ins. Do we really want to upset him?'

Sophie shook her head and sighed. 'No, you're right, as usual. And, as usual, I'm being too bloody impatient. I'll get in touch with Sandie Blake up at HQ. She might have someone spare.' She looked at Barry more carefully. 'Sorry. I should have been more understanding. You've been on the go since early morning, haven't you?'

'It's okay. As I said when you first arrived, we've hit some kind of barrier. Maybe you can get to the bottom of it. How was your day? Has Jade settled in?'

Sophie nodded, frowning. 'You know what my problem is, don't you? Envy. I can't admit it to anyone else, Barry.

I kept thinking this is me thirty years ago. Starting out on life's first big adventure. New friends, new experiences, new possibilities, and I was ready for it all. It was like a whirlpool, drawing me in. I had the time of my life. And there she is, at that same point. I'm so proud of her, but there's a bit of resentment too.' She sighed. 'I can't believe I feel this way. It's so . . . ridiculous.'

Barry thought a change in subject matter was needed. 'Do you want a rundown of how far we've got? It won't take long. Because, basically, our victim doesn't seem to have existed.'

Sophie looked at him with renewed interest. At last a sparkle was back in her eyes. 'So, he was in hiding, was he? Sounds fascinating.'

CHAPTER 3: AUTOPSY

Sunday morning

Benny Goodall, West Dorset's senior pathologist, was in his office pouring boiling water into three coffee mugs when Barry and Rae arrived.

'Sorry, it's instant,' he said. 'My coffee machine's on the blink and it's all I have. That's unless you want to try the hospital cafeteria. I wouldn't recommend it though.' He pulled a face. 'Good job it's you two and not your boss. She might have thrown the stuff at me.'

Barry smiled but Rae looked puzzled.

'I'll explain later,' Barry said to her.

'I always like to have a coffee or tea before starting,' Benny said, sipping at his mug. 'The five minutes I spend slurping it down helps to clear my mind. I can't afford to do a post-mortem if I'm preoccupied with anything. It works better for me if my brain's a clean slate with nothing else on my mind. What music do you want on?'

'Sorry?' Barry said. Rae looked bemused.

'Music. I'm experimenting with a new idea. Have calming background music on while doing the examination. It's meant to help normalise the atmosphere. Apparently, it's been really successful during surgeries up and down the country. It helps to keep the tension down.'

'Mozart's Clarinet Concerto,' Rae suggested. 'How would that do? Do you have it?'

'Everything's available. I use an online streaming service. So, whatever takes your fancy. Even Led Zeppelin.'

Barry frowned. 'Surely not? Do you mean some doctors have that playing while they're doing a delicate operation?'

Benny nodded. '"Dazed and Confused." "Communication Breakdown." Not sure they'd help me to remain calm and in control. We'll stick with Mozart.'

They finished their coffees and walked through to the theatre where the body lay waiting on the bench.

'I'd guess he was in his early forties,' Benny said. 'Average height and weight. Hair just starting to turn grey and recede at the temples. No obvious distinguishing marks on his skin. Fairly tanned, but to me it looks more of a weather-beaten tan rather than sunbathing on a beach. I could be wrong though. He's about five ten in height. We weighed him earlier and he came in at just over eleven stone. He looks fairly fit and healthy on the whole, apart from one thing. His right ankle was strapped. It looked very much as if he'd damaged it sometime and it had never totally healed.'

'Is it possible to say how bad it was and how it happened?' Barry asked.

Benny shook his head. 'Not really. We're not miracle workers. It was serious enough for him to get treatment and it might have affected his ability to do manual work. The strapping was done professionally.'

'Would he have been able to walk okay?'

'I would have thought so. That's partly the function of the support strapping. It bears some of the strain. He might have limped slightly. And other activities like running or cycling would have been out for a while. Really it all depends on how long ago he did it. Anyway, that's all from an external perspective, apart from the stab wound.' Benny moved closer and shone a light on Bunting's chest. He probed the wound. 'Two things. It looks as though it was intended for the heart. The entry point is exactly right. But the blade slid off one of the ribs and it got diverted. It did damage to the blood vessels, so he was losing blood at a fairly rapid rate, but it never reached its intended target.'

Barry frowned. 'Do you think he might have been struggling, or moved somehow? Is that what it looks like?'

Benny shrugged. 'It's impossible to be sure, but it could have been something like that. The end result was the same though. There was enough damage to the blood vessels to cause a fatal loss of blood.'

'If he'd got to A and E quickly, could he have been saved?' Rae asked.

'Very much touch and go. If the right personnel had been in the hospital and got him to surgery quickly, there might have been an outside chance.'

'We think he climbed over a wall at the station to get away from his attackers, then managed to cross the platform and crawl onto a train,' Rae added.

Benny shook his head. 'That would have opened the wound and increased the blood loss.' He paused. 'We'll get measurements for you when I open him up. Penetration depth and angle, along with what vessels were damaged. I'll get the lot to you late tomorrow. Do I send it to you or your boss?'

Barry made a face. 'Me. It's part of my new role now I'm a DI. I think she's secretly glad.'

Benny gave a wry smile. 'She always left before the gory bit. You can stay if you want. The gowns are over in that cupboard.'

Barry looked at Rae. 'Shall we give it a go?'

She nodded. 'Why not? I'll try anything once.'

An hour later the two detectives were in their car, heading back to the incident room.

'I think that goes right to the top of my *things not to do on a Sunday morning* list,' Rae said. 'Did I really choose to stay of my own free will?'

Barry, grey-faced, was driving rather more slowly than normal. 'I think I might follow the boss's lead in future. How do pathologists do it?'

Rae shook her head. 'I don't know. There was a girl in my class at school who caused a stir in a careers lesson once. She said she'd always wanted to work as an undertaker, embalming dead bodies. You can imagine the reaction. But she was serious. Maybe some people just don't get affected by it like the rest of us.' She nodded at the approaching sign for a pub. 'I could do with a drink.'

Barry turned into the car park. 'That's the most sensible suggestion I've heard today.'

* * *

Having been off duty since Friday, Sergeant Rose Simons listened to PC George Warrander, her regular sidekick, recount the previous day's events as they made their way downstairs to the squad-car pool.

'Glad I wasn't there, Georgie boy. All that blood would have put too much strain on my delicate mental constitution. See, us girls just can't cope in the way you tough blokes can. The sight of blood brings me out in a rash.'

'Yes, Sarge, I've often noticed that. I've never mentioned it though, just in case it made you self-conscious.'

Rose stopped dead and turned to face George. 'First rule of policing, George. It's the job of the sergeant to make the jokes. The role of a rookie cop is to listen in an agreeable way and laugh at the appropriate moment. You know that. What's got into you? Has the enforced absence of the love of your life turned your brain?'

'I'm wondering about putting in for detective training. It's been on my mind for a while. What do you think? Seriously, I mean.'

Rose sighed. 'Tell you what, George. I've guessed it was on the cards for a long time. You're too good to keep doing this kind of rubbish for the rest of your working life. You've got a good brain so you should use it. If I had my time again, I'd be with you like a shot, but at forty-five, I guess I've reached my peak. I'm not gonna rise above chucking drunks, thugs and assorted lowlifes into the back of vans now.'

George smiled. 'You love it really, Sarge, don't you?'

Rose gave him a grin. 'Dead right, Georgie boy. You've got me sussed. Which is why you'd make a good 'tec. And I'll say that to anyone who asks. You can depend on me for a good reference when the time comes. We've made a good team, haven't we? Bugger it, not just a good team — we've been a great one.'

George was speechless.

'But a bottle of gin wouldn't go amiss if you want a really good appraisal. One of the good ones?' She winked at her protégé. 'You've booked next weekend off, I see. Let me guess. Off to Oxford?'

He looked at her warily. 'Yeees.'

'Go for it, George. She's perfect for you. People like you and her are nuggets of gold. So rare in this world. Or maybe I'm being a wee bit prejudiced there. We only see the low life in this line of work.' She stopped at the car and took her usual walk around, examining it closely and finishing with a glance underneath. They climbed in. 'Apparently the knife used to kill that guy on Saturday still hasn't turned up, so they're sending in their top team to double check. That's us.' George started the engine. 'There's always a bonus to a morning on the streets of Weymouth,' Rose continued. 'Ham, egg and chips in that great seafront café. My stomach's rumbling already.'

CHAPTER 4: NEW RECRUIT

Monday morning

Sophie walked into Sandie Blake's office at Dorset police headquarters and sat down. Sandie ran the HR department and had always worked wonders matching people with positions.

'It hasn't been easy, Sophie. To be honest, the whole staffing situation is a shambles. It's an inevitable result of the budget cuts, I suppose. Anyway, I've got someone for you but . . . well, it's a case of take it or leave it, I'm afraid.'

'Listen, Sandie, you found me Barry and Rae. You're obviously a magician, so why should I be even remotely worried?'

Sandie pulled a face. 'Because the good old days are gone. I can't work that system anymore. I just don't have the flexibility. Between you and me, I'm beginning to wonder if my own days here are numbered. Everything to do with placements and gaining experience is much more programmed than it used to be, and the staffing cuts have made it so much harder. I can imagine myself being replaced by a computer system.'

'Well, if you're serious, why don't you design it? You could suggest it to the chief, get Home Office funding, team up with a programmer, and Bob's your uncle. I don't want to pry, Sandie, but weren't you talking about looking to retire in a few years? Introduce a system to replace you and then go for redundancy. You'll get more money that way.'

Sandie looked at Sophie through narrowed eyes. 'You're a hard woman, Sophie Allen. Cruel.' She laughed drily. 'If you must know, I've got at least ten more years to go. No, I told you that a couple of years ago when I had my cancer scare. I've got the all-clear now, so I want to keep working. The last thing I want is to be stuck at home all day with Roger. He'd drive me barmy with his constant neediness. I feel like murder some days.'

Sophie smiled. 'Well, if you have to kill him, please do it while you're on holiday somewhere else. I don't want to be the SIO on that particular case.' She paused. 'So, who do you have in mind for me? You sound a bit worried.'

'Tommy Carter? He's a young DC in Weymouth CID, as it happens, but he put in for a transfer to a different unit a couple of weeks ago.'

Sophie frowned. 'I know him. He was part of Bruce Pitman's team. We worked with the local Weymouth squad on the Andrea Ford case. I don't know, Sandie. You know my feelings about the way Bruce worked. Has Tommy been influenced by him?'

'I can offer you a bit of reassurance there. He'd only been with them for a couple of months when that all blew up. I know he can appear to be a bit too easy-going, but he's all I have. I'm afraid it's take-it-or-leave-it time.'

Sophie stood up. 'Well, in that case, I don't have much choice, do I? At least he'll be useful on the current case. It's Weymouth-based, so his local knowledge should prove useful.' She paused. 'You know that my long-term wish is to get George Warrander into the unit, don't you? Can you do what you need to smooth the path? He's got just the right mindset for the kind of work we do.' She turned and left.

Sandie Blake watched her go. She'd heard the rumours about young George going out with Jade Allen. That could have the makings of a disaster, if he were to work in Sophie's own unit. Better to avoid any possibility of a future meltdown and put the idea into cold storage.

* * *

Despite the number of search personnel out on Weymouth's streets, no trace of the murder weapon had been found. Every bin and skip was examined, every hedge and bush scrutinised, every litter-filled nook was inspected and every drain cover lifted. All to no avail. Barry, allocated a temporary office in the railway station complex as search HQ, listened to the reports from the returning team leaders in disappointed silence. There were several logical explanations, but one was particularly worrying. Whoever carried out the murder still had need of the knife. And what was the obvious conclusion to draw from that?

He thanked the station manager for the temporary use of her office and made his way back to the incident room at the local police station. Rae looked up as he entered. She too seemed worried.

'Boss, we need to talk.'

Barry made himself a coffee and went across to her desk. 'Nothing good, I take it?'

'Not really,' she replied. 'You remember how surprised I was at the lack of information on our victim? Well, I decided to attack it from a different angle. I looked at the house rather than the person in it. It's owned by the government — the Home Office, I think.'

Barry stood stock still. 'What? How did you find that out?'

'Well, the owner is officially recorded as a Corinne Lanston. I checked the property records, and she also owns a house in Poole. So, merely out of curiosity, I went further afield. She's also got houses in Exeter, Southampton and Portsmouth. All port towns.'

Barry frowned. 'Yes. What else?'

'So, I googled the name. And nothing came up. There isn't anyone with that name listed anywhere in the public domain.'

'Okay, I think I know where you're heading.'

Rae gave him a thin smile. 'Yes, you'd be right. I used some of the systems open to us for security checks. There is a Corinne Lanston. She works for the Home Office in London and all records about her are locked. Only people with high-level security clearance can get further. It seems we're not even meant to know that she exists. I wonder if I've set off any alarms by trying to access information about her. Hope I'm not for the high jump. Is the boss around?'

Barry nodded. 'She's just back from HQ. I'll get her.'

Sophie listened to Rae's account, frowning. 'I knew this would happen one day. It was inevitable.'

'Do you know about this Corinne, then?' Barry asked.

Sophie shook her head. 'No, not her specifically. Only that we might get tangled up with one of the intelligence agencies at some point. I'm pretty sure that's what it might be. The place is some kind of safe house. Which begs the question. Who really was Robert Bunting?'

'Can we keep going with the investigation?' Barry asked.

'Yes, on a routine level. But we can't follow Rae's avenue of investigation until I've spoken to Special Branch. Well, this is a real turn up for the books. Great work, both of you. Let's take a break until tomorrow. I'll get on the blower right now to lodge Rae's discovery and fix a meeting at HQ. You two need to leave this angle well alone until I tell you otherwise. Understood?' She looked at her watch. 'By the way, our new DC should be here any minute. Don't mention Rae's discovery to him until we get it sorted. As far as he's concerned, it's just a normal murder inquiry.'

'Who is it?' Barry asked.

'Tommy Carter. We already know him and have a rough idea of his capabilities. He'll be useful on this occasion because he's a Weymouth local. He'll be on probation with us for three months, and then we'll need to make a decision. He'll report to you, Rae, because you start officially as DS in the unit next week. But keep Barry posted.'

'You don't sound too thrilled, ma'am,' Barry said.

Sophie shrugged. 'Maybe you're reading me wrongly. I'd have liked to have a choice but, on this occasion, there isn't one. It was either take him or leave the position unfilled. It's the cheap solution, you see. Now, I need to get on the blower to Matt Silver and Jim Metcalfe about this safe-house business. It'll be up to HQ for me first thing in the morning, I expect. Can you get a summary prepared for me, Rae? I'll need all the facts at my fingertips. Barry, can you stay a moment?'

Sophie waited until Rae had left her office. 'I just wanted to warn you. Joel Kennedy is in hospital after having a heart attack last week. He's our resident Special Branch person. Apparently, he's in a bad way. It means we can't tap into his background knowledge at the moment, so we're operating in a bit of a vacuum. His second, Karen Brody, may know something but she's unlikely to have Joel's pool of background knowledge and know all of his contacts. There's also the fact that we have different priorities. We're investigating a murder. She'll be investigating a possible security leak.'

* * *

Tommy Carter arrived about an hour later. He stepped through the door looking around nervously. Rae gave him a wave, and stood up to greet him.

'Hi, Tommy. Welcome to the Violent Crime Unit, currently on location in your own cop shop. You've only had to walk up some stairs, haven't you? I'll be your immediate senior officer from next Monday when I officially become a detective sergeant, but the boss wants us to start the way we intend to go on. Let's go and meet the others. They're ensconced in the broom cupboard that is laughably referred to as the

SIO's temporary office. The boss suggested I bring you along when you arrived.' She noticed Tommy's anxious expression. 'No need to worry. They're both great to work for. You're at an advantage anyway. You've worked with us before on the Andrea Ford case.'

'That's what worries me,' Tommy admitted. 'I don't know whether I came up to scratch then. She's a bit intimidating, isn't she?'

'You'll be fine, Tommy. Just be prepared to work hard. Don't expect this to be a cushy number, because it sure isn't one. We're Dorset's top team, and that's something to be proud of.'

Rae tapped on Sophie's office door and they went in.

CHAPTER 5: RECOLLECTIONS

Tuesday morning

Jim Metcalfe, Dorset's Assistant Chief Constable, chaired the meeting in his office. The four officers sat around a table, notepads in front of them, glasses of water to hand. Matt Silver, Sophie's boss, sat to his left, Sophie opposite. Karen Brody, sitting to his right, looked nervous in the presence of such senior officers, which was understandable considering that she'd only been in the post for six months.

Sophie started by giving a summary of the case and Rae's discoveries of the previous day. Karen listened in silence, making an occasional note.

'So, you have the details as they stand, Karen,' the ACC said. 'What can you tell us? Were you aware of the existence of these houses in the county? And their use?'

Karen sat up straighter. 'It's possible we were aware of them, but not their specific locations, their purpose, nor who was in them. That's Border Force stuff, while our main business is with internal security and the terrorist threat. Joel may have known more but, if he did, he didn't share it with me. Sorry, sir.' There was a short silence.

‘This is a bit of a problem,’ the ACC continued. ‘We need to get a grasp of what might be going on. We have an ongoing murder inquiry and, in my mind anyway, that’s a high priority, particularly if it looks more like an assassination, as it does in this situation. What always worries me in a case like this, is that there could be more. So, we need to discuss this as a group, make some decisions and meet regularly to monitor the situation. That’s what the chief has decided. It’s my job to make sure we’re all up to speed on the background, and my decisions will be the final ones if we can’t agree. The only other person to be in on the loop will be the chief herself. She’s aware we’re meeting this morning and will want a report, including our plans. I’ll try to find out a bit more from the Home Office and colleagues in neighbouring counties because Sophie’s team can’t be left to blunder around in the dark not knowing what they’re getting mixed up in. The fact is, with this Robert Bunting, if that’s his real name, now a murder victim, it looks as though someone might have found a loophole in the security framework, whether the powers that be like it or not. We’re duty-bound to investigate a murder. They have to recognise that. Any ideas, anyone?’

‘They may have secure safe houses available in other port towns along the south coast,’ Karen added.

‘That fits with what we discovered late yesterday,’ Sophie said. ‘Rae Gregson, my DS, did a bit of clever digging in various different property records, then matched the details with the security records we have access to. It wasn’t difficult. But if she can do it, you can bet your life others can too, and maybe people we don’t want probing around in that way. We need a clearer picture of what we’re dealing with.’

Karen still looked troubled. ‘I don’t know anything else for sure. My guess is that Special Branch haven’t been officially informed, because Joel would have told me. I checked as much as I could but couldn’t find anything else.’

‘Well, we can try to make a guess,’ Sophie said. ‘You can tell me your thoughts. These are port towns on the south coast, which means it's something related to the Channel. Crossing it maybe? Right now, smuggling migrants across from France and the low countries is a very lucrative business. The sums of money involved must be enormous, the kind of huge amounts that might explain a cold-blooded murder like this. Any migrants intercepted crossing the Channel are put into special holding camps, so these houses are not for them. The Home Office is trying to put a stop to the smuggling, so will be actively attempting to identify weak links inside the smuggling gangs and using them for information, maybe even turning some of them. So, maybe these properties are to house those people, possibly on a temporary basis. Other scenarios, like drugs or weapons, are a possibility we have to consider but I'm not sure they fit the facts as closely. And if it was terrorism, Special Branch would be in the mix and Karen would know all about it.'

There was a silence. Finally, Jim Metcalfe said slowly, 'You could be right. As I said, I'll do some checking around, both officially and unofficially. I know there's a gossip grapevine and that my opposite numbers in Hampshire or Sussex might be aware of something. Joel would have picked up on it if he'd been here.'

'I'll be going to see him once he's well enough to receive visitors,' Karen said. 'Do you want me to ask him, sir?'

The ACC shook his head. 'No. We have to make it official and on the record because of the security implications. I'll do it. But we'll need to hold off until the medics think he's well enough.'

Matt Silver, Sophie's immediate senior, was quick to point out another puzzling observation. 'I can't understand why no one's been in contact. It's now been more than three days since Bunting was murdered. Surely that triggered some kind of alarm. What are they doing, for goodness sake? Why hasn't someone been in touch with us?'

Jim Metcalfe shrugged. 'I'm worried that this could all blow up in our faces, so I'll get the go-ahead from the chief and then, as I said, try to find out exactly what's been going on. We need to pin down who was operating that house and why. We might think it was MI6 or a special unit from the Border Force, but we can't be sure at the moment. God knows what we do if we find it isn't them.'

'It's got to be some such organisation,' Sophie said. 'And remember that someone's been seen watching the house, according to my team. The neighbours saw men or a man in a large BMW several times in the week prior to the murder. Who might that have been? Security keeping an eye on Bunting, or the killers tracking his movements?' She deliberately kept quiet about the youth on the bicycle that Barry had seen. That was still being followed up.

* * *

Back in Weymouth, Rae was taking the new boy, Tommy Carter, through the Violent Crime Unit's procedures.

'When we're on a case, it's like we live out of bags and boxes in someone else's home. We've got an office up at county HQ but we're always in some kind of temporary incident room when an investigation's on. We're all waiting for a murder to happen in Wool or Winfrith, so we can use our own base as the incident room, but what are the chances of that happening? They're pretty small places. I live in Wool and I know it's got its fair share of nutters, but most of our cases are going to come from the big towns. You put Bournemouth, Poole and Christchurch together as a single block, and you're talking about half a million or more people. What's the rest of the county? About a half of that?'

Tommy shrugged. Rae guessed he'd never done any population analysis. Maybe he'd never had the need to, based as he'd been in Weymouth's small CID unit. Because the VCU's operating region spanned the county, and often beyond, she had a much clearer idea of the spread of population. Added to which, they'd expanded into neighbouring counties in recent years, both in the investigation of specific crimes and because the unit's expertise was increasingly being called on by other forces in the south west. Rae sometimes wondered if there were long-term plans afoot to initiate a totally regional unit to investigate serious and violent crimes, one that would cover the whole of the south west. It was the way things were going in other parts of the country, with local units feeding into a wider command structure. She could see the sense in it, though problems would arise if bureaucracy triumphed over practicalities. Such a scheme would work if someone like Sophie Allen were in charge, but not some of the other senior officers that Rae had come across. She wondered if that was one of the reasons for Sophie's recent promotion. Indeed, her own promotion to DS might be a pointer to a different approach.

Rae realised that Tommy was watching her. Here she was, lost in thought, and there was a murder to solve.

'Why don't we head out?' she said. 'I've got the names of a couple of people to visit who were in or around the train station late on Friday evening at about the time that our man got stabbed. We need to jog their memories a bit. The problem is, Tommy, people often see something that might be relevant, but they don't realise it. We have to get them to remember Friday night in precise detail — who they saw, where, what people were doing, what cars were moving out of the car park. We're starting with one of the taxi drivers who was just finishing his shift. He claims that he didn't spot anything out of the ordinary, but we need to push him a little.'

Tommy looked around him. 'Where is everybody?'

'The boss is at a high-level meeting at HQ. She'll fill us all in on that later once she's got to the bottom of the puzzle. Barry, that's DI Marsh to you, is back at the house we visited. He's trying to follow up his sighting of the youth on the bike on Saturday afternoon. It's a bit of a puzzle, you see. Here we are thinking that Bunting's murder might have some kind of connection with security, but what was a young guy on a bike doing watching the house? That doesn't seem to fit, does it? So, if he was keeping an eye on it, why? And who was he? Anyway, time for us to move.'

* * *

Darren Pike had been a taxi driver for more than twenty years. That made him a bit of a veteran as far as the younger cabbies were concerned and they joked about him among themselves when he was off duty or out on a job. Nonetheless, they were glad to tap into his pool of knowledge when they needed to. And new cabbies were quick to realise that very little escaped his observation or his dry wit. It was Darren who Rae and Tommy were talking to now over a coffee in the station café. Scratching his greying, short-cropped hair, Darren was thinking back to late Friday evening.

'It was a bit drizzly earlier, but it'd dried up when that last train got in. I don't usually do the station late on Fridays. You get more jobs in the town centre with people coming out the pubs. But the place was a bit dead. I thought I might strike lucky up here, but the station was pretty quiet too. Only a few people got off the train.'

'Do you remember seeing anything unusual that night? Either before the train came in or just after, as the people came out of the station?' Rae asked.

'Well, I saw your guy come out, if that's what you mean. The thing is, I've had him in my cab a couple of times but that was before he got his bike. He came in on that train a few times. Not every week, mind. He never said much but he did tell me that he was getting a second-hand bike because he couldn't afford the cab fares. I asked him why he didn't just walk — after all, his place wasn't that far, but he said he had some kind of leg injury. I don't really see how a bike could be any better than walking, but he never explained. Odd sort of guy. He had a vague kind of accent, but I couldn't pin it down.'

'Foreign, you mean?' Rae said.

Darren shook his head. 'Not sure. He didn't talk much.'

'What did you notice on Friday?'

'Nothing much. I'd picked up a fare, someone from that same train who was out pretty quick. But I caught sight of your man just as I was heading out of the taxi rank. He was walking across to the bike racks, limping slightly, like he always did.'

Rae noted this down. 'Nothing else unusual going on, was there? No one behaving oddly or anything else suspicious?'

'Not really. There were a couple of cars waiting to pick people up in the drop-off bays. There was a middle-aged woman in a dark coat waiting for someone. She appeared just before the train arrived.'

Rae looked up from her notebook. 'Was she alone?'

'I can't be sure. There may have been a guy with her. But it wasn't obvious they were together.'

'Can you remember anything about him?'

Darren chuckled. 'Nah. When I've got a good-looking woman to look at, I don't bother with the blokes. It was a bit dark to be sure and she was standing in a shadowy area. But him? No, nothing I can recall.'

Rae thought for a few moments. 'Well, we've finished our coffees. Let's go back out to your taxi and park it in the same position you were in that night. You can point out where they were, as far as you can remember.'

The trick worked. Once Darren was sitting in his cab and they were roughly in the right spot, his expression cleared.

'She had a hat on and gloves, I think. Maybe trousers? All dark. I think she had fair hair — a bit was peeping out from under the hat. I still don't remember anything about the bloke.'

'Where were they standing?' Rae asked.

He pointed to a spot by one of the walls of the station building. Rae and Tommy got out of the taxi and walked across to where Darren had indicated. Rae looked around her.

'This wouldn't be a particularly good spot to wait for someone if you were down here to pick them up from the train. You'd be missed too easily. But if you're watching someone it's useful for keeping an eye on the two key places — the main exit from the station and the bike rack. And Darren was right. It'd be in shadow at night. Look where the car park lights are. Now, if the two people Darren spotted happen to be the same ones that were seen on the station the next morning, we're onto something.'

'You mean that they came back the next morning to check, because he'd got away from them?' Tommy asked.

'Wouldn't you? Something went wrong. Maybe he took them by surprise, and they didn't see where he went.'

'Do you think he fought back, and they weren't expecting it? He might have hurt one of them.'

Rae smiled. 'That's good thinking, Tommy. Let's have another chat with the station staff who saw the couple on Saturday morning. We'll prod their memories a bit in the same way we did with that taxi driver. You never know, we might get lucky.'

Their luck held. One of the station cleaners who'd been working the early shift on Saturday morning did now recall a couple of very useful facts. The man who'd been briefly seen alongside the woman with the wheelie case, had a sticking plaster across the bridge of his nose. And there'd been a large black BMW 4x4 parked in a near-empty area of the car park for a short while. Rae looked at the cleaner with interest. That last fact might help Stu Blackman with his search for vehicles that had possibly been in the area. Definitely worth following up.

CHAPTER 6: SELFIES

Barry Marsh was also out on the streets of Weymouth, with Stu Blackman in tow. Barry was keen to trace the young cyclist he'd seen on Saturday but didn't want to flood the area with uniformed officers whose presence might well send the youth into hiding. This was why Barry was dressed more informally than usual, and he'd asked Stu to do the same. They wore dark jeans, zipped jackets and trainers. Barry even had on a flat cap in an attempt to hide most of his ginger hair. His partner, Gwen, had teased him about his appearance when he'd set off from home earlier.

'I could really fancy you in that garb, Barry. Are you sure you haven't got a secret floozy lined up at work?'

As usual, he'd been unable to think of a suitably witty reply and had merely given her the customary hug. It certainly made a change from his usual tailored jacket, collar and tie. He liked his ties and so did Gwen. He'd always owned ties in a range of colours, but Gwen had added several with much livelier patterns and styles and made sure he wore them. Today, though, his shirt was open-necked, with a thin, blue jumper over it.

The two detectives strolled around the neighbourhood of Bunting's house, getting a feel for the geography of the area.

Old terraced houses lined tidy and well-maintained streets. A network of narrow paths gave access to the rear of most of the properties, dating from the days of coal fires when the houses all had coal sheds in their back gardens and the delivery merchants needed access. It was in one such lane that Barry had spotted the young man watching the rear of Bunting's house. Barry would not have attached so much importance to his observation of the watcher, if not for the way he had run off when he realised he'd been spotted. He might have been there for any number of reasons, but it was his panicked reaction on seeing Barry approach that was so suspicious. Barry guessed that he was about seventeen, tall and gangly, but his face had been obscured by the hoodie he'd been wearing.

'This could be like a needle in a haystack,' Stu grumbled. 'If he was really up to no good, what are the chances of finding him?'

'Better than you might think,' Barry replied curtly, irritated by the remark. 'He's local, I'm sure. The way he made off and skidded around the corner at the far end of the lane meant he knew this area as likely as not. Lads hanging around on a bike one day will probably be doing the same on other days. Come on, Stu, don't be so negative. This is what the job's all about, trudging around somewhere, looking and listening. I'm trying to spot where he could have gone once he reached the road at the far end of the back lane. Turning right would have brought him back to the street with Bunting's house on it, so I reckon he'd have gone in the opposite direction. He'd have turned left, which brings him out just here, so let's have a wander.'

The side street took them towards a busier road with some commercial premises about fifty yards along — a local shop, a launderette, a pub and a café. A play park was situated further on, in front of the local primary school. In the opposite direction the road headed south towards the town centre and the seafront. The two detectives walked towards the shop and Stu went in to buy a newspaper. He glanced at the sports pages and went to rejoin Barry.

'Sergio Aguero,' he said as they walked towards the park. 'Scored again. What a player.'

But Barry had spotted several youths on bikes, weaving in and out of the bushes in the park. 'Look.'

'They should be at school,' Stu said.

Barry shrugged. 'Maybe. But we're here to watch and learn. The guy we're looking for isn't one of them. My guess is that he's a bit older. Let's have a seat for a few minutes and listen to what they're talking about, if anything.'

But seeing the two men entering the park put an end to the three boys' aimless cycling. They rode out through the narrow gate, turned and gave the detectives the finger, then sped away.

Barry sighed. 'So much for that bright idea. Do you think they realised we're police?'

'Doubt it,' Stu said. 'I think they'd react like that whoever we were. We've invaded their space.'

'Where have they gone?'

Stu Blackman walked back onto the street and looked along its length.

'Heading down towards the front. That's where kids sometimes used to hang out before we started getting tough with them for skiving off school. Worth a look?'

'Why not? It's not often I get a chance to have a wander around a place like this. But maybe we should be a bit more careful if we spot them.'

It took the two detectives ten minutes to arrive at the seafront gardens. The sun had just peeked out from behind the autumn clouds and instantly what had been a stretch of somewhat tired green grass, dull flowers and grey sea now almost vibrated with colour. The sea, now blue, was flecked with the white of wave tops. Even the air seemed to have more life in it. Barry put on his sunglasses, took a deep breath and inhaled the salty breeze. He was about to say something but stopped. He laid a hand on Stu's arm. He had spotted a group of teenagers in the distance.

'Is that the same three?' he asked.

Stu peered past the nearby shrubs towards the narrow, landscaped gardens beside the beach promenade.

'Looks like it. There's a couple of others there too. They look older.'

The two detectives descended a couple of steps onto the promenade and walked slowly in the direction of the group. Barry took a small map out of his pocket and pretended to study it as they approached. The three younger boys from the park rode away, leaving two older youths leaning against the wall, smoking.

'That's lucky. We can afford to get a bit closer now.' Barry led the way back into the gardens and approached the pair. He pretended to point out a couple of landmarks on the map.

'Is the sea-life centre much further?' Stu asked the lads when they drew level.

The untidier of the two answered. 'Nah. Couple of minutes.'

'Is it worth visiting?'

The youth snorted. 'Yeah. If you like that kind of thing.'

'Okay. Thanks.'

Barry had stayed back during the exchange, surreptitiously inspecting the two bikes leaning against the wall. There it was, the same model he'd seen on Saturday, propped against the fence at the rear of Bunting's house. He took another glance at the youth who hadn't spoken. He looked about eighteen, and the height was right, so was the build. The same hooded jacket and shoes. Barry indicated to Stu that they should move on, then stopped after a few yards.

'Let's get a selfie with the sea in the background,' he said.

He took out his phone, manoeuvred into a good position, then took a snap. Not bad, but the two lads were a bit blurred. He adjusted the zoom and took another two. Much better. They walked on.

'Did you notice the bikes?' Barry asked. 'What did you think?'

'They were very different,' Stu replied. 'One was a bit battered and grubby. It looked like a pretty ordinary model and had been through the wars. The other one looked flash and expensive. Why?'

'Just curious to get your view. The good one was the one I saw on Saturday afternoon, behind Bunting's house. I reckon the quieter guy, the one who didn't speak, is the one we're looking for. I want him identified and watched. As soon as we're out of their sight, I'll head back to the car. Can you hang around and keep an eye on him until I get back? I'll get Rae and Tommy to take over from us. What do you think of Tommy, by the way? You'll be aware that he's joining our unit on a trial basis.'

Stu shrugged. 'He's okay. He's reliable and works hard when he has to. He's not got a lot of initiative, though. I can't see him going much further unless he gets to grips with the job.'

Barry was silent. That wasn't what he wanted to hear.

* * *

By mid-afternoon, DC Tommy Carter was still out on the streets, trying to track the meanderings of Barry's teenager. He'd been following him since midday, time largely spent around the promenade and its landscaped gardens, wandering, seemingly at random, from one location to another. The young man seemed rather guarded with the people he met. Some of them were flamboyant and loud, others, like him, seemed more restrained and cautious.

Tommy lost sight of him late in the afternoon when the lad went inside an amusement arcade that suddenly filled up with schoolchildren. He'd followed Barry's instructions and not hurried about peering into corners and behind pillars. That was too much of a giveaway. So he waited outside, hoping to spot the youth coming out. By the time the young man finally appeared, Tommy was in a state of near-panic, having convinced himself that he'd failed miserably on his first assignment for the VCU. Things got better after that. The youth made his way to an upmarket house in a quiet residential street and went inside. He didn't appear again. His home? Tommy hoped so. He was tired, hungry and cold. His immediate boss, Rae Gregson, was due to take over for the evening if required, but when she arrived to collect him, she told him further surveillance was probably unnecessary. The address that Tommy had radioed in showed that the family in residence had an eighteen-year-old son. Tommy's afternoon had not been wasted after all.

CHAPTER 7: KNIFE

Late Tuesday morning

The hostel's front door was just like any other in the rundown street — faded and chipped, its deep red surface dull and streaked. The whole frontage was shabby and could have done with a lick of paint. The only clue as to the building's occupancy was a small plaque screwed to the wall beside the door, *Beechwood Women's Refuge*. A dark-haired woman in a nurse's uniform rang the doorbell, stepped back and waited. The door opened a crack, a security chain across the gap, and part of a face appeared, peering at her suspiciously.

'Yes?'

'I've come to visit Louise Bennett,' the nurse said. 'I'm the replacement district nurse, Charmaine Cookson, come to check on her progress. I may need to change her dressings. I've also brought her some cakes for her birthday.'

'Wait a tick.'

The door closed, the safety chain was disengaged, and it opened just wide enough to admit Charmaine. She walked as far as the small reception desk, where the woman stood blocking her from moving any further.

'You'll need to sign in,' she said. 'I'm Bella Fisher, the warden. I'll need all your details. What's happened to Julie, our regular? She always comes in the afternoon.'

'She's gone down with a nasty bug. Some of the others have too. This is the first time I've done this area, and it's more convenient if I do the calls in reverse order.'

'Louise can't manage the stairs very easily,' Bella said. 'You'll have to go up. She's in room fourteen. I'd normally come up with a new nurse, but I'm the only person on at this time in the morning. Can you find your way? It's the door second from the end on the first floor. If you can't wake her, come back down and I'll bring a key.'

Charmaine opened her carrier bag to show the warden the small collection of cakes. 'It's her birthday tomorrow, isn't it? I'd have brought them then, but she isn't due for another visit till the end of the week.'

Bella used her swipe-card to unlock a door to the left of her desk and gestured for Charmaine to go on up. The stairway, lit in a dim, pale yellow, was steep and narrow, as to be expected in an old terraced property like this. At the top, a corridor opened up in front of her with several doors along its length. She made her way along the carpeted floor and knocked on the second from the end, then took her thin gloves off, putting them into her pockets.

'Yes?' a weak voice said.

'It's Charmaine, from the district nurse service.' She spoke with a broad Irish accent. 'I've just come to check on how your injuries are healing. And I've brought you some cakes for your birthday tomorrow.'

The sound of shuffling feet could be heard inside, and the door opened.

'Hi, Louise. I'm the temporary replacement for Julie, your usual nurse. I've bought some goodies for your birthday, but let's have a quick look at you first.' She held out the carrier bag for inspection, its tempting contents visible even in the poor light.

The door opened wider, and Charmaine stepped inside. The small room was rather like a cell, an impression reinforced by the cheap, amateurish artwork on the walls. She placed her medical bag on a small table set against the wall and flipped it open.

'Well, you're looking better than I expected,' she said, sliding on a pair of latex gloves and securing a thin nylon apron around her waist. 'Sorry about these new hygiene requirements. I wouldn't think you're infectious, but I've been told these are a necessity now on all house calls. Where shall I put the cakes?'

Louise, still half-asleep, looked at her somewhat suspiciously but indicated a shelf above the table. Charmaine started to empty the bag, watched by Louise.

'Look, eclairs, cupcakes and Viennese whirls. We knew you'd like those.' She continued to remove items from the bag. 'And some really nice chocolate biscuits. They're everyone's favourites.'

Louise stepped closer to examine the items.

'And there's this,' Charmaine said, lifting a long, slender-bladed knife out of her medical bag. She slid it smoothly between Louise's ribs, twisting it as it reached her heart. Louise uttered a shuddering sigh. Charmaine lodged her arm around Louise's back to support her weight as she toppled, allowing her to slide onto the bed. 'I'll just leave the cakes with you. No charge. Not the blade, though. I still have need of that.'

Charmaine glanced around the room and spotted an old towel on the back of a chair. She pulled it towards her and held it tight around the handle as she carefully drew the knife from Louise's chest, then used it to wipe the blade clean of blood. Perfectly calm, she took a look around the room. Everything was as it should be. She covered Louise's body with a thin blanket, and then spent several minutes searching through the two drawers and the small cupboard. She glanced at the mattress, now beginning to look decidedly damp and sticky with blood, and wiped the few surfaces she'd touched with a surgical wet wipe. She removed the apron and slipped it into her bag, replaced the latex gloves with her own and left the room, closing the door gently behind her.

Charmaine smiled at the warden as she rejoined her in the downstairs lobby. 'She's not looking too bad, is she? She was very appreciative of the cakes. But she's really tired and was ready for a nap. Maybe don't disturb her for another hour or two?'

She turned towards the front door. The warden let her out and closed the door behind her. Charmaine walked unhurriedly along the road to a parked car where a man was waiting in the driving seat. He already had the engine running and in seconds the shiny black BMW was driving away, heading towards the nearby main road. It was late morning and the sun had just come out.

CHAPTER 8: RIGHT UP THEIR STREET

Early Tuesday afternoon

Detective Sergeant Gwen Davis from Southampton CID was the first detective to arrive at the scene. She was greeted by a uniformed constable at the hostel's front door. Inside, the hysterical warden was being comforted by a second uniformed officer who'd arrived a few minutes earlier in one of the squad cars that was outside. She indicated for Gwen to go up the stairs. She arrived at Louise's room to find another uniformed constable standing guard outside.

'Nasty,' he said. 'Nothing's been touched but there's a lot of blood soaked into the bed underneath the body.' He looked at Gwen and shook his head slightly. 'It's not a natural death, Sarge. It looks like a stabbing to me.'

Gwen stepped into a protective suit and entered the room. She could smell the blood, that unmistakable taint to the air that always accompanies a violent, bloody death. The victim was lying on her back, seeming to gaze at the ceiling, with her mouth slightly open and her eyes filmed over. It was a thin, pinched face, even after death when the muscles usually relax and tensions vanish. Did it look as though she'd had a troubled life? Gwen couldn't tell. She took a look around, checking for signs of a struggle but not finding any. She returned to the corridor, closing the door behind her, and removed her nylon hair cover, which always made her feel too hot.

'We'll just wait for my boss to arrive.'

Gwen's immediate senior was DCI Jack Dunning. He arrived within a few minutes, looking unconcerned. 'You said it looked like an assassination. Are you having me on, or do I need to refer you to the funny farm?'

Gwen shook her head, her dark curls brushing her shoulders. 'I'm serious, boss. The victim's name is Louise Bennett. A woman masquerading as a district nurse came to see her, saying she was here to change her dressings. Middle-aged and well-spoken, according to the warden. She even had some cakes for Louise and showed them to the warden. She went upstairs and was back within ten minutes. The warden went up at lunchtime to see what Louise wanted to eat and found her. She was lying dead on the bed, covered by a loose blanket, but the blood had soaked through. I lifted the corner with a pen and the wound appears to be right over the heart. If that isn't an assassination, I don't know what is. It sounds as if it was planned, and very cold-blooded.'

Her boss grimaced. 'Okay, I take your point. What was she doing here, this Louise Bennett?'

They climbed the stairs.

'That's the strange thing. It's a women's refuge, so most of the residents are victims of domestic violence. You know, thumped by their partners. According to the warden, Louise's injuries fitted that pattern. A couple of bruises around the face that were healing, a fractured wrist and a bad cut near her right knee. But she didn't arrive by the normal referral route, from a surgery or A and E unit. Someone got her in here, but Bella Fisher — she's the warden — never got the paperwork. She doesn't know anything about Louise's background. It's a mystery. I had a quick look at the inmates' records and it's true. She was admitted late on Saturday but there's no other information. The whole thing's weird.'

They entered Louise's room. Gwen stood back to let her boss peer around the somewhat gloomy interior. Like her, he raised the thin blanket with a pen and looked at the blood-soaked jumper that Louise was wearing. He backed away.

'We'll have to wait for forensics to get to work in here,' Jack said. The two detectives left the room and made their way back down the stairs. 'You're right. It doesn't make a lot of sense, does it? Why would anyone kill a hostel resident in such a cold-blooded way? It just doesn't fit the pattern.' He shook his head slowly from side to side, and ran his fingers through his cropped, sandy-coloured hair. 'And someone posing as a nurse did this? It's almost beyond belief. I'll need to get on the blower to the chief. It's distinctly odd, and I don't like that.'

Gwen couldn't help thinking of her fiancé, Barry, who worked in a Dorset unit that specialised in unusual murder cases. He and his boss, Sophie Allen, would relish a crime like this. It would be right up their street.

* * *

Gwen and her boss decided to interview the warden while they waited for the forensic team to arrive. Bella Fisher had calmed down somewhat, although her shoulders still shuddered regularly.

'The woman fooled me totally,' she said. 'I was completely taken in. She spoke and acted like a nurse and her uniform was perfect. If only I'd suspected something, I'd have phoned the clinic to check up on her. This might not have happened.'

Gwen grimaced. 'Oh, but it would have. Once she was inside, what happened was inevitable, except that you'd have been added to the casualty list, either dead, injured or left locked in a cupboard. Don't beat yourself up about it. That woman was a killer and you'd have come off second best if you'd tried to stand in her way.'

'We've checked with the clinic,' Jack added. 'There's no nurse Charmaine Cookson. So we need a good description from you, whatever you can remember.'

Bella slowly shook her head. 'I don't know. It's all a bit blurred and I can't think straight. I suppose she was about my height, about five foot five.' She closed her eyes. 'She had very dark hair, in a bob. She had quite a lot of make-up on, especially round the eyes, and that's not common in the nurses we see. I think her eyes were blue.'

'Did she have a coat on?' Gwen asked.

Bella opened her eyes suddenly. 'No. I've just realised. And it was quite chilly this morning.'

Gwen turned to Jack Dunning. 'Maybe she came in a car parked nearby?'

He nodded. 'We can check for any CCTV in the vicinity. Anything else you remember about her, Bella? The way she spoke, maybe?'

'Oh, it was a fairly posh voice. Sort of correct, like. And she knew it was Louise's birthday tomorrow. That's what she brought the cakes for.'

'Useful. And she knew Louise had a dressing on an injury? Where was that, by the way?'

'She had quite a bad cut on her right leg, just near her knee. She couldn't bend her leg easily, which is why she struggled with the stairs. To be honest, I didn't know she was due for a dressing change. She was only admitted on Saturday and had a fresh dressing on then.'

'What was her reason for being here? Did she fit your normal pattern? A victim of domestic violence?'

Bella shook her head again. 'I don't know. We're run by a charity and we get money from all kinds of people and places. One of the trustees rang me on Saturday afternoon and asked if we had a spare bed for a woman in an emergency. I said we did — someone had left that day. But we had a waiting list and we'd already earmarked her room for the next person. But the woman pulled rank on me and told me that if we housed

Louise for a few days, we'd get a big grant coming in. I was left with no choice but to take her. We're really scraping the barrel for cash at the moment.'

'Who was it who called you with the request?'

'Cleo Cathcart. She's one of the people who helped set this place up. I didn't dare turn her down. God knows what would happen to our funding. Most of it comes in because of her efforts.'

That was the extent of the warden's recollections. The detectives left contact details with her in case she remembered more, and then left.

'The women in here are usually penniless, boss. If they get killed or assaulted, it's by paranoid ex-partners who are usually paralytic, lose their rag and lash out. This is as far from that pattern as it's possible to get.'

'Agreed. It's not just a question of tracing the killer to find out why she did it, but also of finding out why anyone would go to these lengths to kill someone who, on the face of it, wouldn't normally generate that level of interest. I mean, who was she really, our Louise? We need to find out.'

'That back story makes me uneasy,' Gwen said. 'Why was she brought here? From what the warden said, it looks like procedures were conveniently ignored. And then this happens.'

Getting into his car, Jack said, 'There's something very fishy about the whole thing. Let's set up the incident room and get busy.'

Gwen noticed that he looked worried, which was rare for her boss. Jack Dunning was well known across the region for his cool, calm approach to investigating serious crime. She was about to return to her own car but stopped.

'Is there something you're not telling me, boss?' she asked.

He remained silent for a few moments, examining his hands. 'Cleo Cathcart,' he finally said. 'She's the wife of Gus Cathcart.'

Gwen looked blank. 'Who?'

'Before your time. He held the rank of DCI in West Sussex. Nominally Special Branch but he had fingers in lots of security pies. They live on Hayling Island, moved there when he retired about six years ago.' He paused. 'I don't like him. Not one bit.'

* * *

Jack Dunning was one of the most well-regarded detectives in the Hampshire force. It was something of a puzzle to members of his team as to why he'd taken so long to progress to his current rank, but he'd once shared the reason for his reticence with Gwen.

'There's too much politics in the senior ranks,' he'd said. 'I want to stick with what I can cope with and am happy doing. Look at some of the people above us, they're all looking over their shoulders, wondering where the next stab in the back is going to come from. It's just not for me.'

Gwen recalled these words as she checked procedures back in the local police station, where an incident room was being set up. Notices were being pinned to a whiteboard setting out areas of investigation and lines of responsibility. Photos taken at the crime scene were added, as were some of the initial forensic assessments. It was all go, part of a system Jack had set up several years ago.

She realised that Jack had appeared at her shoulder. 'It's all good, boss.'

He smiled. 'Sophie Allen and I put this approach together after we attended a joint planning course about five years ago. I've added a few new touches, and she probably has too, across in Dorset. But it works. Well, let's just say it's worked up to now.'

'Barry seems happy enough with it.'

Jack looked puzzled.

'Come on, boss. Surely you haven't forgotten. My fiancé? He's a DI now, second in her unit.'

He shook his head, as if trying to clear it. 'Of course. A temporary lapse. I think I need a holiday.'

She laughed. 'Well, you're not going to get one now, are you? Not with this going on. What's first on the agenda?'

'We'll get across to Hayling Island and speak to Cleo Cathcart. Finish your coffee. I could do with a good slug of scotch myself, to prepare, but unfortunately that's a no-no.'

'Is it going to be that bad?'

He rolled his eyes. 'You have no idea. Let's hope the great man is out playing golf or something. We might get somewhere if it's just her. With a bit of luck and a following wind.'

CHAPTER 9: NO NEED TO GET BULLISH

On a chilly autumn day, Hayling Island appears to be a relatively quiet backwater. Outside the peak summer months, the road bridge from Havant was free of heavy traffic, and the two detectives pulled up outside the Cathcart's luxury villa within forty minutes of leaving the incident room in Southampton.

Gwen stood back and took a look at the house. It was of a modern design, beautifully maintained with an attractive, landscaped garden full of neat shrubs. A large upstairs balcony would give a panoramic view across the grassy dunes to the sea. Gwen could imagine evening barbecues up there, with chilled wine at sunset. Glorious. With a sigh, she followed her boss to the front entrance.

The woman who opened the door was tall and slender, her pale-blonde hair perfectly cut. She was elegantly dressed in expensive looking, slim-cut trousers and a cashmere jumper. She appeared to be in her mid-forties, but Gwen knew how deceptive looks could be. There were no obvious signs of cosmetic surgery but . . . The woman blinked when she saw Jack Dunning, evidently puzzled. Gwen smiled to herself. *She's recognised him but can't think who he is.*

‘Mrs Cathcart. Sorry to disturb you. It’s DCI Jack Dunning from Hampshire police. This is DS Gwen Davis. Can we come in for a brief chat with you, please?’

The woman smiled. ‘Of course. It’s nice to see you again.’

They followed her into a spacious lounge. ‘Please call me Cleo. We have met before, after all. Can I get you a coffee? Tea?’

‘That would be good. Tea, please,’ Jack said.

Gwen indicated with a nod that she would have the same. She and her boss had agreed a strategy on their way here. He’d take the lead and she would only jump in if she thought he’d missed something. She looked around. There was artwork on the walls but no family photos on display. A newspaper and two magazines lay neatly stacked on a low table. There was not a single item out of place. The room looked like an illustration for an interior design magazine.

The woman returned, carrying a tray of delicate, expensive looking chinaware. Gwen, who came from a working-class family in Cardiff, was beginning to feel on edge. She was glad her boss would be taking the lead. He was good at tailoring his approach to suit the situation.

‘Now, what’s this about? Gus is playing golf and won’t be back until later.’

‘That’s not a problem, Mrs Cathcart. It’s you we’ve come to see. I understand you’re one of the trustees of the Beechwood Women’s Refuge in Southampton?’

‘Yes, I am. One has to do one’s bit for the less fortunate. Why?’

‘We’ve spent the last couple of hours there. One of the inmates was found dead at about noon. The death is extremely suspicious.’

Cleo frowned. ‘That’s tragic. But what does it have to do with me, Jack? I’m a trustee, involved only with funding matters. I leave the day-to-day running of the place to the employed staff. Are you saying there’s been a security breach or some kind of financial problem?’

Jack didn't answer her question. 'The dead woman is Louise Bennett. I understand you pulled a few strings to get her in. At the weekend, I think. Is that correct?'

Cleo put a hand to her mouth. 'Oh, my goodness.'

'Why did you ask for the rules to be bent to get her admitted, Mrs Cathcart?'

'Well, I wasn't aware of that, to be honest.'

Her voice was weak and shaky. Gwen sensed rising panic.

'My understanding, from talking to the warden, is that there's a waiting list. And I believe you asked her to bypass it to get Louise in. Can you tell me why you did that?'

Cleo took a sip of tea, her hand shaking visibly. She put the cup down hastily. 'She needed somewhere safe to go in a hurry. Look, I admit I used some leverage to get her admitted. But she was in danger.'

'Who from?' Jack asked.

'Well, as far as I know, the usual. Some ape of a man who was after her.'

'Did Louise tell you this herself?'

'I didn't actually meet her. I was acting on behalf of someone else. Did some drunken lout find her, then? Despite what we did?'

'Well, not exactly. It wasn't some crazed ex-husband or boyfriend who killed her. It was a woman. Louise was stabbed through the heart in cold blood and it looks as if it was carefully planned. So, who were you acting for? Who asked for her to be admitted?'

They were interrupted by the sound of the front door opening. Gwen looked up to see a burly, grizzly man come into the room.

'What's all this?' he asked. He looked at the two detectives, his eyes narrowing.

'We're talking to your wife about a serious incident at the hostel in Southampton, Gus. An inmate was murdered there this morning,' Jack said.

'Well, I don't want her interviewed without me or a lawyer being present. Is that clear?' the man snarled.

'This isn't a formal interview, Gus,' Jack said. 'There's no need to get bullish about it. We just need to clarify why the victim's admission was fast-tracked and normal procedures circumvented.'

'Piss off, Dunning. You come into my house only at my invitation. I'm not some bit of skanky lowlife you can push around, you know. Who do you think you're dealing with here? Show some respect. Now, get out.'

Gwen decided it was time for to intervene. 'I can carry out the interview, sir, if you'd both prefer, at a time and place of Mrs Cathcart's choosing. Either here or at the local station.' She passed her contact card to Cleo, who was looking even more shell-shocked than before.

Cathcart's gaze swivelled around to settle on Gwen, as if he'd spotted her for the first time. 'And who are you?'

'DS Gwen Davis. Hampshire police.'

'Well you can piss off too, DS Gwen Davis. Who the hell asked you to speak? Just get out, both of you.'

Gwen glanced at her boss, who signalled to her that it was better for them to leave. She deliberately took her time to finish her cup of tea. 'That was very nice, Mrs Cathcart. Thank you. Very refreshing.'

'What was that all about?' Gwen asked as they returned to their car.

Jack shook his head. 'I don't know. He was far worse than I expected. I never liked the man, as I said earlier, but that really was beyond a joke. He acted as if we were accusing Cleo of a crime.'

'What if that's what we were doing?'

Jack turned to face her. 'What do you mean?'

'We came to see her to find out why she'd bent the rules to get Louise admitted. What if the reason is connected to something shady? What if it wasn't her at all? What if it was him who was somehow behind Louise's admission? I watched him from the moment he came in. I tell you, he knew something. She was genuinely puzzled when we questioned her, but he didn't seem particularly surprised. It made me suspicious.

His bluster was just an attempt to put us off. That's why I gave her my card. I've a feeling she'll contact me.' She started the engine.

'Isn't that a bit fanciful? He's got an aggressive streak, that's all.'

'Trust me, boss. There's something not right back there. I think she'll phone.'

'Well, I hope you're right. I don't particularly relish the thought of going back again if it's only going to end up in another confrontation.' He smiled. 'But it was rather satisfying to see him getting so wound up. As I said earlier, I could never stand the man.'

'Well, leave it with me. If there's dirt, I'll find it. Then we can wind him up some more. What an insulting bastard. No man speaks to me in that arrogant, rude, patronising way and gets away with it. It was the way he looked at me, as if I counted for nothing in his eyes.'

'You have my blessing.'

'What makes you think I need it?'

They both laughed.

* * *

Gwen was home late that evening. She'd received a brief phone call from Cleo Cathcart just as she was about to leave. Cleo confirmed that her husband had wanted to move Louise somewhere safe but hadn't told her the reason. Barry's car was already on the drive and as Gwen stepped into the hallway, the aroma of warm cheese and tomato reached her. She walked through to the kitchen where Barry was setting cutlery on the table.

'I've made a quick pasta bake,' he said, looking up. 'It's just gone in the oven, so it'll take about twenty minutes. Do you want a drink?'

She gave him a hug. 'A cup of tea would be brilliant. Have you been in long?'

He shook his head. 'About half an hour. Has something cropped up at work?'

'Oh, yes.' She told him of the unusual murder case, then realised he was looking at her in a strange way. 'What is it? Why are you looking at me like that?'

'You need to sit down,' he said. 'I'll pour our teas then tell you something really interesting.'

CHAPTER 10: COMPLETE SLUG

Wednesday morning

'Have you ever come across Gus Cathcart?' Jack Dunning stirred his coffee and took a sip. It was very good. Maybe he should visit this café more often. It was less than ten minutes' walk from the CID offices. He knew he wouldn't though, certainly not on a regular basis. He was always too pushed for time. He was only here this morning for an off-the-record meeting with Sophie Allen.

She grimaced. 'Oh, yes. I slapped his face once, right in front of his own chief constable. I know some men can get a bit frisky when they've had a couple of drinks, and I can usually fend them off and stay on friendly terms with them afterwards. But he was something else entirely. His hands were all over my backside, squeezing, and I can't repeat the stuff he was whispering into my ear. We were in the queue for the buffet at a police charity reception. What he didn't realise was that his chief and deputy were behind us. Even I was only dimly aware of them approaching. I snapped when he started licking the back of my neck. I turned around and hit him as hard as I could. The whole place suddenly went silent. He walked away with this big red weal on his face. I didn't see him again that evening. He must have left immediately afterwards. In fact, I haven't seen him again, ever.'

'When was this?' Jack asked.

Sophie shrugged and took a sip from her own mug. 'About three months before he retired. I'd just landed the DCI job in Dorset but hadn't yet started. I spent a few days in Sussex with their unit, studying their methods. The ACC invited me to their Christmas charity function at the end of my visit. I have no idea what was going through Cathcart's head, but he'd been pestering me for the previous hour or more and wouldn't take no for an answer. I could only think he imagined I was a low-ranking bit of fluff invited along to keep the likes of him amused. He was a total tosspot. I got an apology from the chief who'd seen what he was doing.' She took another sip of coffee. 'Look, Jack, I've never told anyone about it and Martin must never know. Don't even mention it to Gwen, please.'

'Of course not. Cathcart married Cleo just after he retired, when his divorce papers came through. Apparently, he used to show her off at social events, even when he was supposedly still happily married to his previous wife.'

'Like I said, he's a complete slug. I don't expect he ever wants to see me again. I heard through the grapevine that it was his behaviour that night that helped to make the chief's mind up about pensioning him off,' Sophie said.

Jack looked thoughtful. 'So, if we ever wanted to really rattle his cage, we could send you in? Would you be up for that?'

She smiled widely and happily. 'Oh God, yes. Particularly after the way he spoke to Gwen yesterday. It doesn't sound as if he's changed at all. I pity his wife. Anyway, Jack, we mustn't get side-tracked. These two murders are worrying. Have you been digging into the background of the victim and hit the buffers like us? Nothing to be found?'

He nodded, playing with his coffee cup. 'We just can't find any information about Louise Bennett at all. It looks like someone's been doing a clean-up job. Either that or it wasn't her real name. Of course, we're a couple of days behind you. How are things going?'

Sophie frowned. 'Bloody slowly. We only have two leads. The couple spotted on the railway station on Saturday morning and the young guy Barry saw watching the back of the house. A few other things have cropped up but they're pretty weak at the moment. Then this, across here. It might give us the breakthrough we need. Rae spotted that one of the safe houses was in Southampton. Any connection so far?'

'I've got Gwen working on it. As yet, all we know is that it had a single woman occupant. No other details, but they'll come.'

'I did get a message from Jim Metcalfe, my ACC, this morning. It looks as though we might be on the right track with our people-trafficking connection, though he hasn't had it officially confirmed yet. But it's pretty close to what we thought. All he's found out so far is that there's an operation on to identify and infiltrate the gangs who are running the system. It's probably a joint effort with security units from France, Belgium and the Dutch. But Special Branch haven't been directly involved because it comes under some new security unit. It's all very hush-hush. We don't even know if the Border Agency are involved or whether it's just MI6. It's all just rumour. And that's it. I don't know anything else.'

'So, this connection to Gus Cathcart might be the best lead we currently have?' Jack said. 'Right. Should we do it now?'

'Absolutely, totally, yes. Let's go and skewer the bastard.'

'I'm just a bit bothered by going to see him without any leverage. He might well just slam the door in our faces, and then where will we be?'

Sophie finished her coffee and stood up. 'Jack, you should trust me. I thought you knew that by now. I got Rae, my DS, to do a bit of her expert digging first thing this morning and she came up with a nugget.'

He smiled happily. 'In that case, I'm convinced. His treatment of Gwen and me yesterday was several steps too far.'

* * *

The villa's front door opened, and Gus Cathcart glared out. His gaze landed on Jack Dunning and his face turned puce.

'What the hell . . . ?'

He stopped, seeming to realise that the woman standing beside Jack wasn't the same as the one who was with him the day before. His eyes flickered over her in puzzlement then, as realisation dawned, his face turned pale.

'Good morning, Mr Cathcart,' Sophie said. 'May we come in, please?'

Cathcart stepped out, pulling the door to behind him.

'Absolutely not. What kind of trick is this? What are you up to, Dunning, bringing her along?'

Jack said quietly, 'I didn't *bring her along*. Sophie Allen is a detective superintendent, and heads up Dorset's VCU. She's the senior officer here.'

'I don't care who the fuck she is. What I said yesterday still stands. Piss off.' He turned to go back inside.

'Better for you if you cooperate. You really won't like what will happen if you shut that door on us,' Sophie said.

Cathcart sneered. 'Yeah, well, you've got no leverage over me. Not now. I'm out of the force and very comfortable with it, thank you very much. You can do your worst and it won't make the slightest bit of difference to me.'

'Comfortable? Does that assessment take into account the fact that you've remortgaged the house without your wife's knowledge? And wasn't it her money that bought it in the first place? I can't imagine her being at all pleased when she learns about that. My guess is that you forged her signature.'

Cathcart stopped dead. His shoulders drooped.

'You always were a total prick,' Sophie went on. 'Everyone in the division knew it. That's why they kept shunting you around, trying to keep you out of harm's way. Desk job after desk job. Well, *ex*-Detective Chief Inspector Cathcart, now's your chance to do some good and set the record straight. May we come in, please?'

He pushed the door open and stood aside. They went in and found themselves facing Cleo, who was standing at the far end of the hall, staring at them.

'What's going on?' she asked.

'Detective Superintendent Sophie Allen, Dorset police. You've already met DCI Jack Dunning from Hampshire. We're investigating separate murder inquiries, but we've spotted a possible link. You, Mrs Cathcart, and your husband can help us. Can we find somewhere more comfortable to talk?'

They followed her into the room she and the two Hampshire detectives had used the previous day. Sophie turned to Cathcart, who was following them into the room.

'Maybe you can go and put the kettle on or something. We want to talk to Cleo alone for a couple of minutes.' Sophie took a seat and stared hard at Cathcart until he stalked out of the room. Cleo raised her eyebrows in surprise and sat down too.

Jack Dunning began. 'I'd like to thank you for calling DS Davis yesterday evening. It couldn't have been easy for you. I know it was only a few words, but it's opened a couple of avenues for us to explore.'

Cleo merely nodded. Despite the strained look on her face, her appearance was still flawless. Sophie speculated on her motivation for working so hard on her looks. Did it come from her own background, a mask covering an underlying insecurity? Or did it derive from her husband's bullying demands?

'We haven't met before, Mrs Cathcart, but I too want to thank you for the help you've already provided.' Sophie was speaking in her gentlest, most seductive tone. It was so different to the one she'd used a couple of minutes earlier, talking to her husband out on the front porch, that it took

Jack by surprise. 'These have all the hallmarks of a particularly difficult case, so any help you can give us is really appreciated.'

Cleo smiled weakly but said nothing. Jack sat back in his chair. He had the feeling that he was about to be treated to a masterclass in manipulation.

'You have a lovely house, such tasteful decor. Have you been here long?'

Cleo was visibly relaxing and brightening up. 'Nearly five years. I bought it when we married. I'd just sold my previous property in Wimbledon. I really love it, especially its views out to sea.'

'I can understand that completely. Now, in your call to DS Davis, you confirmed that it was your husband who wanted to get Louise into the hostel at the weekend. Did he explain why?'

Cleo shook her head. 'He just said it was complicated but that she needed somewhere safe in a hurry.'

'Were you happy about being asked to bend the admission rules? Even for a supposedly good cause like Louise's?'

'Not really. And Bella wasn't happy either. She said she already had a waiting list.' She looked puzzled. 'What do you mean by *supposedly good cause*?'

'Neither of you had met Louise or any of her case workers. You must have had doubts, surely?'

Cleo merely shrugged.

'Whose idea was it to suggest an increased donation to hostel funds?'

Cleo looked worried. 'That was Gus, beforehand. It was a fallback position, he said, in case my request was turned down.'

'Does that mean he was prepared for some resistance from the warden? Didn't that concern you? That what you were requesting was somewhat dubious?' Sophie's voice was still soft and conversational.

'Of course it did. I hate manipulating people. And being manipulated myself.'

They looked up as the door opened and her husband appeared, carrying a tray of mugs. He still looked sullen. He offered the mugs around, but Sophie refused hers, having seen the way her mug was carefully located on the tray, separate from the other three. 'No thanks. I wouldn't put it past you to have spat in mine.'

Cleo started. 'Have you two met before?'

'Yes,' Sophie replied quickly. 'At a charity function, as it happens, just a short while before your husband was offered early retirement. I think he made a major misjudgement about me and why I was there, so maybe the two events weren't unconnected.' She turned to face him. 'You need to tell us about Louise Bennett and why you pressured Cleo into getting her into Beechwood refuge.'

'I got a phone call, late on Saturday morning. I was asked if I knew somewhere a woman could hide, safe, for a few days. They said it was important.'

'Who's "they?"'

He shook his head. 'Just someone I know.'

'You need to be more specific. I'd like a name.'

He bristled with frustrated tension, fidgeting in his seat and running a hand across his head. 'Peter Zelinski. He's someone I knew in the old days. He's doing some kind of below the radar work for a government department. He said they'd had a security breach and needed to get this woman to somewhere secure in a hurry. He leaned on me quite hard. He knew about Cleo's role at the refuge. That's why he called me.'

Sophie watched him carefully. He didn't meet her eye. There was more, she was sure of it. 'He pressurised you, didn't he? You wouldn't have agreed to that without leverage being applied. My guess is that he threatened to spill the beans about something or other. And there's so much to choose from, isn't there? You are a walking, talking disaster area, Angus Cathcart. This Zelinski character, I bet he was someone else who was in and out of security work back in the old days. Am I right? Probably he's now doing some kind of freelance agency work and was hired by a senior civil servant for a few months. Well?'

He didn't respond.

'Honestly, you're all just kids playing games. Meanwhile, Jack and I are left to sort out the mess.' She sighed. 'I need to warn you both that the Official Secrets Act applies. Neither of you are to breathe a word of this to anyone, not until we get to the bottom of it. And Zelinski, whoever he is, is right. He does have a security breach on his hands. A bad one. Now, how do we get in contact with him?'

Cathcart checked his mobile phone and read out a number. 'Can you please not let on that you got it from me?'

'I'll do my best. What reason did he give for his request?'

'He didn't, and I didn't ask.'

Sophie stared at him. 'I don't believe that for one moment. You're an ex-cop, for goodness sake, and you were being asked to go to a lot of trouble to help them out. What was in it for you?'

He didn't answer.

'You got a backhander for it, didn't you?' Sophie said. She shook her head in exasperation. 'A woman in difficulties, maybe facing violence, and you had to be bribed to help her out. Unbelievable. There's something else that puzzles me. How did Louise get to the refuge? Who took her?'

Cathcart shook his head.

'There would have to be arrangements of some kind made beforehand. What day and time she might be expected, any immediate medical needs she might have, that kind of stuff. And some basic information about her for the hostel records. Who handled that?'

Sophie looked across at Cleo, who had her head in her hands. Was she crying?

'It was you, wasn't it? Both of you. The warden wouldn't have opened the door to just anybody. You'd have needed to be there, Cleo, having made the arrangements. So, tell me about it.'

Cleo finally looked up. 'We collected the woman from a house somewhere in Southampton. I stayed in the car while

Gus fetched her. There was a man in the house, but I only caught a glimpse of him. As soon as she and Gus climbed in, I drove off. We headed straight to the refuge and I went with her to sign her in. We came straight back here afterwards.'

'Did you talk to her?'

'Not really. She was very uncommunicative. She didn't say more than a dozen words.'

'Did she have an accent?'

Cleo shook her head. 'Not really. She was tense. Nervous.'

'She was probably scared,' Sophie said. 'She realised she was being moved in a hurry and guessed there'd been a security leak. Who else was at the house other than Zelinski?'

Reluctantly, Cathcart spoke. 'Nobody. And he was in a bit of a panic too.'

Sophie shook her head wearily. 'And it was all a waste of time. They got to her anyway.'

'Who? Who was it?' Cathcart asked.

'Do you think I'd tell a plonker like you, even if I did know? Get real.' She looked at her watch. 'We obviously need a full debrief somewhere more formal than this, and with someone of senior rank sitting in. I'll contact my ACC across in Dorset and we'll go either for this afternoon or tomorrow morning.'

She stopped and looked at the Cathcarts, both of whom were staring at the floor despondently. 'Have you considered the possibility that the two of you might be in danger? Once we've got all the facts from you, it might be wise to disappear for a few days. As long as we know where you are. And as long as it's not too far. Look at it this way, we're giving you an excuse to have a holiday. What's not to like?'

CHAPTER 11: UNDER THE RADAR

Thursday morning

'I just don't get it. Why would they set it up like this? Why bypass all the normal agencies?' Matt Silver, who was speaking, was one of the same four senior officers who had met two days previously. Then, they'd been blundering about in the dark. They now knew rather more, but it made them even more uneasy than before. 'It just doesn't seem credible. Why would whoever's behind this business choose to construct a unit from people on the fringes of the intelligence services and retired Special Branch personnel? Why not use the usual security channels?'

Jim Metcalfe sat back in his chair. 'That's what we're here for, Matt. To piece together what's been happening. One thing seems obvious to me. By doing it this way, they avoid the normal scrutiny that usually accompanies an operation like this. No parliamentary committees, no detailed record keeping, nothing that might leak out to the press.'

'Do we know who *they* are?' Sophie asked.

Karen Brody cleared her throat. 'Umm, it's beginning to look as though it might be the junior minister at the Home

Office. The one in charge of the "immigration crisis," as it's called.'

'Mad Ken Burke,' Matt said. 'It figures.'

'And possibly his Parliamentary Private Secretary,' Karen added. 'That's all I've been able to track down. It's based on little more than rumour, though.'

'Yauvani Anand,' Matt added. 'Just a tiny bit reactionary. Subtlety isn't exactly a strong point with either of them.'

'I'm aware that they don't like the chains of command in the orthodox security services,' Jim said. 'I remember going to a conference a couple of years ago at the start of the refugee crisis in Europe. The two of them were there and they were openly hostile to the somewhat hands-off approach being followed at the time. Neither of them was an official speaker. After all, Burke didn't hold a government post back then. But the questions they posed made their views obvious. Hard-line in the extreme. That's all very well, but when it leads to a policy that would result in hundreds of people being left to drown on the open seas, then it's questionable. He's toned down his rhetoric since he took up the ministerial job, but . . .'

'So, by setting up this special unit in this way, they're operating under the radar? And they can employ people whose views match their own and whose methods might be questionable?' Matt said.

'Looks like it. But remember we're only speculating. The trouble is, I can't think of any other explanation. Nothing else makes sense.' He looked across the low table to Sophie Allen. 'You've been quiet, Sophie. Anything to add?'

She shook her head slightly. 'It's the deliberate ignoring of the law that gets to me. All these countries signed up to international treaties decades ago. We did too. The basic human rights of all individuals are enshrined in those treaties. They're protected by them. Yet in the eyes of these kinds of people, we can just conveniently ignore those rights when it's advantageous for us to do so. That's the line peddled by people like Burke and Anand. Which means leaving people to starve or be bombed to death if they stay at home, or drown if they try to escape. And do you know? That's just the kind of person Cathcart is too. That's his approach to life exactly. Life's brutal, so if you fail, tough shit. You're not from my neighbourhood or family or tribe, so piss off and die. It's not my problem.'

'That's as may be, but it doesn't help us, Sophie. We've got to come up with a workable plan. That's what the chief wants.'

'Sorry. I was a young and idealistic law student once. A workable plan? Let me sweat Cathcart and Zelinski. Cathcart thinks he's such a tough guy. I love needling macho men like him.'

Jim frowned and glanced at the paper in front of him. 'Have you got anywhere with this other name? What was it? Corinne Lanston? The name the properties were registered to. Didn't you say she was at the Home Office somewhere?'

'*Was* is the operative word. Apparently she's gone on prolonged sick leave. It smacks a bit of tidying up loose ends. But I've got one of my team working on it, so we'll find her soon.'

'But Burke and Anand are government ministers. They wouldn't be involved in anything criminal, like murder. They're just doing what they think is right,' Karen said.

'I don't think we're saying that they're involved in these killings, Karen,' Jim said. 'My own guess is that progress was too slow in identifying the criminals running the trafficking operations. So, Burke and Anand came up with their own scheme to get things moving. Maybe they tried to infiltrate these gangs, but someone blew the cover on their operatives. They pulled them back to these supposed safe houses that weren't as safe as they should have been.'

'I wonder if they've got a mole,' Matt added.

'What I can say is that we're joining forces with Hampshire on this case. The quick work of Sophie's squad in hotfooting it across there has given us these two insiders, Cathcart and Zelinski. I'm not implying they've done anything seriously wrong either. They're not the killers. As for interviewing them, you can take Zelinski, Sophie, but not Cathcart. You've obviously got too much negative history with him. The Hampshire people want to deal with him and I'm happy with that. Does that seem a fair split? Meanwhile, Karen, you use your contacts to trace the whereabouts of this Lanston woman. Work alongside Sophie's DS, Rae Gregson. She's already started on it.'

Sophie was annoyed at having someone else allocate tasks to the members of her unit but felt it wise not to object at this point. The ACC was having to tread a tightrope without a safety net. Better to let this one go.

* * *

Peter Zelinski was as far removed from Gus Cathcart in both appearance and manner as it was possible to be. Controlled and watchful, he peered at them through rimmed glasses. He reminded Sophie of World War Two photos of Himmler — short, slim and in his late fifties. He'd voluntarily agreed to an interview, so Sophie had driven across to Southampton CID and, accompanied by Gwen, set off to see him at his home. He lived alone in a semi-detached house close to the city centre. From the outside the building was nondescript, but the interior was a different matter. Zelinski showed the two detectives into the living room and asked them to wait while he made some tea. Sophie gazed at the very minimalist furnishings. Usually, she took advantage of such moments to look at the photographs on display. Not on this occasion. There were no pictures. Nor were there any shelves to put them on. The room revealed nothing about the personality of the man who lived here. Did he have something to hide, or was he totally self-contained?

Zelinski came back into the room with a tray of chinaware and deposited it on a low, glass-topped table.

'A few things we should get clear before we start,' he said, settling himself into a chair. 'I've done nothing wrong. I'm doing a special job for the Home Office immigration unit and everything has been agreed by the minister. I'm co-operating because of the murders you're investigating. I want to make it clear that I'm on your side. I want the killers found. If you in any way imply that I'm some kind of suspect, I will terminate the meeting and ask you to leave.'

'I'm sure we share the same interests, Mr Zelinski,' Sophie said. 'So, what can you tell us?'

The story he told was exactly as the ACC had suspected.

'I'm working for the Home Office in a unit set up to investigate the people traffickers bringing migrants across the Channel.'

'Who heads up this unit?' Sophie asked.

'I can't tell you that. I'm sticking to an agenda agreed by my boss, and that isn't on it. We've had a couple of operatives in France, trying to identify the main traffickers. We're convinced some of them are Brits, out to make a quick buck. We know some routes are run by foreign gangs but not all. Our people were trying to get some of the junior gang members to give us information in exchange for a promise of a future here if they're from elsewhere. We had someone ready to spill the beans. Then all this happened.'

'So, how did the information about their locations leak out?' Gwen said. 'Have you traced that leak?'

Zelinski shook his head. 'I haven't been told and I think I would be if the leak had been identified.'

'But you were told that the address of the safe house this so-called Louise was in had been compromised. That's why you had to move her in a hurry. Where did that information come from?' Gwen asked.

'You've got that wrong. It didn't come from above. I got wind of what had happened to Robert Bunting through other channels and the press, so I made the decision to move Louise. I told the powers that be, rather than the other way around.'

'Did you pass on the information about her new location?' Sophie said.

'Of course. It had to be in the official record in case anything happened to me.'

'Do you know anything more specific about these two, Mr Zelinski?' asked Sophie. 'Maybe what the Home Office was hoping to get from them?'

'Nothing more than what I've already told you.'

'That's what I have difficulty in believing, Mr Zelinski,' Sophie said. 'From what you've told us, you were Louise's main contact. Surely you found out something about her background?'

He shrugged. 'I can't discuss anything with you that's classified. Those are my instructions.'

'You've acknowledged that it's our job to solve these murders, but you don't seem aware that we can't do that without an understanding of the bigger picture. So far, it's all rather minimal, little more than we'd already guessed,' Sophie said.

Zelinski shrugged again. 'I'm telling you only what's been cleared from above. Nothing else.'

'Who's your boss?' Sophie asked.

'I can't tell you that.'

'Where does Corinne Lanston fit into this?' Sophie asked.

Zelinski paused. 'I can't talk about personnel. It would breach my instructions.'

'Were Louise and Bunting the only ones? Do you have any others?' she asked.

'I'm not permitted to tell you that.'

Sophie was beginning to find it hard to hold her anger in check. 'For pity's sake, Mr Zelinski. This isn't some kind of game. People's lives are on the line here.'

'Nevertheless, that's my answer.'

Sophie thought hard. Time to change direction. 'Why was that refuge chosen as a safe location for Louise?'

'It's got good internal security, and it's pretty nondescript and below the radar. It seemed a good choice at the time. I was in a hurry to get her somewhere safe, as I said.'

'How did you know about it?' she asked.

'I phoned Gus Cathcart and asked him for advice. I knew he could be trusted.'

Sophie thought it wise not to question his assertion, not yet. Even though she had her doubts about Cathcart, they related to him as a person. They had no evidence that he was a security weak link. 'What's your relationship with him, Mr Zelinski?'

'I've known him for a long time, since he was a Special Branch liaison officer in Sussex. Since he retired, we've been meeting fairly regularly for a game of golf.'

'Is that where you learned of Cleo's links with the refuge?'

He nodded.

'So, the idea was yours but not the final decision?' Sophie asked.

'That's right. Look, don't you think I feel bad about what happened there? It was my idea and it went spectacularly wrong. That woman died. But if we'd left her where she was, she'd have been killed anyway.'

'I'm glad that makes you feel better,' Sophie said dryly. 'So, can you assure me that people are trying to trace the leak?'

'Of course. We're not amateurs, despite what you obviously think. Again, that's all I'm allowed to tell you. But we are doing all we can.'

'I need a contact person, Mr Zelinski. I'm running a double murder inquiry, and so much that could help us is tied up with the leak of their whereabouts. We need to work together. I suggest you consult your boss again, and then contact me. You're a material witness and obviously know a lot more than you're letting on. I find that reprehensible, and I won't tolerate it. Let your boss know that and we'll speak again tomorrow.'

Though he looked troubled, Zelinski refused to say anything else, so the two detectives rose to leave. As they did so, Zelinski's phone rang. He listened, his previously impassive face growing tense.

On their way to the car, Gwen said, 'We didn't get very far, did we, ma'am? What do we do now?'

Sophie made a wry face. 'Maybe we got more than he intended. The name Corinne Lanston definitely set off a nerve. It wasn't just that he clammed up after that, he reacted when I mentioned her by name. So, she's clearly more important than a mere administrative assistant. Then there's the fact that they weren't really prepared for anything to go wrong. I got the feeling that panic might have set in and they've been making decisions on the hoof. That's not good for an important initiative like this one. I think the whole thing was too rushed and badly thought through. Which begs the question, who or what is driving the agenda? And something in that phone call upset him badly. Did you see the way his face went pale? It looked like really bad news. Maybe we'll hear something from him by tomorrow.'

'That was really useful,' Gwen said. 'I'm interviewing Cathcart in an hour or so, with Jack, so I can compare what the two of them say. Exciting times!'

Sophie pulled out into the traffic. 'Something else has occurred to me. The so-called nurse knew that Louise's birthday was the following day. She also knew that Louise was due a dressing change and where the injury was. Interesting, don't you think?'

* * *

Gwen looked at Gus Cathcart and smiled. 'I'm sure this is going to be a much more productive interview than the brief conversation we had a couple of days ago, Mr Cathcart. DCI Dunning and I just want to get to the facts.'

On the drive over, she and Jack had agreed that, initially, Gwen should take the lead, if only to obtain some recompense for the insults she'd endured during their previous visit.

'You see, I'm a logical kind of person, so I'd like to get the facts straight. All of them. So, shall we start with when and how you first met Peter Zelinski?'

Cathcart still seemed sullen. 'A long time ago. I was with Special Branch and liaised with the other security services in the county. That was my role. He was doing some work for MI6 on the terrorist threat. He needed some local knowledge, so I was asked to step in.'

'And you kept in contact with him? How?'

He shrugged. 'We played golf a few times a year. It gave us an opportunity to exchange views. That kind of thing.'

'Has he been with MI6 ever since?' she asked.

'You'll have to ask him that.'

'No, I'm asking you.'

Cathcart fidgeted in his chair. He was clearly uneasy about something. 'No. He went freelance for a while. I don't know the details, but he did some press work at one time. Look, why don't you ask him about it?'

'That's in hand, Gus,' Jack Dunning said. 'You know how it works. We crosscheck the fine detail.'

'Yeah, and make me feel like a criminal in the process. He's alright. He'll have official protection from someone on high. I feel as if I'm being hung out to dry.'

'There's no need to feel that way, Mr Cathcart,' Gwen said. 'You're a retired police officer. That carries some standing, certainly with me.'

'Well, that's reassuring to know. And I'll tell you why. Because I suddenly feel very alone and very exposed here. And it's not right.' Cathcart was almost whining.

Gwen decided to put the conversation back on track. 'Are you aware of how this unit he works for has been set up, and who by?'

Cathcart shook his head. 'I didn't meet anyone else. Pete plays his cards close to his chest. I did jobs he asked me to do and he paid in cash.'

At last he'd let something slip. Gwen kept her voice even. 'What jobs did he ask you to do, Mr Cathcart?'

Cathcart shrugged. 'Information mainly. What was going on in my neck of the woods. Local extremist organisations. Animal rights. Environmental groups that are considered a threat. Anything really.'

'You said *mainly*. Were there a couple of jobs that weren't just information?' Gwen asked.

'He asked me to go along to a couple of meetings of these groups. I think he wanted to know whether some of the threats were real.'

'And?'

Cathcart laughed. 'Most of them are just disorganised rabbles. They make a lot of noise but never get much done. The meetings are like that, full of young hotheads who couldn't organise their way out of a paper bag. He wanted reassurance in that regard, and I supplied it.'

'Do you know what he did with the information?' Jack said.

'Fed it on up the chain, I guess. Someone wanted it. It was all pretty low level until this latest one, smuggling people in from across the Channel. That's when it got serious.'

'Have you heard the name Corinne Lanston?'

There was a pause. 'I don't think so. I can't recall it.'

Gwen closed her notebook. Interesting. He'd suddenly become more alert on hearing that name but had tried hard not to show it.

Jack indicated that they should leave. The front door was just shutting behind them when his phone rang. 'That was the forensic guys,' he said to Gwen. 'Something odd. They've found a couple of dark hairs on the cakes left in Louise's room. They're synthetic, from a wig. It looks as though the killer was in disguise.'

'I think we knew that, boss, didn't we? We'd already decided she wasn't a real nurse.' She raised her eyebrows.

'You know what I mean.'

CHAPTER 12: RITCHIE

Friday morning

Tommy Carter was puzzled by the activities of the youth he was keeping on his radar, the young man Barry had spotted lurking behind Bunting's house. There wasn't the time to spend more than an hour or two catching up on his comings and goings, not with the way the case had recently opened up, but Rae had suggested that he should still try to build up a picture of him and his life.

Ritchie Finn lived with his ageing parents in a large semi-detached house in one of Weymouth's leafier districts. Except that they weren't his birth parents. A childless couple, they'd adopted Ritchie when he was young and they were already in their late middle age. This had puzzled Tommy when he'd first discovered it, until he found that they were blood relatives, his aunt and uncle on his father's side. Ritchie spent some time in the middle of each day out on his bicycle, meeting with various friends. He didn't seem to have a job, nor did he attend college. This was a puzzle. Surely a young person like him should be doing one or the other? Tommy knew that some young people took a year off between school and university to do voluntary work of some kind, but Ritchie didn't seem to be involved with any charity work. So, what did he do with his time, and why had he been watching Robert Bunting's house?

Tommy had yet again spent a fruitless hour keeping an eye on Ritchie Finn's house before returning to the incident room to get on with other tasks. Surely there were more important things to do. He decided to speak to his boss about it.

'I think you're right,' Rae said. 'We need to speak to the lad. Keeping him under surveillance is going nowhere. I'll check with the DI and then we'll go and see him.'

'Do we need a parent there?'

Rae shook her head. 'No. We would if this were a formal interview, but it isn't. Anyway, if we catch him at home, one or the other of them might be around. Didn't you say they were quite elderly?'

The two detectives drove to the Finn house, knocked on the door and waited. It was opened by a petite, grey-haired woman in her sixties.

Rae introduced them. 'Good morning, Mrs Finn. I'm DS Rae Gregson and this is DC Tommy Carter. We'd like to speak to Ritchie, if he's in. He isn't in any trouble, but we have reason to believe he may have witnessed something suspicious and might be able to offer us some help.'

'Come in,' said Ritchie's mother, looking anxious. 'He's up in his room. I'll get him.'

They followed her into a sitting room and, while she went to call Ritchie, studied the few photos on display. All featured Mrs Finn with a man of similar age, presumably her husband. In a few, Ritchie was with them.

The woman returned with Ritchie. 'Do you want me to stay?' she asked.

'It's entirely up to Ritchie,' Rae answered, with a questioning look at the youth. 'As I said, he isn't in any trouble — at least we don't think so.'

'No, I'll see them on my own, thanks.'

'Well, call if you need me.' Mrs Finn retreated from the lounge, still looking worried.

'Shall we sit down?' Rae said.

They seated themselves on the couch and Ritchie sat in an armchair facing them, looking anxious.

'Ritchie, we're following up on an observation a colleague of ours made last weekend. We believe that you were outside the back of Robert Bunting's house last weekend. You appeared to be watching it. Robert had just been found dead in suspicious circumstances and we're investigating his death. We want to know why you were there.'

Ritchie shrugged. 'I dunno. I just was.'

'He was murdered, Ritchie. We have to follow up every lead, if only to eliminate people. We think you were there for a reason. Did you know him?'

Ritchie looked at the floor. The penny dropped. Rae told herself to be extra delicate.

'I think you did know him, Ritchie. It's possible that you knew him better than anyone else in Weymouth. He was in hiding, living in a safe house. He should have been out of harm's way, but someone got to him on Friday night, at the railway station. So why were you hanging around the back of his house on Saturday?'

Ritchie, silent, kept his eyes fixed firmly on the floor.

'Look, Ritchie. We promise to be discreet. I'm transgender, and I do voluntary support work for the LGBT community here in Dorset. Am I likely to blab about you? And DC Carter here knows that his career will be on the line if he talks about either of us, you or me. Isn't that right, Tommy?'

Tommy nodded vigorously but couldn't hide his surprise. 'Sure, boss.'

'We were due to meet for lunch,' Ritchie began slowly, 'but he didn't turn up. I was worried about him.'

'Did you meet him on a regular basis?'

'Just a couple of times a week. He shouldn't have been out, not really. But he said staying in was driving him mental.'

'I need to make this an official interview, Ritchie, with DC Carter taking notes. What you say could be really important to us.'

Ritchie nodded, albeit somewhat reluctantly.

'How did you meet?' Rae asked.

'In a bar in town. It's a place where gay people go. It was only a month or so ago and it was my first visit there. It was Rob's first time there too, he'd only just arrived back in the town. We got talking. He seemed to like me, even though he's ten years older.'

'Did you visit him at his house?'

'Yeah, a couple of times. He only came out occasionally, when being shut up there really got to him. Look, what happened to him?'

'I can't give you the full details, but he was stabbed late on Friday night, at the station.'

'Was it a hate crime, you know, 'cause he was gay?'

'No, we don't think so,' Rae said. 'It was more likely to be linked to the reason he was under protection. We're pretty sure he was stabbed just after he got off the last train. Apparently, he'd used that train a couple of times before. Did he ever say why?'

Ritchie was silent for a few moments. 'He never really said. I kind of thought it might have been an ex-partner, but I never knew for sure.'

'Did he travel all the way from London?' Rae asked.

'I don't think so. He let slip once that he was about to visit a woman he knew in Southampton. He clammed up about it though, and never said anything else.'

'Do you know what his line of work was, Ritchie?'

'He used to work on the fishing boats, here in Weymouth. Then that all stopped, and he did something else. He never told me what it was, just that he'd walked out on it, and he was keeping quiet until things settled down. That was all he said.' His lip quivered. 'He was a really nice guy. I liked him a lot.'

Rae saw that he was really distressed. 'This is off the record, Ritchie. Was he your first boyfriend?'

'Yeah. I feel a bit lost now, to be honest. I never knew what I really felt about him until he wasn't there anymore. I feel a lot worse than I thought I would.'

Rae handed him her card. 'Phone me if things get too bad. I'll be back in touch anyway because we need you to make a formal statement. And, please, think through everything he told you. There'll still be some little clues that might not seem important to you, but could help us a lot. By the way, we think he was limping when he got off the train. A witness at the station said he'd seen him before, and that he was limping then. Is that right?'

'Yeah,' Ritchie said. 'He'd hurt his leg while he was working on one of the fishing boats. That's what he said happened. That's why he'd given it up and found different work. Whoever took him on said that his leg injury didn't really matter. He wouldn't talk much about that work though, except that it obviously didn't work out. He clammed up when I asked him about it.'

CHAPTER 13: OXFORD

Friday evening

Jade Allen stood in the ticket hall at Oxford railway station, craning her neck and trying to spot George in the crowd of people coming through the ticket barrier. She was taller than average but was finding it difficult to pick him out among all those people. She breathed a sigh of relief when she recognised the familiar dark, spiky hair and cheerful face. He'd seen her too — not difficult considering the coat she was wearing, her favourite bright red, crushed velvet one that had been a birthday present from her grandmother. Her father teasingly described it as being made from curtain material.

At last, George was standing in front of her. She flung her arms around him. 'I'm so glad to see you,' she said. 'I've missed you.'

He grinned at her. 'I've missed you too. Work has been a bit mad this week and I've been really looking forward to this weekend. So, what's the plan?'

Jade grabbed his hand and pulled him towards the exit. 'We'll head back to the college and check you in. I've got you one of the guest rooms for the weekend, like I said. Dump your stuff, do what you need to and then I thought we could head out for a Thai meal in this great place off the High, with a couple of friends I've made. Then we'll maybe do one of the pubs and head back to the college. There's a sort of social and disco in the common room, and I ought to show my face.' She paused. 'I'm so glad to see you.'

He kept smiling. 'Anything you want to do is fine by me. So, you've already made some friends?'

'Oh, yes. Not just the other medics at Keble, but some of the students who've got rooms near mine. I'm lucky, I've got a really lush room.' She pulled him close again. 'Listen, I know you've officially got a guest room, but we can be flexible about that. It'll take us about twenty minutes to walk there. Is that okay?' Jade was almost jumping up and down in her excitement.

'I've been sitting on a train for a couple of hours. A walk will be good. A walk with you will be even better. And I especially like your idea of being flexible.'

Jade was so full of happiness that she thought she might burst. Her first week had gone really well, on both the work and social fronts. She'd joined several Keble-based clubs and societies, including a salsa class, and Oxford SU Womcam, a feminist group that spanned the whole university. She'd enjoyed several ice-breaking parties, had got off to a good start with her tutor, had already managed to visit a couple of good pubs and sent reports about them back to her parents, and had still found time for several long phone conversations with George. True, it often felt that she was trying to balance too many balls in the air, but wasn't that what life was about at her age?

'Have you ever been to Oxford before, George?' she asked as they strolled towards the city centre.

He shook his head. 'No. And it wasn't even worth thinking about trying here when I was doing my university applications, not with the grades I was likely to get. I'm a bit overawed by it all, to be honest.'

Jade poked him in the side. 'Don't be. Most of the students here are very normal, though some can be a bit intense. The Hooray-Henry types are in a minority now, in most of the colleges. And we wind up anyone who sounds too posh or snobby. Anyway, I've always been brought up by Mum and Dad to value a person for qualities like kindness and empathy rather than status. And you've got those in bucketloads. That's unless you've been kidding me for the past few months.'

He poked her back. 'Yeah, that's me. A wolf in sheep's clothing. Seriously, Jade, I do sometimes feel a bit of an outsider in the police. Your mum didn't exactly talk me into it, but she gave me a lot of encouragement. It wasn't something I'd ever thought of doing when I was growing up. I sometimes worry about how well I'm doing.'

'Yeah, well, you've got mad Rose for your boss, haven't you? She's famous across the whole of Dorset, though everyone seems to think a lot of her.'

He smiled. 'I wondered what I'd let myself in for at first, but you're right. She's very human and warm-hearted underneath. As well as being a total nutcase. She told me you were a nugget of gold and I needed to treasure you.'

'Well, I hope you do everything your boss tells you. Actually, there is someone you might be interested in meeting if there's a chance, though she might not be around much at the weekend. She's one of the law tutors and her speciality is in the international treaties and declarations that apply to political asylum and refugees. She was at one of the fresher shows and I had a chat with her. She was interested in all the FGM stuff that Hannah and I do.'

'Are you doing the right subject, Jade? I mean, here you are set to study medicine, yet all your activities are connected to civil liberties and human rights. I've thought that before, but I've never been brave enough to say anything.'

Jade snorted. 'What, and do Law, like my mum did? You must be joking. No, it might be important to me, but I really do want to be a doctor. It's what I've always wanted to do, ever since

I went to stay with my gran when I was small. She's not a doctor but she's the practice manager of a surgery in Bristol. I went in with her a couple of times and she found me little things to do. It was great. But it would be perfect if there was a way to link the two things.' She gripped George's arm tight. 'We're just coming up to the Martyr's Memorial. It was built to commemorate three bishops who, in Tudor times, were burned to death for their beliefs. Queen Mary wanted the country to revert to Catholicism, and these bishops resisted. The actual spot where they were executed is just round the corner outside Balliol College.'

George looked up at the monument and shook his head. 'Bad times.'

'I wonder if I'm in the wrong college,' Jade mused. 'I knew vaguely that Keble was named after someone famous in the nineteenth century but didn't bother finding out what this John Keble stood for. He was one of the leaders of the Oxford Movement, which wanted a partial return to Catholicism, though not a full-blown merger with Rome.'

George turned to look at her. 'Does it matter that much these days? My dad was a lapsed Catholic. He spent most of his life resenting the indoctrination he'd been subjected to as a child. It doesn't really mean much now, does it?'

Jade nodded. 'And quite right too. Protestants aren't really any better either. Every religion tries its best to brainwash children when they're at their most vulnerable. Their fairy tales about heaven and hell and the creation appeal to young children. It's such rubbish.'

'Yet people fall for it,' George added.

'Well, it's a comfort blanket, isn't it? But one that too often ends up leading to prejudice, torture, abuse and even murder. Almost anything is justifiable if it's carried out in the name of some religion or other, and it's hard to argue with people who think they're in possession of the truth.' She paused. 'Anyway, it's time we got moving. I'm getting hungry.'

* * *

Jade had been right about Professor Alice Linklater. She held several positions in the university. As well as being a tutor in Jurisprudence at Keble, she was a prominent expert on human rights law, particularly in an international context, and she spoke at seminars and conferences across the world. Her current concern was the plight of asylum seekers and refugees fleeing conflict in Africa and the Middle East, people who had no choice but to take flight from their homes but who were all too often treated with contempt by comfortably-off westerners with their saloon bar opinions on migrants. It was a term that she herself used in discussing the crisis. An issue that was complex and involved real human suffering was dismissed out of hand, as if people had no right to seek to escape violence and destitution. Was there still such a lack of imagination among so many British people that, despite the media coverage, they couldn't see the human turmoil and misery that went on in much of the world?

Alice also acted as a counsellor to women students who felt themselves at risk from the predatory behaviour of a few of their male counterparts. She worked with male students too, advising on what was acceptable, helping to write leaflets and pamphlets that were distributed in common rooms across all the colleges of the ancient university. Everyone gains from being non-exclusionary, she often said. Men and women all benefit from a better understanding of the issues surrounding human interaction, no matter what their gender.

She had popped into the college, along with her husband, on their way home from a concert in the Holywell Music Room. After chatting with several of her own law students she was on her way out from the common room when she met Jade and George, who were just arriving. Jade gave her a cheery smile.

'So, who's this, Jade?'

'My boyfriend, George, Professor Linklater. He's visiting for the weekend.'

'It's Alice, not Professor, particularly on a Saturday night in the JCR.' Alice turned to George. 'Are you a student somewhere else, then?'

George laughed. 'No. My student days are long gone. I'm a serving police officer in Dorset, though I did a degree in Business Economics at Bournemouth University. Not quite as illustrious as this place.'

'A police officer in Dorset?' Alice frowned, and then her expression cleared. 'Jade, does that mean . . . ?'

'Please don't ask me, er, Alice. It just gets too embarrassing sometimes.'

Alice smiled. 'Yes, I can understand that. We're all a bit touchy when it comes to our parents. But we do know each other, even if these days we just exchange Christmas cards.'

'I know. It was me that addressed the envelopes last year. Um, there was something I was wanting to ask you, Professor. Next year I can choose an option towards my degree. Would there be anything in medical jurisprudence, do you think?'

'I expect so. I think we've run something like that a couple of times in the past. Leave it for a few weeks and then check with the Dean. Let me know if they say no, I can always try to cobble something together for you. But right now, you need to get yourself in there and enjoy the evening.' She cocked her head in the direction of the thump of music inside. 'That's Frankie Goes to Hollywood. Come on, Teddy, we can do this, can't we?'

Her husband, silent up to this point, rolled his eyes. 'If you insist, dear.' He turned to Jade and George. 'This was her favourite in the days when we went clubbing, what, some twenty years ago now.'

Alice poked him in the ribs. "Don't pretend you didn't like it too. I recall you had some special moves to this one. "Relax. Don't Do It . . ." She grabbed his arm and pulled him towards the door.

Jade and George followed them into the JCR and onto the small, packed dance-floor. Jade still glowed with happiness.

CHAPTER 14: THE BOAT

Friday night

Out on the water, the night was cold. At least the wind wasn't particularly strong, the waves not particularly high. So Kamal Bahrami kept telling himself, huddled down against the side of the boat alongside his younger sister, Arshi. She was whimpering. He could feel the tremors that ran through her small body, followed by the occasional heaving sob. Kamal tried to be brave, but it was hard not to cry. He must not break down in front of all these other people, though from the look of them they were all frightened, every single one of them packed into the overcrowded boat. Back on shore, he'd heard his father asking how long the crossing would take. Just two or three hours, according to one of the men pushing the boat out to sea. But that man had remained ashore, which from the worried frown on his father's face, could mean he was lying. Only one of the trio of men had come with them. Kamal wondered if this was normal. Was one crewman enough on a boat like this, packed as it was?

The men had provided everyone in Kamal's family with a lifejacket, which he knew had cost his father more money.

He'd seen the anger on the faces of some of the other migrants. They'd all been told lifejackets were included in the original payment, but when they were about to board the boat the men had demanded more money. Some of the families had already spent all their cash and were forced to travel with no protection. Even the few jackets that were provided were of poor quality, and Kamal, young as he was, guessed that the vests he and his sister had been given wouldn't be of much use if they ended up in the cold water, swamped by waves. They were already taking on water. It was carrying so many people that the boat was sitting far too low. Every time a bigger wave struck the side, water would slop into the vessel where it mixed with the muck already sloshing around Kamal's feet. At least the stiff breeze blew away some of the smell — sour body odour, vomit, shit even. Some of the men tried to scoop the foul liquid out with tin cups and whatever containers they could find. But the wind blew some of the muck straight back at them, mixed with sea spray. This fine mist soaked everything on board, including the passengers. No wonder Arshi had spent the entire sea crossing in tears. This was hell, and it was getting worse.

He tried to remember his geography lessons. Didn't the gap between England and France get wider further west? So, why hadn't they crossed at the narrow part? He recalled a conversation between his father and another man during the journey through mainland Europe. That man had argued that it would be better to take the shortest route, but Kamal's father had seen newspaper stories that told of boats being intercepted at sea and the people on board taken back to France. He thought there was a better chance of getting to England further west, even though the Channel was much wider there. Kamal's father was an engineer and had spent time at the university in Southampton, so he knew that part of England well, along with people who lived there. He'd know where they were when they landed. Kamal's uncle and aunt lived in a coastal town called Weymouth. They'd offered to help, once the Bahrami family were ashore.

Arshi's tremors had ceased. Kamal looked down and saw that she was finally asleep, though her face was still pale and pinched beneath the damp blanket. Maybe she'd sleep through the rest of the trip. He had a feeling they were only halfway. No one was allowed to shine a light, so he couldn't check his watch, but they seemed to have been in the boat for more than two hours. He took off his glove, pulled a grubby handkerchief out of his pocket and blew his nose. His mother, Roya, turned to look at him, so he gave her a weak smile. Kamal had listened to some of his parents' late-night conversations when they'd thought he was asleep. He had heard his father imploring her to please agree to leave Iran, and his mother resisting those pleas. She'd finally given in when a neighbouring family had been rounded up for taking part in a protest. They'd never been seen again, and reports reached the neighbourhood that they'd all been killed. His mother finally agreed to go.

At first the trip had been exciting. They'd made out they were flying to Serbia on holiday. Kamal's father had explained that Serbia was trying to build links with Iran and encouraged holiday visits. Once they were in Serbia, they slipped out of their hotel one night and made their way to the first in a series of hostels in Belgrade, then across to the west of the country. That was when Kamal first realised the true power of money. There were people of other nationalities also trying to move west, but many of them had very little cash, certainly not enough to pay for rail and air tickets. Kamal's family were among the favoured few because they could pay. His father's professional status as a graduate engineer, and his ability to negotiate deals in English, meant that the family moved relatively quickly through central Europe and into France. They travelled on false passports purchased in Iran and sewn into a pocket hidden in the lining of one of their suitcases. France wasn't their final destination however. His father was one of Iran's top bridge construction experts and his year in Southampton, studying for a master's degree in civil engineering, had decided him that England was where his family would settle. He'd admired the freedoms open to people in Britain: to work, study, think, vote, read and even worship in any way you chose. Of course, France had these freedoms too, as did the other countries of Western Europe, but Kamal's parents both spoke fluent English, and the rest of the family were almost as good. His Uncle Saman, Roya's brother, ran a café and his Aunt Jenny, who was British by birth, managed a garden centre. Kamal's family would have a place to stay with them. His father explained all this to Kamal as they moved slowly westwards, from city to city, country to country.

Kamal idolised his father. To Kamal he was everything a good father should be — wise, calm and principled. He loved his mother too, but she was quieter and more nervous about the upheaval. She was also well-educated, with a degree in agricultural science. But she'd never been outside Iran before, and she came from a devout Islamic family. Leaving the country in the way they had meant that she was turning her back on her family and the tight-knit society of the mosque.

So here they all were, hunched up in a small boat that was starting to pitch and roll as it made its way towards the supposedly safe shores of southern England. The journey seemed endless to Kamal, and he started to pray. At last, he too fell into a light doze.

* * *

Kamal awoke with a start as the boat lurched and a mass of water crashed over the side, soaking him and filling the bottom of the boat. He felt Arshi slide away from him in the swirl of water, but he managed to grab her leg. He thought his father was holding onto her from the other side, but it was impossible to be sure in the dark. Where was his mother? She'd been sitting on his other side, but she wasn't there now. The boat lurched again, and someone crashed into him. He heard his mother's voice shouting in his ear. 'Kamal, is that you?'

He reached forward, felt her arm and squeezed it. What was going on? He managed to turn his head and peer over the side. A line of white foaming surf was visible in the moonlight and the sound of crashing water seemed to drown everything. They were making landfall on a wave-lashed beach with the boat sideways on to the shore. In the dim light he could just make out shapes lurching about as people in the middle of the boat were thrown from side to side. He gripped the edge of the boat even tighter with his free hand. Some people had already been thrown out of the boat and were floundering in the deep water, even the adults were up to their necks. They were hampered by the bags they were trying desperately to hold onto, and weren't making much progress, even the ones closest to the shore. As each wave retreated, it would suck at their legs causing them to topple. Several small children were being tossed about in the rough surf like rag dolls and were in danger of drowning. There was a continual grinding noise, as if thousands of teeth were being gnashed together, drowning out many of the screams and shouts. Was it the sound of rough water on small stones and pebbles?

Belongings and people alike were soaked. He felt his father's lips at his ear, shouting. 'Kamal, we must move. Keep your backpack on. Cross the boat. Climb out the other side. Stay with your mother. I'll take Arshi.'

But his mother already had his arm in an iron grip. She hauled him upright and across the narrow boat, bumping into the people still floundering in the middle of the vessel. She pushed him up to the rail and told him to hold tight, and then she jumped out, pulling him after her. In her youth she'd been a strong swimmer, so the waves held no fears for her. The water was icy. Cold and soaked as he was, it was still a shock. She began to move slowly, step by step, braced against the suck-back of the retreating waves. Kamal followed suit, pushing his feet down hard onto the seabed. Amid the people floundering in the crashing surf, Roya remained upright, hauling Kamal after her. He couldn't see his father and Arshi. It was like a nightmare, a hellish dream, people falling over, gasping and shrieking all around them. As they reached the shallows, he could see a man wade back into the water in an attempt to rescue some of the drowning children. People lay sprawled across the shingle, exhausted and gasping for breath. He spotted his father over to their right, carrying a petrified, sobbing Arshi. The family of four embraced and huddled together for a few moments.

Kamal heard more shouting. He turned just in time to see the boat swing around again, lurching wildly. A larger wave struck the boat just as it listed to one side under the weight of the people preparing to jump off. Several were flung into the water, including a couple of small children, and were then dragged under by the backflow as the water from the retreating wave sucked their legs from under them. Kamal's parents returned to the water and began to haul the children out. From where he was sitting, it was impossible to see what was happening. All the while, Arshi was crying at his side.

Trusting in his parents' ability to swim, Kamal breathed more easily. But his relief was short-lived. Several things happened in quick succession. His parents had waded back to the boat a second time to rescue the remaining children when a huge wave bore down on them like an express train and hit the boat sideways on. It rose up, and then toppled onto the two rescuers, the deck rail catching them both and knocking them under. Kamal stood up, shouting, and ran into the water. He couldn't see where his parents had gone. Then something hard struck him on the head, and he lost his footing.

* * *

Someone was shaking him. People in uniform. Police? And nurses and doctors. He struggled to sit up and looked around for his parents. A little further on was a row of lumpy shapes laid out on the shingle, each covered by a blanket. Arshi was beside him, coughing. Someone, a hazy figure, seemed to be talking to him.

'I'm Kamal Bahrami. This is Arshi,' he said in English. 'Where are my parents?'

The paramedic glanced at a police officer standing nearby, who shook her head. Kamal caught sight of his mother. Lying on a stretcher, she was being carried towards an ambulance. Her eyes were closed, and she had blood on her face.

'Umi!' he called. Then in English, 'That's my mother.'

The police officer bent down to him. 'Your mother?' She took his arm and helped him to stand. 'She's alive but we think she's badly injured.'

He craned his head, looking around frantically. 'Where is my father?'

She shook her head. 'We haven't checked everyone yet. Do you want to go in the ambulance with your mother?'

'Yes, but where is my father? Where is he?'

'Go in the ambulance just now. We'll find you in the hospital.'

* * *

Sergeant Rose Simons watched the last of the ambulances leave and then leant on the shoulder of her boyfriend, a member of one of the paramedic teams also in attendance at the beach.

'I can't cope with this, Tony. Dealing with drunks and thieves is one thing but a tragedy like this is something else. It's the sheer bloody hopelessness of these poor people that gets to me. I mean, think how far they've travelled to get here, only to have this happen. Do you think the mother of those two poor kids will pull through? Her injuries looked pretty bad to me.'

He grimaced. 'I reckon she's got a fifty-fifty chance, Rose. She's got a couple of broken ribs and a fractured pelvis. It all depends on the damage the ribs have done to her lungs and whether she's got other internal injuries. I really didn't like the look of her. There was something seriously wrong. That's why we got her off in the first ambulance. And then there's her mental state if she does pull through. She probably doesn't know her husband's dead. Still, just think, Rose. These people have crossed most of Europe to get here. They're pretty tough. Jesus, I wish I could get my hands on the people who organise these boats.'

'Me too,' Rose growled. 'They're nothing but cold-blooded killers.' She pointed to the upended boat, which had been pulled clear of the roaring surf. 'That thing's not fit for crossing the Channel with half a dozen people on board, not at night when the sea's like this. And how many were packed into it? Thirty? It makes my blood boil. It's sheer bloody murder. Putting young kids through that. I can't put my anger into words.' She shook her head in despair. 'Four people dead. Four desperate people who gambled with their lives and lost.'

She was finding it hard to clear her brain of the scenes of raw emotion she'd witnessed when some of the migrants realised they'd lost loved ones to the cold, foaming water. The man who'd lost his wife. The sets of parents who'd each lost a child. The two children who'd lost their father and might yet lose their mother as well. The injured, with broken bones, head wounds and internal injuries. The desperation of such people, causing them to risk everything to seek a haven away from the wars and disputes that ravaged their homelands. It was all too much. She turned and trudged back to the line of vehicles. At least George, her young protégé, had been spared this awful experience. Rose had developed an almost maternal feeling for the young man and was glad he was off for the weekend, visiting his girlfriend in Oxford. She spotted a familiar car pulling in at the back of the line of vehicles and went over to it. But when Sophie Allen climbed out, she couldn't think of anything to say.

Sophie looked at her. 'Was it that bad, Rose?'

She shook her head. 'Worse. But there may be something useful for you to go on. There's a young lad called Kamal.

Some of the others told me he took photos of his journey from Iran on a small camera he had with him. The thing is, ma'am, his father died trying to rescue some other kids and his mother's in a really bad way. You'll need to go easy on him.'

'Rose, I'm not that much of a blunderbuss, am I?'

'No. Sorry, ma'am. Spoke out of turn.'

'It's okay. The first forensic unit will be arriving any moment now. Once you're happy that the place is secure, go get some sleep. I'll visit the hospital with you later in the morning. Will you be alright for that?'

Rose nodded. 'I had a few words with this boy Kamal last night before he went in the ambulance with his mum. He speaks English really well. He doesn't know about his father, though he may have guessed.'

'Has there been any sign of whoever crewed the boat?'

'No. They expected a crew of two or three but there was only one on board. From what we could tell, he was the first out of the boat, well before the passengers realised that things were going wrong. There's no sign of him.'

'Any description?'

'Short, bearded. He's got a squint.'

'Well, we need to put out an alert for him.'

'Already done, ma'am. Abandoning those people in conditions like that is tantamount to murder.'

'I'm not disagreeing with you, Rose.'

* * *

Dorry O'Brian was cold, hungry and in a state of near-panic. He'd been first off the boat, jumping into the sea as soon as he'd realised that they'd been driven further east than the planned landing spot. Instead of a relatively benign sandy beach with a shallow approach, the stiff breeze had driven them onto the steep shelf of Chesil Beach. Eighteen miles of pebble. He knew what that meant. Almost certain disaster. Most of the migrants on board had their eyes shut and weren't aware of their proximity to the shore. He'd checked his life vest, the only professional quality one on board, grabbed his backpack with his personal belongings in it, waited until the boat had turned side on, and slipped over the side.

The water came up to his chest, but his life vest kept him from going under. He'd timed it right. There was a lull between waves, and he made rapid progress through the water. He was in the shallows when the waves started getting bigger again. Even so, the strength of the backflow was frightening. He reached the shingle beach and looked back. The people on the boat were starting to panic. One was pointing to him and shouting something. Did they really think he was stupid enough to go back and help? It'd be suicidal. He'd done the best he could for them. They were on their own now.

He headed up the beach and found a rough path among the dunes. He couldn't see much in the darkness but if he kept the sea directly behind him, he reckoned he'd be okay. He was moving up a shallow rise, trying to follow the narrow track. He thought he could see the dark shape of trees ahead and to the left, but he decided to keep on going for another few minutes. He was still cold and wet and wasn't getting any warmer, despite his rapid pace up the incline. Finally, he stopped beside a clump of bushes, only just discernible in the weak moonlight. He trudged around to the lee side, dropped his pack on the ground and removed a carefully wrapped plastic binbag. He pulled out a bundle of dry garments and a towel, stripped off his sodden clothes and laid them close by, then quickly towelled himself dry before pulling on the new ones, topped off with a windproof jacket. He was nothing if not well-prepared. He quickly gathered his wet things, feeling for them in the dark, and stuffed them into the backpack, hoping they were all there. He hurriedly ate a biscuit, took a gulp of water from a bottle, slung his backpack across his shoulders and set off westwards.

Within five minutes he'd found the official coast path, its occasional way-markers visible even in the dim moonlight. He was making faster progress now, starting to set more distance between him and the chaotic scene he'd left behind on the beach. There was no point thinking about what was happening back there. In a situation like this, it was every man for himself.

He kept going, walking west until he was well beyond Bridport, and the grey light of dawn had started to seep into the eastern sky behind him. He reckoned that he had, at best, another hour or two before people began to appear with their walking poles, rucksacks, dogs. An hour in which to find somewhere hidden to shelter during the daylight hours. By now he was exhausted and needed to rest. Thank God the weather was dry, though chilly. He spotted a ramshackle barn in a field off to one side of the path. Was that hay piled up inside? Perfect. He crossed the field, checked that no one was about, and entered the small building. He wormed his way behind some bales of hay, pulling some out to cover his body. Then Dorry O'Brian lay down and fell asleep.

CHAPTER 15: HOSPITAL

Saturday morning

Kamal opened his eyes and sat up with a jerk. Where was he? He saw cream-coloured walls and a white ceiling fitted with rails for curtains, but these were pulled back tight against their frame. Medical equipment was neatly lined up against the bed. He turned his head. There were three other beds in the room. Arshi was still asleep in the next one and the two opposite beds were empty. There was a window to his left, the curtains still closed. Even so, he could tell that the sun was out. A stray beam of sunlight had made its way through a gap in the curtains and illuminated an area of the wall behind Arshi's bed. She began to stir, then yawned and stretched.

'Where are we?' she whimpered. But Kamal was just as confused. After weeks of travelling across Europe, moving from room to room in hostels, cheap hotels and the homes of parental friends, his brain was struggling to keep up.

'We must be in hospital,' he said. 'I think it's in England. We came across the sea on a boat last night.'

He stopped speaking as the memories started to crowd in and tears rose to his eyes. He squeezed them shut. He mustn't cause Arshi to panic. He had to stay calm.

The door opened and two people dressed in blue scrubs came in.

'So, you're both awake,' the man said. 'You've slept for more than ten hours — not surprising considering what you've been through. I'm Doctor Shaw and Staff Nurse Shepherd here is in charge of the ward. Would you like something to eat?'

'Where's my mum and dad?' Kamal asked, his stomach a knot of anxiety.

The two medics glanced at each other.

'Well, your mother is in intensive care after having surgery last night. Your uncle and aunt are outside, waiting to see you. I think they should come in now.'

The man left the room, returning in a few seconds with two adults and a girl. Kamal recognised the two adults from photos that his parents had shown him — his Uncle Saman and Aunt Jenny. The girl must be his cousin, Soraya. They all looked upset.

'What's happened?' Kamal said. 'What's happened to Dad?'

'We were expecting you and then we saw the boat accident on the news. Your father didn't survive, Kamal. He died trying to rescue some children. We think a huge wave threw the boat on top of them. He was a hero.'

Kamal felt the first tear trickle down his cheek. His head dropped to his chest and he began to sob. Arshi looked shocked.

'Where's Mummy?' she asked in Persian.

Aunt Jenny was already across at her bed and had her arms around the thin girl. 'Your mother was operated on last night for injuries she got when the boat fell over, but there's every chance she'll recover. We have to keep hoping. We're all so sorry about your father. He was such a good man.'

'What will happen to us?' Kamal whispered.

'You'll be staying with us while your mother's in hospital,' Jenny replied. 'That was always the plan, anyway.'

'We were hoping you'd feel well enough to get up for an hour or so, to get something to eat,' the doctor said. He indicated the two empty beds. 'That's where the other two children have gone. They were in the boat with you. Your mother rescued one of them before she collapsed. That's what we've been told.'

'Can we see Mum?' Kamal asked.

'Of course. But how about getting something to eat and drink first? Your mother is still under sedation.'

'I want to see her first, please.'

The doctor murmured something to the nurse by his side. 'Fine. But promise me you'll take some nourishment afterwards.'

Kamal nodded. The small group took the lift to the Intensive Care Unit. Roya Bahrami seemed to be connected to so many displays that it was a wonder anyone could get to her bed. Kamal and Arshi crept through the mess of tubes. Each put a hand on one of hers and spoke to her in whispers. A nurse explained that Roya was responding well after her surgery.

'She might be in hospital for a while longer,' the nurse said. 'Her injuries were severe, but she should make a full recovery. We should go soon.'

There were too many tubes for them to hug their mother, but they kissed her before returning to their ward.

'Do you want some food in here rather than going to the sitting room?' asked a nurse.

'Yes,' Kamal murmured. Hearing of his father's death had left him feeling numb, empty, though he had half-expected it. Fragments of memories, images of the disaster, had flashed through his brain as he'd woken, as if preparing him for the news to come.

He looked up to see two women at the entrance to the ward, one in police uniform. Kamal vaguely recognised her, but from where? Last night?

'I've just popped in to see how you both are,' she said. 'We chatted briefly last night on the beach. I've brought one of my bosses with me. She's a detective.'

'They've just learned about their father,' Saman said. 'I hope this won't be stressful for them.'

'No, we're just calling in to see how they are and if they have somewhere to go when they leave hospital. Are you their uncle?' She waved to the two Bahrami children and went across to their beds. 'This is Detective Superintendent Sophie Allen. She's the boss of the team that's investigating what went on last night.'

Sophie squeezed the hands of each of the children in turn.

'The doctor says you need to rest, so I just have one question to ask you, but it's important. Rose here told me that you were keeping a photo diary of your journey. Is that right?'

Kamal nodded. Close to tears, he couldn't speak.

'Did you take photos of the people you were with on the trip across Europe?'

'Yes, some.'

'Would you have photos from the beach in France, the people that went on the boat with you?'

He nodded.

'Would there be pictures of the men who organised the boat and got people on board?'

'I think so.'

'Where's the camera, Kamal?'

'It's in my jacket, in the inside pocket.' His voice shook. 'I don't know where my jacket is.'

Sophie turned to the nurse who opened the bedside cabinet. There was no jacket inside.

'I'll need to trace it,' the nurse said. 'The people who came in last night were soaked to the skin. They were stripped of their wet clothes in the ambulances and put into warmer things. It's possible their clothes still need to be sorted and identified. I'll get someone to check. What colour was your coat, Kamal?'

'Blue. Arshi's was red. We had backpacks as well.'

'Once it's found, do you mind if we take it, Kamal?' Sophie asked. 'I promise to look after it. It needs to go to some people who'll try to recover the photos. I expect it got soaked through while you were in the water, so it may not work anymore. But we have experts who might be able to fix it. If they can't, we'll get you a new one. We need those photos to catch the people who crowded so many of you together in that boat. Do you understand? Why did you have a camera, by the way, and not a phone?'

'Our parents won't let us have phones yet. They say we're too young. But the camera might be dry. I put it in a plastic bag when we got on the boat and into a zipped-up pocket in my coat.'

'That's very sensible of you. I'll be back to see you soon. And thanks for your help.'

The two police officers left.

* * *

'He's special, that one,' Sophie said to Barry as they waited at the ward's reception desk. 'He's just found out that his father's dead and his mother's life is hanging by a thread, but he could still talk about the camera. I think they're worth speaking to again. They might be able to tell us more about what happened on the beach in Normandy before they set out on the crossing.'

The nurse reappeared carrying a damp blue anorak. 'I think this is the one. I can feel something in the inside pocket.' She was about to open it, but Sophie stopped her.

'Let me,' she said, slipping on a pair of latex gloves.

She unzipped the inner pocket and lifted out a small, crimson camera, well protected inside a plastic bag. 'I'll get this across to forensics right away. Can you keep all the other possessions secure, please? Everything will need to go for forensic examination. I'll arrange for someone to collect it all later today. I'll also get a couple of uniformed officers down. I'd like all these people kept close together and we'll put a watch on them — it's for their own safety.'

The two detectives headed towards the hospital manager's office, to discuss security. It was going to be paramount here. There was no knowing how the traffickers would react once they realised that some of the migrants might be willing to testify against them in a possible murder trial.

The detectives drove to the forensic unit at police headquarters and handed the small camera over to Dave Nash.

'How important?' he asked.

'I don't know, Dave,' Sophie replied. 'A young lad with a camera, travelling across Europe — the photos might all be rubbish. You know, poor exposure, blurred, no use at all. On the other hand, there might be something there, particularly if there are some shots of the beach in Normandy, which is what he claimed. We can but hope.'

A gloved technician extracted the camera from the plastic bag. She removed the memory card and took it to one of the computers. Images started to appear on the screen, most of scenes in Europe, taken as the family moved west. Many had the boy's family posing, either singly or as a group. Sophie recognised the small girl. What was her name? Arshi? And the mother, now in intensive care at the hospital. The man must be the dead father. He had an anxious look about him, even in those photos where the rest of the family seemed relaxed. No wonder. What an undertaking, to smuggle his family out of their home country under threat, then across several thousand miles, in search of sanctuary.

Finally, they came to the last set of photos, taken among dunes on a beach at dusk. Even in the low light, the boy had done remarkably well. In most of the photos he'd managed to keep the setting sun behind him, so faces and figures were clearly defined. The last two photos showed a small group of men deep in discussion with Kamal's father, who looked angry.

'Zoom in on that group,' Sophie said.

Dave watched closely. 'Very useful. They're good enough to be used as evidence in court.'

'Move across to that figure on the left, the one hanging back slightly,' Sophie said. She squinted at the image. 'Is that a sticking plaster on his nose?'

'Looks like it,' Barry replied. 'I don't know what else it might be.'

Sophie reached forward for the mouse and zoomed back out, looking at the photo carefully. There was another figure, standing well back from the group and leaning against a spindly tree, only partly in shot.

'Zoom in there,' she said, pointing. She leant forward, screwing up her eyes.

'That's a woman, isn't it? Blonde, do you think? Come on, someone. Am I imagining it?'

'No. I think you're right, Sophie,' Dave replied. 'But we need to do some work on the image before we can be sure. How important is it?'

'A man with a sticking plaster on his nose. A blonde middle-aged woman. This might be the couple we're looking for. That little boy has just given us the link we need. We need to talk to him again, Barry. In fact, we need to arrange for everyone on that boat to be interviewed. And soon, before they start to forget.'

CHAPTER 16: AMBITIOUS POLITICIANS

Late Saturday morning

The big cars arrived, sweeping to a halt in the turning area at the end of the narrow lane. The press were already there — journalists, photographers, film units, standing in a broad semicircle on the shingle and all looking cold, miserable and windswept in the stiff breeze that was blowing in from the west. The Home Secretary got out of his car, accompanied by his security unit, and made his way to the appointed position, where he was to speak, along with Dorset's chief constable. Sophie Allen was in the accompanying police entourage with her boss, Matt Silver, having just arrived from Dorchester hospital.

The Home Secretary shook hands with some of the police and ambulance personnel. His quiet words seemed genuine enough. He then made a short speech about the evils of people trafficking and the gangs that made a fortune out of the misery of others.

'Rest assured,' he went on, 'we will catch the people responsible for this tragedy. And we will strive to keep the numbers of immigrants down. People trying to enter the country illegally need to know that we are not a soft target. We'll be working with our friends across the Channel to stop this wicked exploitation.'

He and his junior, the Immigration Minister, exchanged a few more words with the chief, smiled for the cameras and left.

The chief turned to Matt and Sophie. 'He's okay, really. His own parents were immigrants, so he has some understanding of the issues. Not like that idiot of a junior minister. He's a total knobhead. Far too aggressive and rude for my liking, and only interested in his own political ambitions. He wants a report on his desk on Monday. I ask you. Haven't we got better things to do over the next couple of days?'

'Do you know anything else, ma'am? About what's been going on here without our knowledge?' Sophie asked.

'I'm not allowed to tell you, apparently. I don't have permission to confirm what you both suspected has been happening. So I'm not confirming that the Home Office has set up a special unit in an attempt to counter this kind of trafficking, but without telling us, and without involving many of the agencies that already have some expertise. And I also can't confirm that it's the brainchild of the junior minister, Ken Burke. Sorry, did I use the word 'brain' somewhere in that sentence? A mistake there, I think. And you can imagine how disorganised this special unit is with him in charge, can't you? Not that I can confirm that, either. It's non-confirmation all round, I'm afraid.' She stopped and looked at Sophie closely. 'You've got that eureka look in your eye, Sophie Allen. Are you planning to enlighten us?'

'I can hazard a guess. Whether it's right or not . . .'

'Come on, out with it, woman. I haven't got all day.'

'Ambitious politicians. To be more specific, the junior minister at the Home Office. He's angling for the top job. It's autumn, ma'am. We're just coming up to party conference season. Just imagine the kudos he'd have gained if he could have announced a successful action against the people traffickers in the middle of his speech. I think he was pushing that unit a lot faster than they wanted to go, just for his own personal ends.'

The chief constable smiled. 'You cynic, you. But I have no doubt you're right. Have a million brownie points and keep up the good work.' She turned and headed for her car and was soon being driven away. Matt turned to Sophie. 'I think we've just got her blessing to continue, wouldn't you say?'

'Bloody good thing too, Matt, if this special unit is as useless as she implied. Maybe it'll be down to us after all.'

'Isn't it always?'

* * *

An hour after the last member of the press had departed, a shiny, dark blue BMW four-by-four drew up on the headland overlooking the long sweep of Chesil Beach, about a mile from where the tragedy had occurred. Two people got out and stood looking down.

'What a complete shambles,' the woman said. 'Why do those cretins always have to squeeze extra people in? We agreed on a maximum of fifteen, didn't we? Didn't you hear me say it to them on the beach before we left? They'd have made it in without a problem if they'd stuck to that number. But no, they have to be greedy and go for the short-term gain. And then they only sent one crewman across. How was he ever going to cope alone? And they've been pocketing the extra cash. It's not as though we've been mean with the money, not with the amount they get from us for every trip. It could ruin everything.' She looked through her binoculars. 'Look at the number of cops swarming about the place.' She shook her head angrily. 'The whole setup has gone to buggery.'

'We can just lie low for a while, until things settle down. It's not as though anyone can finger us, is it? We'll be fine like we always are, Charmaine. Haven't we always got through sticky situations?' The man fingered his nose as he spoke. He'd been able to remove the sticking plaster this morning, but the scab still itched.

'You can be a real simpleton sometimes, Phil. Learn your forensic rules. Every interaction leaves a trace. If they've got really good forensic people and the right cops, they'll pick up on something. I think we need to head across to Normandy and sort a few weak links. Permanently.'

'But that will be an interaction, won't it? If what you say is right, it'll leave traces. Is it worth it?'

'It's a judgement call we have to make. Those guys we used to organise last night's trip are morons, basically. They need to be dealt with. It's safer than leaving them over there, because they'll be sure to spill the beans when the cops come calling. Just like those others we've had to remove. Christ. What a nightmare. All we seem to be doing is perpetual damage limitation. How did I ever talk myself into this?' She suddenly fixed her companion with a piercing gaze. 'Who was the crewman who stayed on the boat?'

'Dorry O'Brian, the Irishman. The one with the beard and squint.'

'Things just get worse and worse, don't they? He sticks out a mile. Will he follow the rules?'

The man nodded. 'I think so. He's a bit slow on the uptake.'

'Well, let's go get him.'

CHAPTER 17: THE WAY WEST

Saturday afternoon

Dorry O'Brian opened his eyes, lifted his head and looked around. All was quiet. He'd slept heavily on his straw bedding, which had proved more comfortable than he'd expected. He looked at his watch, rose, stretched and slid around the bales of hay. He peered outside. No one about. Good. He picked up his rucksack and headed westwards. According to the plan, he was to go to Chideock, a short distance inland from Seatown on the West Dorset coast. It would be good to reach there before it got dark. There was a lot more cloud cover today and it looked like rain. Would it hold off for the couple of hours it would take him to get there? He forced his stiff limbs to move faster.

He passed just three or four people on the coast path. They looked to be committed walkers, heading east towards West Bay and Bridport, possibly to a night in a comfortable bed, after a hot meal and a drink. Well, that was not an option for him, not for a while yet. The police would be out in force by now, looking for someone of his description. At any moment, he half-expected to hear the clattering of a search helicopter, but his luck held. Maybe the misty drizzle now beginning to fall was a blessing in disguise. Would a helicopter be able to operate in such conditions? He had no idea.

By the time he reached Seatown the mist was getting thicker and he was walking in a dim twilight. He stopped briefly to eat his last three biscuits and finish the bottle of water. He heard voices and dodged behind a low wall, watching a small group of police and coastguard personnel walk past, heading east. So, there were search parties out. He needed to be careful.

He took a narrow track north from Seatown, heading away from the shoreline but avoiding the lane. He didn't want to be picked out in some car's headlights. The traffic on the lane seemed heavier than he would have expected. Maybe this was it, the start of a concerted search for him along the coast. Well, he was heading inland now with only another ten minutes or so to go.

He ghosted past several cottages and finally came out onto the A35, the main road heading west, a mile or so inland from the coast. According to his instructions, he should cross the road beyond the western edge of the village of Chideock and head up a rough farm track to the emergency rendezvous point. He ducked down behind a wall as several cars passed, then decided to remain in the field rather than walking directly beside the road. He was nothing if not careful.

It took Dorry another five minutes to reach the crossing point. There was the farm and there the signpost. That track must be the one he was looking for. He crossed the main road and made his way up the track. Five hundred yards, that's what he'd been told. He passed a copse of trees on his left. And there, pulled in tight under a canopy of beech trees, was the car he'd been looking for. A dark-coloured BMW four-by-four, only just visible in the rapidly failing light.

He saw the door open and two people get out. He raised a hand to wave, then fell like a stone. He never registered the slight popping sound from the silenced handgun. He was already dead before he hit the ground, shot cleanly through the heart.

* * *

The woman slipped the gun back into her fashionable shoulder bag. 'You know, I could get used to this,' she said. 'I always thought I was a knife girl. I like the close-up nature of it, the intimacy. But that gun is a real power weapon. It kind of appeals to my more mature personality, with my newfound direct approach to life.'

They walked the few yards to Dorry O'Brian's body. She was about to prod him with the toe of her boot but thought better of it.

'Just check his pockets and get his backpack, will you, Phil? Then toss him over the fence into that nettle and bramble patch. It looks as though it hasn't been disturbed for yonks. With a bit of luck, it might not be found for a week or more. It doesn't look as though anyone ever comes up here. I really don't want to get blood on my new upholstery.'

Her companion did as she asked. The only indication of the recent drama were a few bloodstains on the ground, and they might well be washed away by morning if the rain continued.

'I think we need to get moving,' the woman said. 'There's a lot to do and we can't afford to miss that Cherbourg ferry in the morning. Too much tidying up to do over there.'

'What are we going to do about the Corinne Lanston angle, Charmaine?' the man asked.

She frowned. 'It's a bit of a problem, I must admit. A permanent disappearance might be in order. But I can't help liking her approach to life, so it needs some thought. It might be an idea to close the whole operation down, Phil, and follow our dream at last. We've cleared more than a million in the past six months, and that's after expenses.'

'You're the boss,' he said.

CHAPTER 18: TEARS

Sunday morning

'Where are we?' Arshi said, rubbing her eyes.

Kamal had been awake for a while, staring at the ceiling and trying to make sense of everything that had happened. 'We're in England, staying with Uncle Saman and Aunt Jennie.'

'I'm hungry,' Arshi said. She suddenly sat up, wide-eyed. 'I hope Mummy's okay.'

'She's still in hospital, Arshi. That's where she needs to be until she's better.' He climbed out of bed. 'I'll go and see who's up. You stay here.'

Kamal made his way to the door. He was wearing pyjamas that didn't belong to him. Whose were they?

He opened the door slowly but couldn't stop the handle from squeaking. When he peered outside, he found himself looking at his cousin Soraya, sitting on the floor and looking up at him, a tentative smile on her face.

'We've been waiting for you to wake up,' she said. 'I'll go and tell the others. The bathroom's along there but don't be long. Breakfast's nearly ready.' She pointed to an open door at the end of the landing, and then skittered off downstairs.

Kamal went into the bathroom, used the toilet and splashed some water on his face. He towelled himself dry then took a look in the mirror. Was that really him? The face staring back at him looked older and thinner than before. Maybe it was because he'd not really eaten much in days, just some grabbed bits and pieces when food was available. He took another look. Tousled hair, dark circles under the eyes and a serious look. Back at home he'd always been known as the laughing boy. Well, that boy was gone. The long journey and what he'd seen as they travelled had put an end to his laughter. He returned to the bedroom. Soraya was back, talking to Arshi.

'Where is this?' he asked.

Soraya looked at him. 'We live in Weymouth,' she said. 'It's a seaside town with beaches and lovely gardens. I really like it.'

Kamal didn't know how to respond. It wasn't often that he found himself tongue-tied but his brain didn't seem able to think of anything sensible to say. It felt foggy and slow. He wished he could have met his cousin under better circumstances. His stomach chose that moment to produce a loud rumble that tailed off into a pronounced gurgle. He felt his face burning. Soraya didn't laugh, though. She looked concerned.

'You poor thing,' she said. 'I bet you didn't eat much in hospital. Breakfast is still on the table, so don't worry.'

Kamal looked at her, embarrassed. 'I need to get changed.' He still had pyjamas on.

She put her hand to her mouth. 'Sorry. We're just in jeans and T-shirts. Saturday and Sunday aren't school days here. But we have loads of homework. I'll take Arshi along to the bathroom.'

She smiled again and left. Kamal waited until the door closed behind her, stripped off his pyjamas and pulled on some clothes, obviously rescued from his backpack, that he found on his bed. They hung on him loosely now.

He waited until the two girls returned and followed them downstairs. He could hear voices coming from behind a half-open door.

* * *

Soraya lived with her parents and two younger siblings, a sister and a baby brother. Her father, Roya's brother, was the co-owner of a nearby restaurant. Her mother, Jenny, was the manager of a local garden centre. She had met and married her husband while he'd been on a student exchange programme many years earlier.

Kamal was still in turmoil. He knew his father was dead, killed by a massive blow to his head as the upended boat fell on top of him. He knew his mother was in a coma in hospital, injured in the same incident. He knew that both his parents were being praised as heroes for their attempts to rescue those drowning children. Yet he felt cold and empty. All he wanted was his life to go back to the way it was before, to see his parents across the table, eating their own breakfasts as if nothing had happened. Instead, there were the concerned faces of two strangers, his aunt and uncle, looking awkward.

'Try to eat something, you two,' Aunt Jenny said. 'You need to keep your strength up.'

Kamal was ravenous but at the same time the thought of food made him feel sick. In the end he took a glass of fruit juice and a flatbread with some cheese. Gradually, the food began to make him feel better.

'We think we should go back to the hospital to visit your mother,' Uncle Saman said. 'She was being kept sedated yesterday, but that might change today. It's nearly midday so we'll go this afternoon if you like.'

'Yes, we want that, don't we, Arshi?'

His sister looked at him with big, solemn eyes. 'I want to see Mummy. She needs a cuddle.'

The hospital seemed quieter than the previous day. Some of their boat companions had been released and taken to accommodation elsewhere. Two police officers stood talking outside the ward entrance. One of them was the woman from the beach, the one who'd been to visit yesterday. Her face broke into a smile when she saw them approach.

She bent down and opened her arms wide.

'You're Arshi,' she said. 'Come here.'

Arshi took a tentative step forward and the policewoman picked her up. 'I'm Sergeant Simons, but you can call me Rose. Just you two, mind. No one else.' She held out her other hand to Kamal. 'Let's go and see your mum. She's awake now.'

She took them into a side room whose four beds were all occupied by people from the boat, three of them sitting up and talking. The fourth bed, in the corner by a window, was still curtained off. The children's mother was lying partly propped up, her head bandaged and her eyes closed. Was she asleep? The policewoman gently deposited Arshi on the edge of the bed, and Roya's eyes opened.

A look of joy illuminated her face and, struggling to sit up, she opened her arms wide. Arshi wriggled up the bed close to her mother and kissed her damp cheeks. Kamal leant in and kissed her other cheek.

* * *

They were on their way out when two more women met them in the ward's reception area. One was the detective from the previous day.

'Hello, you two. Remember me from yesterday?' She shook hands with the two adults. 'Can I offer my condolences again on the tragic loss of Zaan? He was a real hero, and a great loss. We in the local police will do everything we can to support you and Roya through any difficulties that might arise. It's good to know that you two are in safe hands and living with your aunt and uncle.' She looked at the two adults. 'I want to introduce you to Professor Alice Linklater. Alice is an expert on the legal position of refugees and asylum seekers.'

Alice gave the children a smile and a wave, then turned to their uncle and aunt. 'I've already met most of the other people who came across in that boat on Friday night. I'm not from the government. I work for a charity that helps people who've fled from oppressive regimes. I'm willing to offer everyone advice and lend a helping hand where it might make a difference. In the case of Roya, Kamal and Arshi, nothing much will be done by the Asylum Intake Unit until Roya recovers and is out of hospital. Rose here told me that she's pretty sure all three of them will be living with you for the foreseeable future. I'll leave you with my contact details. Meanwhile, please be assured that you'll have people on your side who can offer advice. I'll be back in touch.'

The two women left.

'Is she really a detective?' Kamal asked Rose. 'Like in films and TV?'

'Oh, yes,' she answered. 'Those people who brought you across committed a crime, but that isn't the main point. People died, including your father. The boat people caused four deaths through their negligence, plus a whole lot of injuries. She's the top detective in the county and she's treating it as possible murder. She'll get the people responsible. I often work for her on a case like this — me and my partner, George. You haven't met him yet, but I'll bring him to visit soon. He's young and handsome, not like me. I'm old and crotchety.'

'We like you,' Arshi said.

'And you're a little sweetheart.' Rose picked her up again and hugged her tight.

CHAPTER 19: CELEBRATION

Monday morning

By eight o'clock the glasses of bubbly were out on a tabletop, along with several dishes of nibbles and a plate of bacon sandwiches from the staff canteen, accompanied by a label stating, 'for Sergeant Rose Simons only.'

'It's that pesky Sylvia in the canteen,' Rose grumbled. 'I mean, look at how many she's made. I suppose she thinks she's being funny.'

'So, can I have one, Rose?' Barry asked, stretching out his hand.

'Get away from them,' she hissed. 'I need to test them first, just to check they meet the quality guidelines. Give me a mo.'

Rae Gregson arrived, to be greeted by a round of applause.

'I might have guessed,' Rae said. 'I had a feeling Barry was up to something. Thanks, boss.'

Sophie proposed a toast. 'To Detective Sergeant Rae Gregson, newly promoted and newly clad by the look of it. That is a new outfit, isn't it, Rae?'

'Yes, well, I've got to spend all this extra cash on something, haven't I? I thought I'd go for the businesslike look this time.' She twirled around, showing off her blue skirt suit and red shoes. 'What do you think?'

'Well, I'm jealous, I can tell you that.' Rose held up her bacon sandwich. 'Maybe I'll start to diet right now so I can fit into something like that.' She hesitated. 'Then again, maybe not right now.' She finished her sandwich and reached for another. 'They're okay, Barry. Could have done with a splash more ketchup, but let's not be picky.'

'Where's George? I thought he'd be here,' Tommy Carter asked. His voice sounded a little too loud.

Everyone in the room seemed to freeze. Barry's glass of bubbly stopped halfway to his mouth, Rose's sandwich halted mid-air. Sophie broke the silence. 'He's on his way back from a weekend in Oxford, visiting Jade. It's alright, you lot. I'm fully aware of their relationship. What do you take me for? Some old-fashioned matriarch? Believe me, she's far better behaved than I was at her age. And George is a great young man, as you all know.' She looked at the clock. 'Five more minutes, everyone, then it's down to work.'

* * *

Sophie and Barry visited Karen Brody in the Special Branch suite at police headquarters.

'Have you got anywhere with that photo identification?' Sophie asked.

Karen shook her head. 'Sadly, no. The image of the man was clear enough to put it through the face recognition system, but he's obviously not on any security database. But only part of the woman's face was visible. Sorry.'

Sophie sighed. 'That'll teach me to get my hopes up too soon.'

Barry viewed it differently. 'It's not that bad. It just confirms that these two aren't on the suspected terrorist list, but would we have expected them to be? In my mind they're probably just a pair of criminals, out to make a fast buck. They're white, middle-aged and don't fit the threat profile. My guess is that, if we do find them, it'll be in our normal police databases. Cold-blooded killers like those two don't just appear out of the blue. They always have previous. And, let's face it, a woman as ruthless as her is pretty rare.'

'Do you think she killed the chap on the train too, and not just the woman in the refuge?' Karen asked.

'It's a good bet. Same knife, in all likelihood. Same method. Different outcome, though. Something went wrong and the victim staggered off to die in the train. So maybe she's not as efficient as we think.' He turned to Sophie. 'Ma'am, maybe we need to start looking for similar crimes elsewhere. Whichever one of them it was, the man or the woman, they were used to handling a knife. And women who use knives with that degree of expertise are pretty thin on the ground. Should we put Rae onto it?'

'Yes. Now we've got an image to work with, however poor, it gives us something to go on.'

'I thought you had a name to work with,' Karen said.

'Just the one she used at the women's hostel, Charmaine Cookson. It's false, of course. Nice name, though . . .' Sophie stopped talking.

'What is it, ma'am?' Barry said.

She frowned. 'It's just a thought, Barry. Rae traced the few real Charmaine Cooksons, and it clearly wasn't any of them. But why would she have chosen that name in particular? Was it just pulled out of a hat, as it were, or could there have been a reason? It's something I've never thought about before — the reason why someone chooses a certain false name above any other. What if there's some unconscious force at work? Some association?'

'So, what are you saying?'

'There's only a couple of them. They might be worth a visit. I know it seems like grasping at straws, but you know me. When I've got a bee in my bonnet about something, I need to follow it through. I can't help wondering if she might have known someone with that name. And if she did, they might remember her too. It's what I've always said, Barry. Every interaction leaves a trace.'

* * *

Rae found three Charmaine Cooksons living in the south of England. One was an eighteen-year-old hair stylist from Swindon. Another was a widow in her late seventies in Basingstoke and the last was a wheelchair-bound thirty-year-old in Exeter, disabled since early childhood.

'I don't think it's any of them, ma'am. I spoke to them all briefly, and none of them could understand why I'd contacted them. None have phoned me back, even though I left them my contact details. There is a loophole, though.'

'What's that?'

'What if Cookson was a maiden name? If she's married, she'd probably have a different surname now. Do you want me to do a check with births, deaths and marriages? It might not take long.'

Sophie sighed. 'Why not? We seem to have reached grasping at straws time, certainly where tracing this couple is concerned.' She stopped. 'I shouldn't sound so negative, should I? We're making some progress with the security unit aspect, and Tommy's sorted the lad Barry saw on his bike. He's been helpful in filling in some of the gaps about Bunting.'

After Sophie left, Rae spent the next hour checking through census and registrar records, looking for the name Charmaine Cookson. The same three individuals appeared but they were now joined by a fourth. The birth records showed a Charmain Cookson born in Poole in 1982. An entry in the marriage register showed that she'd married in 2005 and was now recorded as Charmaine Biggs. A subsequent check of the electoral roll showed a Charmaine Biggs living in Poole. Rae went to pay this Charmaine a visit.

Rae drove east from Winfrith to Poole in bright sunshine. As she approached the town centre, the quiet country roads became busy dual carriageways, the traffic congested. She finally drew up outside a neat, well-maintained house on a relatively new estate on the northern outskirts of town. The small front garden was bright with autumn blooms. A tall freckle-faced woman with pale ginger hair answered the door.

'Would you be able to give me a few minutes, Mrs Biggs?' Rae began. 'I just have a few questions for you, but they are important.'

'I'm intrigued,' Charmaine said. 'Come on in.'

Rae gave her the bare bones of their problem — that a woman using the name Charmaine Cookson had committed a serious crime. Rae was now trying to trace everyone with that name, so as to eliminate them from their enquiries. She didn't elaborate further. Charmaine had a strong alibi for the time of Louise's murder at the refuge in Southampton. She did much of her work as a magazine editor from home, but she'd been at the publication offices in London all day on the Tuesday in question, although she had taken her usual hour-long lunch break. Rae decided to broaden the questioning.

'There is another line of thought, Charmaine. We're pretty sure now that she used a false name, and it's entirely possible that she chose the name at random. But there's also a possibility that she picked it for a reason. Do you know of anyone who bears a grudge against you?'

Charmaine shook her head. The question seemed to upset her. 'No. I try to get on with most people. I really do my best to get to know my work colleagues. And as for our neighbours, they're a nice lot of people.'

'Let me switch focus a bit. She didn't use the surname Biggs. It was Cookson. Can you think back to the years before you were married? Was there anyone then who you fell out with? Even as a teenager?'

Charmaine took a sip of water and sat thinking. All at once she seemed to freeze.

'Surely not,' she murmured. 'It couldn't go back that far, could it?'

'You'll need to explain, Charmaine.'

'There was a girl . . . I was sixteen. I started seeing this new boy. He was supposedly a real catch. What I didn't realise was that he already had a girlfriend. She didn't go to my school and I think she may have been a year or two older than me. Anyway, she came looking for me after school one day. She pushed me back against a wall and said she'd kill me if I went out with him again. I was terrified. It was unlike anything I've ever experienced before, or since. She pulled out a knife and said, *I'll use this on you, pretty Charmaine Cookson. I'll cut your eyes out and slit your throat.* Those were her exact words. I've never forgotten them. She knew my name.'

'I can understand why you were so terrified. Did you ever find out who she was?'

Charmaine shook her head. 'Not really. And I stayed clear of her boyfriend, even though he tried to contact me. He wasn't my type anyway. Apparently, he made a habit of playing the field. I never bothered to find out if she threatened anyone else.'

'That's really helpful.' Rae was about to close her notebook.

'Oh, there is something else. I heard that she was really clever at school.'

Something struck Rae. 'What about the boyfriend? Do you remember his name?'

'Yes. Phil something or other. I suppose he might still be around, but I never saw him again. Why would I want to, with that kind of threat hanging over me?'

'You can't remember his surname?'

Charmaine shook her head. 'It was too long ago, and I only went out with him once or twice. I'll check with one or two of my friends from those days who I'm still in contact with, but don't get your hopes up. The thing is, I can remember thinking at the time that there was something familiar about her, but I never worked out what it was. Maybe she reminded me of someone.'

CHAPTER 20: ABDUCTION

Sophie paid a quick visit to Jim Metcalfe, the ACC. She needed the consent and assistance of someone at the top of the police hierarchy before taking the next step. Jim sat and listened to her, tight-lipped. It didn't take long to convince him that this was the obvious course of action, so he lifted his phone and made a call to the Home Office in London, using his official, direct line.

Sophie sat and listened, though hearing only Jim's side of the conversation made it difficult to understand. One thing quickly became clear. Something unexpected had happened. Jim was frowning rather more than usual and seemed exasperated.

'Can I send one of my senior people across?' he asked. 'She's in charge of the investigation at our end. We need to know how all this links together.'

He listened. 'Of course. It's Sophie Allen, head of our Violent Crime Unit. You know her.' A pause. 'Okay. She should be with you by early afternoon.'

He put the phone down and turned to Sophie, still frowning.

'Well, that didn't go as I expected. You wanted me to smooth the way for an interview with Corinne Lanston. Well, that can't happen now. She's gone missing and her flat's been ransacked. It looks like she's been abducted.'

'Did they tell you what her role was?'

He nodded, still looking serious. 'She was the unit boss, running the operation. And someone's got her.'

* * *

A two-hour train journey took Sophie to Waterloo Station. From there, it was a short taxi ride to the address she'd been given, an upmarket apartment block in Kensington. The side street was full of cars and crime-scene vans, and the cab was stopped by an armed police officer as it tried to turn into the cul-de-sac.

She showed her identity card and made her way towards the building, halfway along the street, where she spoke to two uniformed PCs on security duty.

'I'm looking for AC Paul Baker,' she said. 'Is he still here? I'm Detective Superintendent Sophie Allen. I'm expected.'

The two constables scanned a clipboard list. After speaking into her walkie-talkie, one of them indicated that Sophie should follow her into the building. They passed a forensic team making their way out, carrying their kit in various boxes and cases. Sophie's host was standing in the lobby on the first floor, talking to a local detective. He stepped forward.

'Sophie. Good to see you. This is DCI Steve Lamb. Steve, let me introduce Superintendent Sophie Allen from Dorset. Sophie and I started out together as cops on the beat in this very area, many years ago. I've invited her to be here because of the south coast connection, and because she's a very experienced detective. Shall we go in?'

Sophie looked around her at the high ceilings and ornate cornices of the corridor they were in. No cheap residence, this. The door to Corinne's flat was wide open and showed no signs of having been forced. The three officers stepped inside. The small hallway was sparsely furnished and showed no signs of damage, apart from a mirror on the wall facing the front door that was badly askew and a short trail of blood spots on the floor, still marked by the identification flags left by the forensic team. A bouquet of badly wilting flowers was lying on the floor near the front door.

'Any identification yet?'

'Yes. We rushed it through yesterday evening, after we got into the place. The blood's definitely hers. The DNA matches hairs we took from a brush in the bedroom. There's no other entry route, by the way, so whoever did it came in through that door. Either they had a key, or she let them in. We think the latter. We think she opened the door to someone, maybe the delivery person bringing those flowers, then quickly realised something was wrong. She must have resisted the entrant and got hit.'

The group went through a doorway to their left into a large, well-lit living room, pleasantly furnished in pale gold. A low table was lying on its side, and several drawers in a desk set against a wall were open, with letters and papers strewn around it.

The next room off the hallway was a large kitchen/diner. Sophie gazed around in admiration. Someone, presumably Corinne herself, had good taste. No damage was visible here. They went back out and into the main bedroom, which was furnished in deep red and gold. It was a mess, with drawers open and clothes strewn across the bed and the floor. A jewel case lay open on the dressing table, empty apart from a couple of sets of small earrings.

'Is the missing jewellery valuable, do you know?' Sophie asked.

Steve Lamb pursed his lips. 'Probably. One of her colleagues says she has some tasteful stuff. It's possible some cash might be missing too.'

The en-suite seemed to have been undisturbed. Sophie slipped on a pair of latex gloves and searched through the cupboards, which seemed tidy enough. The group moved through to the main bathroom where she did the same. It, too, looked untouched.

‘Was she on any medication?’ she asked. ‘There’s none here.’

‘We’re still checking,’ Steve Lamb replied, ‘but we don’t think so. According to her colleagues, she never mentioned any health issues.’

‘When do you think it happened?’

‘It looks like sometime on Thursday evening, but that still needs confirmation.’

The second bedroom seemed not to have been searched. One wardrobe door had been left ajar, but everything else appeared as it should — to an outsider anyway. They returned to the lounge.

‘Any thoughts?’ Paul Baker said.

‘The puzzle is why she let them in. But I suppose those flowers can explain that, if they masqueraded as a delivery person. Either that, or it was someone she knew. The blood is a bit worrying. It means she got hurt, although there isn’t much of it, so it’s probably a minor injury. There’s the possibility that the injury might have been more serious, with the blood retained within her clothes, but the spatter pattern doesn’t look like that.’ She paused. ‘Have you considered that the ransacking might have been staged by the kidnappers to throw you off the scent?’

‘Why do you think that?’ Baker asked.

Sophie shrugged. ‘Well, it’s worth considering. The way the stuff is scattered around the place looks a bit staged. The theft of jewellery, cash and bank cards implies it was a burglary, but the abduction might be for a very different reason.’

‘That’s the way our thoughts are going. You’re dealing with the results of a security leak in your neck of the woods. What if that leak stretched all the way back here, to include the addresses of personnel running this unit of hers? We’ve moved everyone else to safe accommodation. Just between the three of us, the organisation was a bit haphazard. I’ve spoken to a couple of people from this so-called internal security unit and I can tell you it was a string and sealing wax setup. Our own security people were a bit scathing about it.’

'Do you mind if I take a few photos, Paul?'

'Go ahead. But I can give you access to all the forensics if you like, as it comes in.'

'That would be good too. But I'll just take a few snaps to look at on the train. What have you found out about the origins and background of this unit?'

'Shall we talk over lunch? There's quite a bit to discuss and you seem to know as much as anybody. I think an exchange of information is called for. I'm bloody angry, Sophie. We all are. I'm the Assistant Commissioner for the Metropolitan police, for God's sake. I should have known about this Home Office unit. It's totally insane that they chose to keep themselves so secret. What kind of people were they, and exactly what were they up to?'

* * *

The two-hour train journey back from London seemed to pass in a flash. Sophie had lots to think about — not just the abduction of the unit leader, but the information she'd been able to share with Paul Baker. London's top priority was clear: to trace the missing Corinne Lanston. Could her life be at stake? The Scotland Yard team certainly thought so. Once she was found, maybe with her help, they could begin to make some sense of what had been going on. But they were all extremely concerned. If Corinne was in the hands of the people traffickers, what hope did she have? Life was cheap in their eyes. Innocent people drowned in their hundreds battling across unforgiving waters in small, overcrowded boats. Whether it was the Aegean, the Mediterranean or the Channel, all were graveyards for people at their wits' end who were at the mercy of anyone out to make a quick buck. With such evident disregard for human life, could the police seriously expect a different set of values to apply to this abduction?

Sophie looked again at the photos of the rooms in Corinne's flat that she'd taken on her phone. Had she missed anything important in her walk through the apartment? That's when crime-scene photos became so useful, you could double-check something only half-remembered. One thing Sophie was fairly sure about, the ransack looked to have been staged. The abductors were probably only interested in Corinne herself and had taken the valuables in an attempt to throw the police off the scent.

She opened the file on Corinne Lanston. Corinne had worked at the Home Office since graduating from university some twenty years ago. She'd never married, and little was known of any relationships she might have had. She'd worked her way up the civil service promotion ladder and had moved into security-based work related to migrants and asylum seekers almost a decade earlier. It was clear that she lacked field experience. Who had chosen her to head this special unit? And why?

Sophie looked at Corinne's photo. It showed an attractive, middle-aged woman with pale ginger hair, freckled skin and broad cheeks. Where was she now? Held captive in a room somewhere? Bound and gagged in a cold, dank cellar? Or dead?

Sophie shook her head slightly and closed her eyes. Too many thoughts.

CHAPTER 21: WALKERS

Monday afternoon

The area around Seatown and Chideock is a favourite among walkers. Not only is it part of Dorset's Jurassic Coast World Heritage site, but it also boasts Golden Cap, the highest point on the south coast of England. Most ramblers stick to the south-west coast path which climbs up one side of Golden Cap and down the other. But there are also paths and tracks radiating to inland destinations, meandering around hills and along river valleys. Alan Boothroyd and Denny Churchill had spent the day on one section of this intertwining network, heading south towards Golden Cap. They were walking from Bristol, having set out four days previously, and were on the last leg of their journey, dropping down the incline from the high ground above Chideock. They were accompanied by their two dogs. Alan's was a border collie, Sammie, who was now getting rather old for such long walks, but she loved being outside on open land and trotted happily beside her owner on these annual autumn walking expeditions. Denny had a much younger dog that he'd bought as a puppy some three years earlier, after his wife died. Jodie was an energetic golden retriever, full of bounce and vigour, keen to investigate every smell, every slightest movement.

The two men were tired. Even though they were regular walkers, the years take their toll and a walk of seventy-five miles in five days was no joke for two recently retired pensioners. They'd broken the walk up into five manageable chunks, with an overnight stay in a pub at the end of each day. This final stretch was the shortest. They were hoping to make it to Golden Cap by late afternoon for the views, then head down the north eastern flank to their final overnight resting place for a celebratory meal and drink. A bottle of champagne might be in order, although they were more likely to opt for a couple of pints of the local ale. Neither of them was particularly keen on bubbly.

'What do you think? About another forty minutes or so before we reach Golden Cap and get to the top?' Alan asked.

Denny shrugged. 'You're the navigator, Al. If you don't know, then I sure don't. What's that pesky dog up to now? Here, Jodie. Come on, girl.'

Jodie had disappeared into a thicket of brambles and nettles at the side of the path. The line of the fence lay somewhere in the middle of the tangled mass, but it looked as if it had rotted away some years before and had never been replaced. Despite Denny's repeated calls, the dog didn't reappear and, surprisingly, Sammie had trotted across to join her younger companion in the thicket. The sound of snuffling and low growling came from the two dogs. Both of them ignored their owners' calls. Instead, the older dog emitted a mournful howl.

'Something's wrong,' Alan said. 'I've not heard her howl like that for years.'

He picked up a dead branch that was lying nearby and started thrashing a way through the tangled mass towards the snuffling dogs. A body lay face down in the middle of the thicket. Alan touched it reluctantly. It was cold and lifeless. Alan shuddered.

'I don't think we'll make it to Golden Cap now,' Denny whispered at his shoulder.

* * *

First, a local uniformed police squad from nearby Bridport arrived. They took one look at the body and moved back, well away from the thicket, made some hurried radio calls and started to stretch bright yellow crime-scene tape across the path, above and below the scene.

Several teams from further afield turned up, bringing sturdier barriers. They erected these across the bottom of the track where it met the main road, then seemed to be working out logistics.

Next to arrive was a unit of forensic officers, who carried out a close search of the thicket, cleared some of it from the immediate area of the body, and got to work erecting a tent over the corpse.

And, finally, the detectives. Denny and Allan were obliged to tell their story several times over. They guessed that this must be a significant find just because of the sheer number of people who were steadily arriving, all looking grim. They seemed to know what they were doing, though, which was reassuring. The two men sat on a nearby log, sipping coffee from a flask Denny had been carrying, the dogs beside them, watching the comings and goings.

A detective arrived, his ginger hair conspicuous in the throng, accompanied by a tall young woman. He came across to them and yet again asked them to recount the story of their macabre discovery. The questions these two asked were more probing and wide ranging. Had they spotted anything else unusual? What had they heard? Had the dogs shown any interest in other places in the vicinity? What had the weather been like earlier in the day? Had they seen anyone else on the path?

The young woman detective walked up and down the track, examining the surface. She showed a lot of interest in a rutted area nearby and pointed something out to one of the forensic people.

Finally, the senior detective asked them where they'd be staying that night. He seemed relieved to hear that their planned destination was so close by.

'We'll be in to see you later this evening,' he said. 'I'll be bringing the superintendent, I expect. She's on her way back from London just now but she should be in the area soon. She'll want to speak to you.'

Alan decided to ask the question that had occurred to the two men while they were watching all the developing activity. 'We're very impressed with the police response. It seems so smooth and well-planned. Were you expecting something like this to happen?'

The ginger-haired detective gave a wry smile. 'Not precisely this, but we were ready for something. And I can't elaborate any further, I'm afraid.'

'We're out of the loop, you see,' Denny added. 'We've been walking from Bristol since the middle of last week, out till late afternoon every day, then into a pub. A meal, a couple of pints and we're so whacked we just flake out for the night. We've no idea what's been happening. We did hear a helicopter a few times as we've come further south. Did that have something to do with this?'

'We couldn't possibly comment. Enjoy your meal and drink. We'll see you later.'

* * *

'Is it him, do you think, Rae? Doesn't it look like one of the men from the boy's photo?'

Barry was taking a final look at the body before it was taken away. Rae checked the image on her phone.

'I think so. That bearded one. It was probably him who came over on the boat. Some of the people said he had a squint. But those aren't the clothes he was wearing. They said he was in waterproofs, and they thought he had a dark blue tracksuit on underneath, not jeans and a jumper.'

'Maybe he expected to get wet and brought a change of clothes with him. In which case his other togs may be back along the coast path somewhere. I'll keep the search parties out until it gets dark, on the lookout for them. What do you think? Not too far from the landing site?'

She nodded. 'If it was me, I'd want to get far enough away to reduce the chances of being spotted, which is what he did. Some of the people on the boat said that he jumped out quick and was off like a shot. But he'd be cold and dripping wet, and probably tired. A mile or two at the most before he'd get changed, that's my guess. If he did chuck any of his wet clothes, they'll probably be fairly close to the beach where they landed.' She glanced at her boss again. He looked worried, and with good reason.

'If it's the same people, they've stepped up a gear, haven't they, boss?'

He nodded grimly. 'A gun. And someone knows how to use it. Right through the heart. No one down in the village seems to have heard anything, according to the local unit, so maybe it had a silencer fitted. That means it was almost certainly a professional job. We're not dealing with a beginner here, Rae.'

'I don't think we ever believed that. The murder of that woman across in Southampton was a cold-blooded assassination, carried out very efficiently.'

'I'd better get on the blower to the boss. She's not going to like this.'

CHAPTER 22: CHERBOURG

Tuesday morning

Sophie was tired. She seemed to have spent the last twenty-four hours doing little but travel. Trains, cars and now a cross-Channel ferry from Portsmouth. She yawned as she clambered into the car beside Barry and they drove off the boat. They'd managed a hurried breakfast in the half hour before the ferry had docked in Cherbourg, but she still didn't feel fully awake. She hadn't slept well — she rarely did when travelling.

'Maybe I'm getting too old for this,' she muttered, as Barry took the car through the port area and out onto the city roads.

He laughed. 'Go on. You love it really, you know you do.'

But for once she wasn't joking. 'Maybe at other times, but when we're dealing with something like this, people who kill so ruthlessly, just as if it's part of a job, I seem to fill up with all kinds of doubts. I worry that I might not be up to it, that there's someone out there who's too clever for us. What happens then? I worry that I'll end up a gibbering wreck, haunted by a massive failure.'

'Maybe you shouldn't take it all on your shoulders the way you do. You've got a good team around you, and a really supportive boss in Matt Silver.' He paused, looking out for the turnoff to the local police headquarters. 'You shouldn't doubt yourself so much. The others don't notice it much, but I became aware of it early on, at the time of your father's funeral, and so did Lydia. We both know the reason, and maybe it's not a bad thing in our line of work. It means you're probably the most thorough detective any of us know. But at what cost to yourself? You always aim for perfection and that comes at a price. What I'm trying to say is, don't beat yourself up so much.'

'Psychoanalysis over, Mr Professor?' Sophie said, but she was smiling.

Barry steered the car into an empty parking slot. Sophie took a deep breath of the chilly air as she climbed out. Maybe, being French, the detectives would have access to good coffee in their offices. That would be a blessing. They reached reception.

'*Bonjour*,' Sophie said. '*Capitaine Henri Dutoit, si'l vous plais. Je suis Detective Superintendent Sophie Allen, d'Angleterre. Mon collègue est Detective Inspector Barry Marsh. Nous sommes attendus.*'

Their host was with them within a minute. 'Hello,' he said. 'You've arrived at the perfect time. I'm hoping to set out for the crime scene in a few minutes. Is there anything you'd like first?'

'*Un café?*' Sophie answered immediately.

Henri laughed. '*Mais bien sûr.* For me, it's any excuse. Let's go to the canteen and I'll see what I can do.'

* * *

The two bodies were lying in the sand several hundred metres inland from the beach, obscured by the tall grass that kept the dunes from eroding. Both had been shot neatly in the chest.

'Were there any witnesses?' Sophie asked.

Henri shook his head. 'We haven't traced anyone. It's an isolated spot, probably where they launched their boats from.

A few local people had seen small groups of travellers making their way here during recent months, and none in the other direction. But this?' He waved towards the bodies. 'Nothing like this has happened before.'

A colleague arrived to join him.

'This is my assistant, Lieutenant Natalie Bouchet,' he said. 'She says that the forensic doctor estimates their death at between twenty-four and thirty-six hours ago. That makes it sometime on Sunday night. Does that fit in with your timescale?'

'We think they killed the third man, the one who came across on the boat, on Saturday evening at a rendezvous across on our side of the Channel, in Dorset. It looks like they repeated it here a day later.'

'Have you given thought as to why they're doing this?' Natalie asked, gesturing to the two bodies.

'Someone made a serious misjudgement about the Friday night trip across,' Sophie said. 'The boat was badly overcrowded and was upturned before it beached. You'll already know that there were four deaths, including two children. That's put the spotlight on the operation, and maybe they don't like that. We've got a couple of other related murders that we're investigating, plus an abduction. We're still trying to make sense of it all, so every bit of information helps.'

'Can you tell us anything about these two men?' Barry asked.

Natalie ran her fingers through her dark, curly hair, removed her glasses and polished them. 'They're local, from a small fishing village a mile or two along the coast. They worked on the boats for some years but drifted into a life of petty crime when the work dried up. We've talked to people who knew them, but no one seems to know what they've been up to in recent months.' She replaced her glasses, which were a bright green, and smiled at Barry.

'If the killers are the same people who shot the boatman, then they probably came across on the ferry on Saturday night or Sunday morning,' he said. 'We're trying to get the CCTV footage at our end, so maybe you could do the same? They might have gone back immediately afterwards so we need to see if there's a vehicle that came across and then made the return journey the next day.'

'Would they have made a simple mistake like that?' Natalie asked. 'We'll check of course, but if these people are as well organised as you seem to think they are, it's unlikely, isn't it?'

'As you say. But we don't know the pressure they're under. They might make a simple error if they're in a panic. We think they'll have returned to England. We also think they've abducted someone important, a government official who was looking for the traffickers. If she's their prisoner somewhere, they wouldn't want to leave her for too long.'

'Unless she's dead too,' Henri added.

'Let's hope that isn't the case,' Sophie said. 'They may be keeping her hostage in case they need a bargaining chip.' She paused. 'Can we agree to keep each other informed of our investigations? My guess is that the organisers have closed down operations as a result of Friday night's fiasco. We know the group had been infiltrated by a special security unit, and at least one previous crew member had turned witness, before being murdered. I'll update you as we make progress. Can you do the same?'

'Of course. Let's talk on the phone regularly. We can email useful documents to each other.'

Henri led them back to the cars. 'Have you got time for lunch before your ferry?' he asked.

'Oh, I think so,' Sophie replied. 'I can always make time for French food. Lead on, *Monsieur Gastronome*.'

* * *

Back in Dorset, Rae, Stu Blackman and Tommy were out with the search units, working their way west along the coast path from Chesil where the tragic events of Friday night had occurred. The team members were fanned out on both sides of the track, searching every thicket, peering behind rocks, poking clumps of heather with poles.

A shout went up. 'Got something.'

Rae hurried across. The discarded item of clothing had been spotted under a clump of undergrowth — dark blue tracksuit trousers, still slightly damp. She held her face close and sniffed. Did they smell faintly salty? They looked to be in good condition, almost new. She gave Tommy a broad smile.

'Isn't this just the perfect end to the day?'

CHAPTER 23: PUZZLES

What was the link between Robert Bunting and Louise Bennett? Or, more fundamentally, was there a link at all? Tommy Carter, the VCU's recent recruit, had been given these tasks to investigate.

He considered what they knew and constructed a spider diagram on a sheet of paper. Bunting had worked on the local fishing boats for some time until he'd injured his leg and had been forced to retire. He was gay, though there wasn't any recent history of violent homophobia in the area, so maybe that could be ignored at present. Tommy listed the conjectures: that he'd ended up becoming a crew member for the traffickers. He'd been approached by an investigator for the Home Office special unit and had agreed to talk, so they'd secreted him away in the safe house in Weymouth. Or was it more accurate to call it a 'supposed' safe house? So, what was missing?

He then tried the same for Louise but didn't get very far, realising that they knew nothing about her. Weren't the Southampton CID investigating her? Maybe he should get in contact, but he'd need to tread cautiously. Wasn't the detective sergeant on the case Barry Marsh's fiancé? If he took a wrong step, or even asked a stupid question, it would get back to the DI right away, and he'd end up with egg on his face and his future in doubt. Oh God. Why were things so complicated? Maybe he should go back to Rae about that part of the task and get her opinion. Meanwhile, he'd just concentrate on Bunting.

The missing item from Bunting's diagram was glaringly obvious. Who had infiltrated the people-trafficking gang and talked him into giving evidence? But the people in the know were all dead or abducted, so how was he, Tommy Carter, meant to find out? Unless, of course . . .

He went to find Rae.

'Boss, what if it was Louise who infiltrated the gang and helped Bunting to escape from them? I can't think of any other possible link.'

Rae pondered this for a few moments. 'It's worth thinking about. But how would it work? She was a woman in late middle age. Have you found out anything new about her?'

He shook his head. 'I'm not sure if I should contact the Hampshire lot, to be honest. Isn't the DI's partner on their team? Suppose I ask some stupid questions and it gets back to him?'

'Well, Tommy, even that's better than asking no questions at all, isn't it? If you must know, Gwen is really nice and very approachable. I don't think she'd knowingly drop you in the soup. Look, shall I contact her and fix up a time for us to go across and see her? I'll try for this afternoon, which gives you the rest of the morning to find out all you can about Bunting. We can then exchange information with her. How about you visiting the docks this morning? See if anyone remembers Bunting from when he worked on the boats.'

* * *

Tommy made his way down to the quayside. He was in luck: several fishing boats had just returned after a night out in the

Channel, although it looked as though the catch had been sparse. He tried speaking to several of the men unloading their catch, but they were all too busy to reply. He ended up leaning against a barrier and watching the scene. Maybe someone would talk to him after the work was done. An old man, also watching the catch being landed, shook his head.

'Changed days,' he growled, chewing the end of his pipe. 'It weren't like this in my day. There were three times as many boats and each one of us would land the same catch as this lot all together.' He shook his head slowly. 'Bloody over-fishing. Those big boats hoover up everything and process the lot. Shouldn't ever have been allowed, if you ask me.'

'You might be able to help me,' Tommy said. 'I'm looking for information on someone who worked on a fishing boat ten years or so ago.'

'Dunno about that. It's been nigh on twelve years since I stopped. Anyways, what's your reason?'

'I'm with the local police, DC Tommy Carter. I'm trying to find out about a Robert Bunting.'

The man looked at him warily. 'Oh aye, Bobby Bunting. We all kent him. Like a fish out of water, he was. I kent him from when he were a lad and he were always in trouble. What's he gone and done now?'

'He hasn't done anything. He was stabbed at the train station ten days ago. Didn't you read about it in the local paper?'

'Naw. Must 'ave missed that. Stabbed, eh? He were a sorry lad. Had no luck, see. You get these people who always come up smellin' o' roses. Well, Bobby were the opposite. Everythin' he did turned to shit. He never lasted more than a few months on any boat. He just weren't cut out for the fishing lark, not him. Wasn't strong enough. He were a scrawny lad. Some of them can be really tough even though they're skinny, but not Bobby.'

'Any reason for that?' Tommy asked.

'Oh, aye. His heart wasn't in it. He only got a job on the boats 'cause of his dad. He were a bully, that man. He worked the boats and wanted Bobby to do the same, even though it were obvious to anyone that the lad weren't suited to it. How is he? After the stabbing, I mean?'

'He's dead, so this is a murder investigation. I don't understand why you didn't know. It was on the front page of the local paper last week.'

The man looked astonished. He shook his head slowly. 'That's a shock. No. I were away until yesterday at me daughter's place in Manchester. I dunno if I should be a-talkin' to you now.'

'It's a murder enquiry, Mr . . . ?'

'Coates. Andy Coates.'

'Well, Mr Coates, that means if you do know something you must let us know. There is something you could help with. How did Mr Bunting get his leg injury?'

'Oh, that were on his last job. It were a bit stormy and he didn't get out of the way quick enough when a loaded crate shifted and it crushed his leg. He had ops on it, but it were never right after that. It were a blessing in a way. He couldn't work the fishing boats anymore, see.' Andy Coates paused. 'He had a stutter, did Bobby. It were that bully of a father. Never give him a chance. Used to mock the lad.'

That would explain the cab driver mentioning that Bunting had a slight accent. If he was trying to control a stutter, his voice might well sound stilted. Tommy handed the old sailor his contact card.

'Get in touch if you remember anything else, please.'

Coates studied the card. 'There were this other thing I heard. Dunno if it were true, though. There was rumours that he was, you know, gay. Is that the word?'

'Would that explain why he didn't fit in with the other men on the boats?'

Coates nodded. 'Aye. We're slow to change, us fishermen. God-fearing, that's what a lot of them is. And some of them can be vicious too.'

'And what about you?'

Coates looked at him coolly. 'My youngest daughter's living with another woman now. Talkin' about getting married once her divorce comes through. And she's got the kids. I don't know what to make of it all. She just laughs. What does she say? *It's all part of life's rich tapestry, Dad.* I just don't get it.'

He shook his head, looking bemused.

'How did you get to know Mr Bunting so well?'

'The Buntings lived along the street from us. Bobby were the youngest and by a long way. His old man never hid the fact that young Bobby was a mistake. There's some that see a late kiddie as a blessing, but not them.'

'Do you know anyone with the name Louise Bennett?'

'No. Who's she?'

'It doesn't matter. Thanks for your help, Mr Coates. I may be back in touch.'

* * *

Tommy felt that he could easily have fallen in love with Gwen Davies, if it wasn't for the obvious problem. She was very pretty, with soft, dark curls tumbling around her shoulders, and her figure, particularly in those tight-fitting trousers, was perfect. Her voice was seductive, slightly husky, with a beautiful Welsh sing-song lilt. And that smile — mischievous, soft and musical, all at the same time. Along with big brown eyes that hinted at a warm personality underneath. To Tommy, she represented the perfect woman. But she was an experienced detective sergeant, he knew, and he'd heard she was really good at her job. And here he was, a novice detective trying to keep his head above water in a unit where everyone seemed to work a lot faster than him. How come he'd never managed to land a woman like this? He only emerged from his confused thoughts when Rae kicked him under the table.

'Tommy's found out some interesting information about our victim, Robert Bunting. But we need to find out if there was a link between him and your Louise Bennett. We wonder if it was her he'd been to see that Friday night. His ticket was a return to Southampton. Over to you, Tommy.'

'Umm, yes. Robert had been in that house for about four weeks. He had a long-term injury to his right leg, picked up in an accident while he was working on a fishing boat. It seems he didn't fit in very well among the local fishermen. He was gay, for one thing. But even before that became clear, he was quite a small, thin man and he didn't take easily to the strenuous work. He'd started seeing a young gay guy. This was the man that our DI spotted watching the back of the house.' Tommy's face coloured as he realised that he was referring to Gwen's partner. She'd already know this fact, although she gave no sign. 'He had a stammer. It's possible that was due to his father bullying him when he was young. People say he was a bit of a nervous wreck, growing up. Anyway, he lost his job on the fishing boats after getting his leg injury, so he did casual work, but still on local boats mainly. He dropped out of that about a year ago. We wonder if that's when he was recruited by the traffickers.'

'If he was visiting Louise,' Rae added, 'we've not managed to find anything to link them, and that's why we thought it would be useful to have a chat.'

Gwen frowned, causing Tommy's heart to flip. 'It's not been easy, finding out Louise's background. Our only link is Zelinski, and he's clearly worried. But he's a Home Office employee, not a criminal, so we have to tread carefully. What we have found is that Louise also had a connection with the Home Office. It's possible she worked there as some kind of temp. If that's right, then there was probably no direct link between her and Bunting. Maybe they'd both come to the attention of the thugs responsible, but for different reasons.'

Tommy was puzzled. 'But we think he was on his way home from Southampton that Friday evening. We haven't found any other reason for him being there.'

Gwen shrugged. 'We might never know. Someone from the Met has already been in touch with our chief constable.

We've been told to pool our knowledge, which has got my boss annoyed. In reality, "pooling" means the information flows in one direction only, from us to them. He's getting frustrated about it. Have you had the same problem?'

Rae shook her head. 'Not that I've heard. I expect they'll be onto us next, so we'd better make some quick moves. But we'll keep you posted.' She checked the time. 'We'd better be off. Thanks, Gwen.'

The two detectives made their way back to the car park.

'What were you thinking back there when we first sat down? You were gawping at Gwen all the time we were talking,' Rae said. 'On second thoughts, don't answer that. I can guess.'

Tommy looked mortified. 'Was it that obvious?'

'To me, yes. For Christ's sake, Tommy, she's the boss's fiancé. Have you got a death wish or something?'

CHAPTER 24: COFFEE, BEER AND SECRETS

Wednesday morning

It was eight in the morning and Sophie had just arrived in the incident room when her mobile phone rang. She looked at the caller display and scratched her head.

'Hello, Alice. This is a pleasant surprise.'

'Hi. Sophie, listen. I think I've stumbled across something quite extraordinary. I need to run it by you to check that I'm not going doolally. Have you got time to listen?'

Sophie was intrigued. Alice Linklater had always struck her as a very controlled, unemotional person, just what you'd expect in a high-profile human rights expert and law professor. Yet she sounded almost breathless.

'Of course,' Sophie replied. 'Our daily briefing doesn't start for another half hour. Is that long enough for you?'

She had begun the call perched on the edge of her desk but when she heard what Alice had to say, she went round to her chair and sank into it. Even when the call was over, she remained sitting, elbow on her desk and her cheek resting on her hand. This was staggering.

Barry knew something was up the moment Sophie appeared for the early morning meeting. Frowning, she made her way to the top of the table without speaking to anyone. He glanced across at Rae. From the way she looked at him, she'd picked up on it too.

'I've just had Alice Linklater on the phone. She's Professor of Jurisprudence at Oxford specialising in refugee and asylum laws. She knew Louise Bennett.'

'I met her on Friday night,' George Warrander said. 'Jade and I were at a college social and she introduced me.'

'Yes. Alice told me at the weekend. She was down here, George, because of those migrants. She's heavily involved in a charity that assists asylum seekers. Apparently, Louise Bennett was an occasional helper with that charity. Alice told me that Louise sometimes did freelance consultancy work for the Home Office in Whitehall and that, as far as she knew, her most recent job had been that of advisor to a special security unit.'

'So, why was she deemed at enough risk for her to be put in a safe house?' Barry asked.

'Alice didn't know. She hadn't seen Louise for several weeks. What she did say about that unit, though, was interesting. Apparently, at their last meeting, Louise told Alice that the unit was dysfunctional, and its aims were muddled. The politicians who swung the cash to set it up kept meddling. Alice wonders if Louise was thinking of quitting, or had possibly already left.'

'Why would that have put her at risk, though?' Rae asked. 'Wouldn't she just be reminded of the Official Secrets Act and allowed to go on her way?'

'That's the great unknown. Clearly, she must have been in some danger. My guess is that the person who knew the situation best is this Corinne Lanston, and she's still missing. I doubt whether she's still alive at this point. After all, why would someone who's already killed two relative juniors have any qualms about doing the same to the top person? It would make sense to silence her permanently. It ensures their tracks are covered and makes it next to impossible for the Met team to piece together what's been going on.'

'Has Zelinski been moved to somewhere safe?' Barry asked.

'Yes, him and the Cathcarts. The problem is, we haven't been told where they are. I have to go through Paul Baker and Steve Lamb from the Met if we need to see him for anything. Apparently Zelinski's undergoing a "deep debrief," whatever that is.' Sophie rolled her eyes.

'You'll be passing this information about Louise Bennett on, ma'am, won't you?'

Sophie looked at him shrewdly. 'Of course, Barry. I'll tell Jack Dunning and Gwen right now.' She paused. 'But I might wait until tomorrow to inform the Met. That gives us the rest of today to follow this up ourselves. You know what the Met will do once they learn of it — they'll demand total control and start to block off our access to anything. If we all spend the rest of the day working on this, maybe we'll have something concrete by the time I have to tell them. But not a word of this to anyone outside these walls, apart from Gwen, Barry. You can yack all you like, as long as it's only between the two of you.' She looked at Rose and George. 'I've included you because of your links to the migrant group, particularly those children, and to Alice. You've both met her. I'm just wondering if she might be in any danger, having talked to all those people from the boat, and because she knew Louise.'

'Is that likely?' Barry asked.

'That's the problem. We just don't know who's under threat, to be honest. I told Alice to be careful, but I may have to contact the local police.'

Barry allocated tasks to everyone and they dispersed.

'I don't get it, ma'am. It just doesn't add up. If she was a volunteer at that charity, why was she also advising the Home Office? Those are two opposing positions, surely, given recent government heavy-handedness in the immigration stakes.'

Sophie grimaced. 'I know. Maybe the politicians are more even-handed than we think and want to know the views of people who support immigrants. But I can't see it. This is mad Ken Burke and Yauvani Anand we're talking about here. When did even-handedness ever play a part where those two are concerned? No, you're right. There was something weird going on, and it's up to me to find out about it. You act as filter for the team here. The best place for Rose and George is across at the hospital and with those two children. I want to know if Louise ever came into contact with the group, maybe while they were waiting in Normandy.' She looked at her watch. 'I'm heading up to Oxford. I need to see Alice Linklater face-to-face. I want to get information from her about Louise that she might not even realise she has. Keep me posted if anything important crops up. Let's aim for a late afternoon meeting to pool what we've got.'

* * *

For once the main roads east and north were fairly clear, so Sophie was in Oxford by eleven. She made her way to the café on the High where Alice was waiting, looking puzzled.

'I still don't fully understand why we need to meet, Sophie. Why drive all the way up from Dorset? What's the rush?'

Sophie ordered coffee and then turned to Alice.

'It's simple really. You seem to have known Louise Bennett better than anyone else we've spoken to so far. And you're shrewd and observant. I know that from the days we were students. And that's what I need. Some insight into Louise and what her problems were.'

'Surely the people she worked with would be a better bet?'

'They're in London, Alice. The Met will have seen them. That's not a problem in itself because it's in the hands of Paul Baker, the assistant commissioner. He's an old colleague of mine and I know he's one of the good guys. But I also know that the Home Office has a habit of meddling in this type of investigation and directing who can be told what. Those types of people think cops from Dorset are a bunch of country yokels, and they'll do their damnedest to restrict what Paul can tell us. Don't worry, I'll tell Paul whatever I find out. I'm not some maverick go-it-alone type.'

'So, what do you want to know?'

'Take me through the first time you met. Where, when, why and what you thought of her.'

Alice was silent for a few moments while she gathered her thoughts. 'It was about two and a half years ago. We always like to keep abreast of current thinking in the government, so we employed someone part-time to do exactly that — analysing speeches, checking documents and government papers, looking at manifestos, that kind of thing. They'd then feed that into our policy meetings. But we lost the person who'd been doing it for the previous decade. He retired because of ill-health so we had a vacancy. We were about to advertise, but Louise contacted us and offered to fill the gap.'

'So, she knew about the vacancy? Even before you'd got around to publicising it? Didn't that strike you as odd?'

'Not really. Remember, I'm only a volunteer, although I'm also a trustee. I sit on the advisory board, but we leave the day-to-day procedures to the full-time staff.'

'Where's your office?' Sophie asked.

'Here in Oxford. The whole thing was set up a decade ago by me and a couple of colleagues. It seemed sensible to keep it local.'

'She must have been interviewed. How did that go?'

'Fine, as far as I recall. We'll still have the paperwork on file somewhere. If I remember rightly, she told us that she started out as a journalist, then worked for a consultancy specialising in analysing demographics. Her area was the mass movement of people across different regions of the world. I think that's why she was picked by the Home Office and did some work for them. That continued while she was with us. We employed her for two days a week.'

'Here in Oxford?'

'Only one day. The other day she worked from home. It suited us because in London she had better access to the people that mattered.'

'Weren't you worried about a conflict of interest?'

'Not when you consider the advantages. We gained information from an insider. And she assured us that she would maintain confidentiality.'

'But how could she guarantee that?' said Sophie, troubled.

'Our chief exec made sure she didn't have access to individual case files. It worked really well, Sophie. We always knew what government policy would be before it was made public. This gave us time to prepare our statements and press releases. We could scrutinise their proposals for any weak points, and really hit hard when the time came. We became much more effective. We were all pleased.'

Sophie was silent. What Alice said might well be true, but what if information was also being transmitted in the opposite direction? What if certain individuals within the special security unit were leaning on Louise to obtain material in return? And leaning hard?

'Listen, Alice, would you agree to a couple of members of my team coming up for a day or two and poking around in your files, looking for any indication that Louise was trying to access information on the sly?'

Alice frowned. 'I'm not sure. Wouldn't that be a breach in itself? Who would they be?'

'I can set your mind at rest there. I'm thinking of Ameera Khan, our police IT networking whizz, and Rae Gregson, my unit's DS. They're both personally committed to supporting minorities and they do voluntary work in the community, Ameera with ethnic groups and Rae with LGBT people.'

'I'll have to consult the others. I should be able to let you know by this afternoon.'

Sophie finished her coffee. 'You haven't yet mentioned what you thought of Louise as a person. Could you describe her to me?'

'To be honest,' Alice said, 'she was hard to get to know. From the way she looked — curvy, always dressed well, almost sexy — you'd expect her to have a lively personality, but she was quite guarded. She was very self-contained.'

'Was she married?' Sophie asked.

'I don't think so. She didn't wear a wedding ring, although I occasionally noticed a thin silver ring on that finger.'

'You never saw her socially?'

'No. The one day she was with us, she travelled up on an early morning train and went directly back to London in the evening.'

'When did you last see her?'

'Let me see. More than a month ago. I popped into the office to collect something, and we had the conversation about her role in this special unit at the Home Office and she made the comment about meddling politicians. But she clammed up quickly. Alan, our chief exec, saw her every week but she never said anything to him about it. She was last in a fortnight ago, on the Monday, her usual day. But the next day she phoned late to say that she wouldn't be in the following week because she'd fallen and hurt herself quite badly. Alan wasn't particularly surprised.'

Sophie looked up sharply. 'Oh? Why not?'

'She was a heavy drinker, apparently. Well, just in recent months.'

* * *

'I just can't get away from you, can I, Mum? Here I am, only in my second week, and you're visiting already.'

'That's right, Jade. Prying into what you're up to, making sure you're behaving yourself and have your nose to the grindstone. The other stuff, the investigation I'm running, meeting Alice Linklater about the role of her charity, is all just camouflage.'

They'd met for lunch in the King's Arms, one of central Oxford's most famous pubs. Each had a pint of beer in front of them, Sophie's a light pale ale, and Jade's an oyster stout. The waiter brought across a ham salad for Sophie and a small spaghetti Bolognese for Jade.

'This place doesn't change,' Sophie said, 'though the beers come from a wider range of breweries now.'

'It claims to be the brainiest pub in the world, with the highest average IQ per square foot of any pub, anywhere.' Jade laughed.

Sophie rolled her eyes. 'So that urban myth is still going strong. I think the Cambridge Blue might dispute that claim, to be honest.' She took a mouthful of food. 'So how have things been going, Jade?'

'Pretty good, though it's still early days, I suppose. Hannah's coming up to visit this weekend, so I'll take her out on the town.'

'Enjoy it all while you can. Other stuff takes over all too quickly.'

'Why are you here, exactly? You said you came to see Professor Linklater. What about?'

'It's the case. That boatful of migrants that upended off the coast at the weekend. Alice is advising some of the people who were on it through the charity she's involved with. I've already mentioned that.'

'But why are you in charge? Surely it was just an accident?'

'Because a deliberate decision was made to pack far too many people into the boat, and people died as a consequence. That means manslaughter at the very least.'

Jade chewed thoughtfully. 'That's detective sergeant level, not you. I saw in the paper that a body was found further west on Monday. Hadn't he been shot? Is there a link?'

'Okay, I'll tell you one thing and that's all. He was probably the boatman. Now, can we change the subject, please?'

'Hmm, okay. Alice seems to think a lot of you, Mum. Were you close when you were here at university together?'

Caught off guard, Sophie stared open-mouthed at her daughter, then realised that the question had been totally innocent. But it was too late. Jade's eyes had already widened in realisation and utter shock. She lowered her eyes and reached for her beer, her hand shaking slightly. Sophie stood up and went to the door. She stood outside, taking deep breaths of cool autumn air and blinking, trying to prevent the tears from forming. She heard the door open and half-turned. Jade pushed herself forward and put her arms around her mother.

CHAPTER 25: CAMOUFLAGE

Thursday morning

Rae and Ameera arrived at the charity premises just after nine the next morning. It was a small set of offices in a converted shop on Holywell Street, a low building almost opposite the historic entrance to New College. The old, perfectly maintained buildings in the street gave Rae the illusion that they'd stepped back a hundred years or more in time.

She rang the bell and they were welcomed by both Alice Linklater and the chief executive, Alan Marchand. Alan was middle-aged and nondescript looking, of average height and with mousy hair. This was offset by an eye-patch he wore over his left eye.

'You look quite piratical,' Ameera said as they shook hands. 'I love it.'

He laughed. 'It's nice to meet someone who's so direct about it. I lost that eye in a skiing accident a long time ago. They've often tried to fit me up with a false one, but I hate the bloody things. They irritated me like fury, so I gave up on them.' He stood back and looked at the two arrivals. 'So, what's on the agenda?' His voice was surprisingly deep and musical. Rae wondered if he sang baritone in a choir.

She explained. 'Ameera is the network security expert. She needs access to your server to run all those checks that we mere mortals don't understand. I do the boring stuff, like talking to staff and looking for discrepancies in documents. But that could change in the light of what we find, if anything. Let's face it, that would be the ideal outcome, to find nothing amiss.'

'Do you really think that's likely?' Alice said. She was clearly worried and sounded almost pleading.

Rae wondered whether to go along with it, just to give some comfort to this anxious woman. But Alice surely must have arrived at the probable truth in the hours since she'd met Sophie for coffee.

'No, sorry, I don't,' Rae answered. 'We think she was probably here for a definite purpose, sent to keep tabs on what you were up to. But the boss also thinks she was torn, which is why she started drinking heavily towards the end. Then again, we may be wrong. Maybe she was able to separate her two roles and we won't find anything.'

Alice said sharply, 'But how can you come to that first conclusion? You never met her.'

'I spent all of yesterday following up the information we had about her. You get a feel for a person as the picture builds up. I can understand you feeling that I'm being judgemental, but that's the role the boss wants me to perform, probing a person and their motives from the information that comes in. Trying to home in on their behaviour and quirks.'

'Yes, she said you had a knack for it,' Alice said. 'What's your plan?'

'We spend the first hour getting to understand how the systems we're each examining work. I'll gather up your business diaries and meeting minutes. Ameera will do the same on the network server. Then we'll get together and look for patterns in file access, emails and that kind of thing from just before or after an important meeting.'

'Clever,' Alan said. 'But if she was up to no good, surely she wouldn't use her charity email address?'

'Your server will keep a log of anyone accessing a web-based account,' Ameera explained. 'I may not be able to see the content, but the record will be there. And that in itself might be suspicious if it formed a pattern. Let's get busy, Rae.'

The two of them had worked on similar cases before and knew what they were doing and what they were looking for. By late morning, a number of suspicious patterns had emerged, exactly those that Rae had identified earlier. After each meeting, Louise had accessed a web-based email account. Ameera couldn't see exactly what had been sent, but several of the transmitted data packets were large enough to suggest that documents had been attached to the emails. Rae went and asked Alan about the meetings held on those dates. He checked against his diary, the agendas and the minutes. In all of them one of their French, Belgian or Dutch volunteers had been present, to discuss the situation in refugee camps across the Channel.

'You're right,' Alan said. 'This is worrying. They'd bring precise details about groups moving towards coastal locations. Our position is clear. We don't help people to come into the country unless their circumstances are dire enough to warrant aid, but we do offer information and advice. We sometimes get to know of a group of, say, Syrians, all moving together and heading for a specific location in the UK because of family connections. That was the type of thing discussed at those meetings.'

'So, the Home Office would be interested because they'd be forewarned of a large group attempting to cross the Channel?' Rae suggested.

'Yes. And I suppose Border Force personnel could be tipped off to be on the lookout, along with security people from these other countries.'

'Well, I can see the logic of it,' Rae said.

Alan looked puzzled. 'The thing is, we put increased network security in place about six months ago which should have stopped anyone accessing web-based email. Are you telling me she found a way round it?' He looked at the dates on the paper Ameera had handed across. 'No. They stopped at about that time.'

Ameera grimaced. 'She avoided using your internal network completely. I looked at the router log. It was about then that she started linking her phone to the office Wi-Fi and sending transmissions that way.'

Alan put his head in his hands. 'It's all too late now, isn't it?'

'It stopped two months ago. Nothing's gone out since then.'

He shook his head. 'I can't think of anything here that would have changed her mind, not at that point.'

'Ah,' Rae said, 'but that was when you noticed that she was drinking heavily, wasn't it? I wonder if she was having a crisis of conscience. Maybe someone was pressurising her for more information, but she was getting increasingly unhappy with the deception.'

'What now?' Alan said.

'Well, that's most of the technical part finished. I need to talk to people and find out more about her as a person.'

Louise Bennett seemed to have garnered mixed reactions from her work colleagues. On the whole they liked her, but never felt that they'd been allowed to meet the real Louise. She contributed little to office chitchat and rarely said anything that would give an insight into the way she thought. That was until the final month or two, when she opened up rather more, probably because of the drink. She began to snap at people, picked arguments and seemed worryingly fragile. Several workmates had found her in the toilet, weeping. Alan, as the manager, had tried several times to talk to her and find out what the problem was, but she'd rebuffed all his approaches.

'Tension was obviously building up, but she refused any offers of help,' he said. 'I can see why now. I wonder if she began to see that our *raison-d'etre* was worthwhile and the morally right thing to do. If she was passing on all our plans, the internal conflict must have finally got on top of her. But I still can't see why she was murdered. No government security unit would go that far, surely?'

'Of course not,' Rae replied. 'What she and they didn't realise was that they had a mole in their midst, who was passing on information to the people traffickers. They make millions from smuggling groups of people in, and, to them, life is cheap. She might have realised that. She might have made her suspicions known to people in the unit and it reached the mole. Maybe that corresponded to the time she started drinking, because of the pressure she was under. We'll get to the bottom of it. I'd appreciate it if you didn't share these thoughts with anyone else, not until we've got it cleared up.'

Rae and Ameera collected their kit and left.

'What do you think?' Ameera asked.

'They all seemed very open and honest,' Rae replied. 'Decent people, trying to do the right thing. But it's too easy to create that impression. One of that lot could still be up to no good. Louise might not have been the only one passing on secrets.'

'So, you think the mole could be one of them?'

Rae shrugged. 'It's something we have to consider. After all, what could be a better camouflage? We have a guiding principle in the VCU, Ameera. Never take anyone at face value.'

They were halfway home, with Rae in the driving seat, when Ameera's mobile phone rang. She glanced at the caller display and raised her eyebrows.

'Hello, Barry. What can I do for you?'

CHAPTER 26: HEAVILY TINTED WINDOWS

Rose and George arrived at the Dorset County Hospital soon after breakfast, well before visiting time. They had the two children, Kamal and Arshi, with them.

'We're giving your aunt and uncle the morning off,' Rose explained. 'We need to be here this morning to review security because most of the people from the boat will be discharged today. Not your mum, though. She'll be needing another day or two here, but she'll probably be out by the weekend.'

'We're starting school next week,' Arshi said. 'I'm scared.'

'No need, pet,' Rose replied. 'I'll be around, along with George here. We're the county's top team, aren't we, George? No one messes with us.'

George laughed. 'They wouldn't dare. Me, I'm just an ordinary policeman, but Rose is a superhero in disguise. You should see her in her Wonder Woman outfit.'

The children giggled. Rose looked at George from under her brow. 'I'll remember that comment, young man.'

Rose gave the officer on security duty outside the ward entrance a ten-minute coffee break and they entered the unit. Most of the patients were dressed, waiting with their bags at the ready. Only Roya remained in her bed, propped up against a heap of pillows. As always, her face lit up at the sight of her two children and she opened her arms.

'I was worried,' she said. 'Everyone else is leaving today.' She turned to Rose. 'Where will they be taken?'

'They all have appointments with the asylum unit today,' Rose said. 'A coach is coming to take them to a residential centre where they'll be seen. A few of them plan to stay with friends or family, like you, so they won't stay at the centre. You'll have to go through the same process, Roya, once the doctors say you're well enough. I'll just keep my eye on what's going on.'

She walked to the window, looking out across the landscaped car park to the tree-lined entrance from Williams Avenue. A coach was just turning in and moving slowly towards the main entrance.

'I'll leave George here with you for a bit and go for a wander.'

Rose left the ward and made for the stairs. She passed the constable on security duty on the way, returning to her post. Rose descended the stairs, heading towards the main entrance. Why was she doing this? She couldn't really identify a clear reason other than the fact that she was nosy and extra-cautious. She always maintained that this vigilance made the difference between a good cop and an everyday, run of the mill one.

She left the building and stood outside, watching the waiting coach, parked a few yards away, tucked in at the side of the approach road. She stood in the shadow of the building as the first of the migrants appeared carrying their meagre possessions in backpacks and carrier bags. Some stepped forward confidently, happy to have finally arrived where they'd striven so hard to be. Others, the more apprehensive, lagged behind.

A large blue BMW that had followed the coach into the hospital grounds was parked in a relatively quiet area close to the exit lane. Rose noted the darkened windows that made it impossible to see who was inside. She made her way slowly along the front of the building, keeping to the footpath and partly obscured by the shrubs and hedges that grew between the different parking zones. Why would anyone park this far away when there were so many free slots close to the building?

She approached the vehicle from the side away from the hospital building. She still couldn't see inside. There were legal limits on the level of tint permitted in vehicles, and this one appeared to breach them. She walked round to the driver's side and tapped on the glass. She could just make out a solitary figure inside, his face now turned towards her.

The window was wound down, revealing a middle-aged man with watery blue eyes and a bony head. He wore a pale blue jumper and a black leather jacket.

'Yes?' he said, sounding wary.

'Just asking you about your vehicle windows, sir. They appear to be very heavily tinted. Are they legal?'

'As far as I know, yes.'

'Is the vehicle yours, sir?'

'Yes, but I've only had it a few weeks. I assumed it was okay. Look, I'll get it checked if you think it's a problem.'

'Very wise, sir. I'm not in the traffic division and I'd hate for you to get a fine because of it. Are you here for visiting time? Because you're a bit early.'

'No, I've dropped someone off for a short outpatient check-up. I'm waiting for them.'

'Okay, sir. I'll leave you to it but remember to get those windows checked.'

Rose moved slowly away, towards the main hospital building. She called George, asking him to join the officer on security duty at the ward entrance, then made her way to the nearest side door into the hospital. That was the problem with big hospitals like this one, too many entrances. She counted four in all, with a couple of them around hidden corners. It made maintaining tight security almost impossible. She went in through the swing doors, looking around her, heading for the main reception area and the lifts and stairs. No one looked particularly out of place, but the corridors were busy now.

She reached the nearest stairs and ran up them two at a time to the next floor. There were a large set of windows near the stairwell, so she looked out. The blue BMW had moved. She glanced down and was just in time to see it much closer to the main doors. Its passenger door closed, and it started to move away, slowly at first and then accelerating rapidly. Rose climbed the rest of the stairs to the upper floor and hurried along the corridor towards Roya's ward. There were George and the duty officer, standing by the doorway, both looking unperturbed. Had someone been on their way to the ward but been warned off by the vehicle driver following her questions about the tinted windows? More importantly, would they have been picked up on the hospital's CCTV?

* * *

Back at the incident room, Tommy was scrutinising all the relevant security camera recordings. Apparently, he'd been the main CCTV guy in his previous job. Barry breathed a sigh of relief. He hated ploughing his way through hours of footage, a sentiment he shared with Rae. Maybe Tommy would prove to be as enthusiastic an inspector of CCTV as Jimmy Melsom had been, years earlier. It was still early days in Tommy's provisional spell in the VCU and Barry had mixed feelings about the new recruit. He could do with another plus against his name.

By midday, several sequences of interest had been identified, extracted and copied. The first was from a camera giving a broad view of the car park entrance and surrounding area. It showed the coach coming through the main entrance from Williams Avenue and making its way towards the building. A blue BMW four-by-four followed it in, turning off towards the quiet section of the car park where Rose had first spotted it.

A minute or two later, a figure climbed out of the vehicle and walked slowly towards the side entrance, glancing around.

This appeared to be a middle-aged, dark-haired woman dressed in black and wearing a headscarf and sunglasses. A few minutes after that, Rose could be seen approaching the dark blue vehicle and talking to the driver. When she had gone, the car moved closer to the main entrance and waited.

'Its engine's still running,' Tommy said. 'See the slight trace of exhaust fumes drifting in the air?'

Soon the woman returned, this time walking rapidly. She climbed into the car and it moved away before her door had fully closed.

'That's suspicious in itself,' Barry said. 'And look at how fast it moves off. Something spooked them.'

'I've also got this from inside,' Tommy said.

This sequence was from the camera inside the side entrance and showed the same woman passing through the foyer and taking the corridor that led towards the main reception desk. Here she was picked up again on a different camera, about to take the stairs, then by a camera on the first floor, this time studying the detailed hospital plan that was on prominent display. She turned to take the second flight of stairs but stopped and extracted a phone from her bag. The woman listened and then went back down the stairs, this time heading for the main entrance doors.

'I've done the sums,' Tommy said. 'The gap between her entering and leaving the building is four minutes, and that's how long the sequences from inside last.'

'So, it looks as though she was contacted by the guy in the car. He must have been spooked when Rose approached him, phoned her and warned her off.' He thought fast. 'We need some biometrics, Tommy. We can't positively identify her, not in those sunglasses and headscarf. But we can get her height, leg length and shoulder width from comparisons with nearby fittings. The lens will be fisheye, remember, so you may have to allow for distortion. Rae will give you a hand when she's back tomorrow. She's an engineer, so she can do the maths. Good work.'

'Why do you think she was there?'

Barry shook his head, worried. 'Not for any good reason. It does mean one thing, though. When the mother leaves hospital, we'll need to keep a security watch on her and those two children. And they won't be starting school next week after all. It would be too dangerous.' He glanced at the clock. 'I'll let the boss know when she gets in.'

At the door, he turned back to Tommy. 'Is there any way we could find out about that phone call?'

'We don't know either of the numbers,' Tommy said. 'Doesn't that make it impossible?'

'Maybe I'll call Ameera. She might know. She should be on her way back from Oxford by now.'

Ameera told him there was a technique called a tower dump, in which a cellphone operator can be asked for a list of all the mobile devices that were present in a certain area at a certain time, and linked to a particular mast. It was only used rarely, in the investigation of serious crimes or terrorism, and strong justification would be needed. Surely this was just such an occasion? Barry waited until Sophie appeared later in the afternoon and went to see her.

'So, what you're saying is that it's technically possible for us to find a list of all the mobiles being used in the vicinity of the hospital during that five-minute spell?'

He nodded. 'I know it might be getting close to snooping, and we've agreed to avoid anything like that whenever possible. But aren't we justified here?'

'Okay, I'll get onto the powers that be right away,' Sophie said. 'I expect we'll need approval from a magistrate. Call Ameera again and ask them to come in here rather than heading straight home, so she can advise us. Let's strike while the iron's hot.' She paused. 'Oh, and there's something else you need to know. Paul Baker's been in touch. Apparently, Peter Zelinski's house may have had an intruder last night. He wasn't there, of course. The Met have him somewhere safe. But a neighbour claims to have seen a flickering light in the early hours. He called the local police and a forensics team are there now, looking to see if they left any evidence.'

'Any thoughts?' Barry asked.

'Well, the obvious one. Someone wanted to ensure Zelinski was silenced. He's the one who knows most, now Corinne Lanston's missing. Thank God we got him away in time.'

CHAPTER 27: RENT

Friday morning

'I never thought it would be instant, but four days? Can't it be speeded up?' Sophie frowned at Ameera Khan.

'It's the sheer volume of network data, ma'am,' Ameera said. 'There are several masts that cover central Dorchester and the volume of traffic is immense. I know we can narrow it down to that five-minute spell, but there are still several thousand calls recorded in that time. It might take a lot less than four days, that was just the timeframe I was given. I think the guy I spoke to was being unduly pessimistic.'

'Well, let's go ahead with it. Though if those two had any sense, they'd have been using burner phones, which won't be traced anyway. I want confirmation of Rose's theory that they were there for a specific purpose. I need the evidence to back up my request for a unit to keep an eye on that family.'

Barry was pleased to see Sophie back to her usual impatient self. She'd been unusually lacking in focus the previous day and he'd wondered what had caused her introspective mood.

'I do have much better news on a different front,' he said. 'A lot of the people on that migrant boat have confirmed that the boatman had a slight squint.'

'Well, that wouldn't be hard to forget, if he was local. Tommy, could you follow up on this down at the harbour? A bearded boatman with a squint? Maybe that old salt you spoke to about Bunting also knew something about this guy. Go and see him. You did very well last time.' She smiled at him encouragingly, and he visibly perked up.

'Sure thing, ma'am.'

'The thing that still puzzles me,' she said, 'is why Bunting went to Southampton. We know it was just for the evening — he left here just after rush hour. We assumed, or maybe hoped, that he was visiting Louise, but that now seems unlikely. So, what other reason could he have?'

'Zelinski. He's my first choice,' Rae said. 'He lives in Southampton. Has he ever cooperated fully in the way we would have expected? I know I haven't been involved in interviewing him, but I've read the notes you both made, and he's obviously holding things back. Could he have been more closely involved with Bunting than he's let on?'

Sophie ran her fingers through her short hair. 'The Met's team have him now, and Jack and Gwen from Southampton don't even have access to him anymore. I'll give Paul Baker a buzz and see if he'll open up. I need to phone him anyway. He promised me a copy of the report into Corinne Lanston's abduction. It should have been with me yesterday but, as always, they need a nudge.'

'Have they found any trace of her, ma'am?' Barry asked.

She shook her head. 'No. Not a sign. And as each day goes by, the chances of them finding her alive drop. They've got hundreds of people out looking for her but there's not been a whisper. I always thought the chances of finding her were remote. We're dealing with a bunch of ruthless killers here. Would they want a live hostage to cope with? It's not as though they were ever going to use her as a bargaining chip. What would be the point? What would they be looking for? The only thing that puzzles me is why they bothered to abduct her in the first place. Why not just kill her and have done with it? That's what's happened to the others who got in their way. But we'll wait and see what the report says. Maybe it will enlighten us.'

'My guess is that they were after information that only she could provide. But the end result would be the same, either way. Once they got what they wanted out of her, she'd be a liability. And if they didn't, she'd still be a liability.' Barry shook his head. 'What motivates these kinds of people?'

Sophie smiled grimly at him. 'Better not to even try to work that one out, Barry. I don't want you getting into their heads and going funny on me. Now, everyone, something else odd has occurred to me, the fact that Bunting was local. He was born in Weymouth and grew up here. If you've got to put him in a safe house, why choose his hometown? That breaks the normal rules.'

'Maybe they were just paying lip service to the notion,' Rae said. 'Or maybe he insisted on staying local. Unless we're making a mistake and it wasn't a safe house, but just somewhere he could live for a few weeks.'

'But it has to be a safe house, Rae. In theory anyway. That's what those properties were bought for. The ones we checked were listed as such on the inventory held in Whitehall. Are you suggesting that it was for some other reason entirely?'

Rae shrugged. 'I don't know. But it might be worth looking into, don't you think, ma'am? Shall I do a bit of poking around?'

Sophie tilted her head, smiling. Clever Rae. 'Why not? I bet no one else has thought of this angle.'

* * *

It didn't take Tommy long to find old Andy Coates. He was in the same spot as before, leaning on a barrier, pipe in mouth, watching the scene. And why not? Tommy found quayside scenes fascinating, and he had nothing to do with the sea. What better way for a retired fisherman to while away the hours?

'I reckon I could do wi' a mug o' tea,' the old man said, seeing Tommy approach. 'I bets you'll be after more information, won't you? So, you can pay.' He tapped his head. 'Stuff I've got in me head don't always come free, yer know.'

'That's fine, Mr Coates. Where shall we go?'

The old sailor looked around him. A nearby quayside pub was just opening its doors.

'Well now, yon's solved a problem. They serve a good pint in that place. We can sit outside in the sun.'

They made their way to the pub and Andy settled himself into a seat that gave a good view across the water. 'Pint, please. An' make sure it's from a handpump. I don't want any o' that keg piss.'

Tommy went in, momentarily blinded after the bright outdoor light. He blinked at the row of handpumps. 'A pint of bitter, please — one of these.'

'Is it for old Andy Coates?' the barman asked.

Tommy nodded. 'He sounded a bit choosy.'

'It'll be this one he'll have, copper.' The barman pulled a glass of a dark gold ale. 'What about you?'

'Oh, just an orange juice, thanks.'

Tommy picked up the glasses and took them outside.

Andy took an exploratory sip and gazed across the quay. 'That's grand. This is the life — sunshine, the boats. A pint o' beer. What could be better, eh?'

'You're right there, Mr Coates.' Tommy took a mouthful of his orange juice. 'But I'm on duty, so I'm stuck with this. Now, I've got something else to ask you.'

'Yeah, well, I guessed that. I dunno if I kin tell you any more about Bobby.'

'It's not him. We've got a problem identifying someone else who we think might have worked on the boats. He's probably in his early thirties. Dark curly hair and a beard?'

Andy snorted in derision. 'That's half the men who work on the water.'

'He might have had a squint.'

'Ah, now you're talkin'.' He swallowed several more mouthfuls and wiped his mouth with his sleeve. 'Sounds like

Dorry O'Brian, the mad Irishman from Donegal. He worked the boats a few years back, was always pickin' fights. I haven't seen him around for a couple o' years. What d'you want him for?'

'We don't want him, Mr Coates. We just wanted to know who he was, er, is.' Tommy sipped at his orange juice. 'Did he live around here?'

'Only when he was working the boats. Someone said he moved along Southampton way after he got his last sacking. Worked on the Isle o' Wight ferries. Dunno if that's true.' Andy stretched out his legs and took another large gulp of beer. 'Ain't this grand?'

* * *

Rae paid another visit to the house used by Bunting and again talked to the neighbours, but she learned nothing new. She then visited Ritchie Finn, the young man Tommy had found. He was at home with his mother and answered her questions at the front door.

'There's something I wanted to ask you about Robert Bunting and where he lived. Do you know if he was paying rent?'

Ritchie looked puzzled. 'Yeah, of course. No one gets a house for free, do they? Though he said his was a bargain, the rent was lower than the other places like it.'

'Did he ever say who the landlord was?' she asked.

'No. Why would he?'

'I have to ask the question. Did he ever say anything else about the house, or the rent?'

Ritchie frowned. 'Just once. He was looking for some cash to buy us drinks. He said he was a bit short, but he had a lot of notes stuffed in the back of his wallet. He said it was for his rent.'

'So, what you're saying is he paid his rent in cash?'

'Yeah.'

'Thank you, Ritchie.'

Rae looked at her watch, thinking. If she hurried, she'd be able to catch the next train to Southampton. She wanted to have a look at the house Louise Bennett had used and talk to the neighbours. If she got the answers she expected, a bit of extra digging was called for. She phoned Gwen Davis.

* * *

Rae and Gwen made their way to Louise Bennett's erstwhile residence and set about interviewing the neighbours. Many had already been questioned, but they hadn't been asked about the house, its previous occupants and anything they might know of the rent arrangements. As expected, most of the neighbours had no idea, apart from two, whose comments bolstered Rae's suspicions. There had been two previous occupants in the house, and they'd complained about having to pay their rent in cash. No one knew who the landlord was, which was hardly a surprise, given that it was a Home Office unit. But if the rent on its properties was being paid in cash, who was taking the money and where was it going? The two detectives speculated on the existence of a secret slush fund, run without official knowledge and with cash coming in as regularly as clockwork. Exactly how many of these properties were there, and where were they located?

Troubled, Rae said to Gwen, 'When I researched them, I found evidence of eight. But I was only looking at the south coast. What if there are more, further inland — London, for example? It could be very lucrative for someone if they're operating under the radar.'

'I'm with you on that,' Gwen said. 'Let's find out a bit more. I'll do the rest of the Hampshire and Sussex ones. You do Dorset and then Devon. Maybe Bristol as well? We ought to check one of the big cities. Have you got any contacts there?'

CHAPTER 28: PALE AND FRIGHTENED

Friday afternoon

Paul Baker, Sophie's senior contact in the Met, emailed the provisional report into Corinne Lanston's abduction at mid-day. It made interesting reading. Corinne still hadn't been found, despite a major effort on the part of Scotland Yard.

Sophie scrolled through the report. It was clear that the operation had been meticulously planned. Two of the internal security cameras, one in the foyer and another on the first-floor landing, had been found not to be functioning, whereas the cameras on the upper floors were still working. A camera on the street outside proved to be much more useful, and several stills from its recordings were attached to the report. The first, from late on the previous Thursday evening, showed a tall, dark-clad man with a hat pulled down low over his brow and a scarf encasing the lower half of his face emerging from a shiny black BMW parked close by and entering the block of flats. He was carrying a bouquet of flowers. Ten minutes later, he reappeared, holding Corinne Lanston by the arm. His other hand seemed to press something into her ribs. The photo showed her looking pale and frightened, glancing around before he pushed her into the vehicle.

Sophie examined the image closely. There were traces of blood apparent on the lower part of her face, possibly from her nose. Several other spots could be seen on her shirt collar, although most of it was obscured by the coat she was wearing. That coat had obviously been put on in a hurry, and she looked dishevelled. Her eyes were wide with fear. No traces of the assailant had been found in Corinne's flat, or the rest of the apartment block, the assumption being that he had worn gloves and had overpowered Corinne quickly.

The report went on to say that the car drove away at speed, heading north. Almost an hour later it was recorded on a traffic camera on the M1, still heading north. It was moving rapidly but within the speed limit. The still extracted from the footage showed two shadowy figures in the car. That was the last visual contact. Despite all efforts, no other trace of the abducted woman had been found.

Sophie looked again at the vehicle, a black BMW four-by-four. It was the same one, surely? She scanned quickly through the rest of the report, looking for its registration details. There they were. The vehicle was registered in the name of Louise Bennett at the address of the Southampton safe house. Sophie swore under her breath. They were going round in circles. But it wasn't the BMW that had been at the hospital that morning — that had been blue — and, as she continued to read on, she discovered that the car used in the abduction had been found early on that Saturday morning, burned out on land surrounding a disused factory close to the M1 near Watford.

Was this abduction linked to the current investigation? The recent events seemed to sprawl more than halfway across the south of England, such that they might be utterly separate crimes. But Sophie was unconvinced of this. Something shadowy was gnawing away at her thoughts, a vague notion that hadn't yet coalesced into a specific idea. But she felt strongly that it was indeed all connected, and that somehow, somewhere, it would all become clear. And sometime soon, with any luck. Her problem was that she hadn't been able to talk to anyone who'd been in direct contact with Corinne. That was being handled by the team from the Met. She needed to find her own contact to gain an insight. A thought struck her. Would Alice Linklater have met her at any time?

* * *

Another trip to Oxford, the second in three days, and very rushed. Sophie left her car in the Redbridge park and ride and managed to leap onto a city centre bus just before it pulled away. She stepped off at Westgate, and hurried through the Queen Street crowds, past Carfax and along the High. She'd promised Alice that she'd try to be there before five, and she only had ten minutes to go. A left turn up Catte Street past the Radcliffe Camera and Hertford College, then right at the Kings Arms into Holywell Street. The door to the charity offices was ajar. Maybe the staff finished early on a Friday.

Alice was in the foyer talking to Alan Marchand. 'You look as if you need a cup of tea,' she said, and laughed.

'That would be lovely. It has been a bit frenetic. Thanks for agreeing to see me at such short notice.'

'It's always a pleasure, Sophie, you know that. Please explain more.'

She accepted the mug of tea that Alan held out to her and took a sip. Lovely. 'Corinne Lanston is the great unknown in all this. She was abducted at the weekend and there's still no sign of her. I have to say that the omens aren't good, but that's between you two and me. I'm not involved in the team out looking for her or looking into her role at the Home Office, though I know they'll be doing a thorough job. But I'm curious to know what she was like, and when you told me that you'd met her at a government reception, I decided to come up and see you.'

'Well, I hope your time hasn't been wasted. There's not much to tell. It was two years ago. I'd been giving legal advice to a working group of civil servants. We had a lunch reception and I found myself next to her in a food queue, and we got talking. I didn't know who she was because she wasn't in the group I'd been working with. It was only a couple of minutes, but I was impressed with her insight into some difficult situations. Too many people think the law is simple, a case of black and white, but as you know, that's often not the case. And it's particularly true in the practical application of asylum law. Corinne seemed to know my background. She seemed very empathetic and I was impressed by her obvious wish to consider the ethical side of the issues. I can remember wishing that all senior civil servants were like this.'

Sophie sipped her tea. 'So, Louise never mentioned her?'

Alice shook her head. 'No. But when Louise applied for the job, Corinne was one of the referees on her application. It was one of the things that swayed my decision.'

'What did she look like?'

Alice thought for a few moments. 'Slightly taller than average, I'd guess. Pale ginger hair, in a neat bob. Some freckles.'

'Clothes?'

'Very businesslike. Quite stylish, actually. I think she had on a blue, pinstriped, skirt suit. I remember because I wondered about getting something like it myself.'

'Personality?'

'Fairly quiet, I think. As I said, she showed understanding. Clever, at least she seemed so from the short time we chatted. I liked her.'

'Did she know who you were?'

'Oh, yes. I had to wear a name badge with my full title. Very grand!' Alice looked at her watch. 'Look, I need to be going. As I said on the phone, I've got an evening reception to attend and I need to get my togs sorted. Lovely to see you. I'll leave you with Alan.'

She picked up her bag and document case and hurried out.

Sophie turned to Alan Marchand. 'Is there something you want to add? It could be my imagination, but you didn't seem all that happy back then.'

'Alice doesn't know, but I also met Corinne once. I don't share Alice's somewhat benign view of her.'

'Can you give me the background?'

'Okay. It was about a year ago, at a conference on the refugee crisis. I was late arriving because of another meeting beforehand. I'd been given my badge but had shoved it into my pocket to put on later because I didn't want to miss the talk that interested me. I was hurrying and nearly collided with her as she came out of a seminar room, and she dropped some papers. I stepped back and apologised, as the British always do, even though it was as much her fault as mine. She told me to piss off. I was about to help her pick her things up, but I changed my mind at that point. My guess is that she confused me with one of the lackeys. As you see, I tend to dress informally.'

'There could be any number of reasons,' Sophie said.

'Of course. She was obviously in a total fizz when she came out and I just happened to be the first person she met. It gave me pause for thought though.'

'Maybe she was under stress for some personal reason.'

'That's what I thought at first. But I asked inside the room when the talk was over. Apparently, she and the speaker had disagreed about some aspect of migrant policy. It had all been courteous, and she'd behaved exactly as Alice has just described, full of empathy and understanding. But it made me wonder if that was all just a mask, and a very different person lurked underneath the surface. She'd held that mask in place until she got through the door, then let it slip. Of course, I might be totally wrong in this. But after she'd gone, the young woman staff member who helped her gather her papers rolled her eyes and said, "typical of her." What I'm saying is that if my interpretation was right, she isn't all sweetness and light. There's a more complex person hidden underneath. She has enough of a temper to make some significant enemies.'

Sophie glanced at her watch as she left the charity office. She was tired and still had to face the long drive back to Dorset. But her hasty visit had been worth it. A simple phone call to

Alice would have picked up on her impression of Corinne but not Alan's, and the latter had been the more insightful.

* * *

That evening, Sophie phoned Paul Baker from home and asked for the latest news, if any, on the investigation into Corinne's abduction. He was able to supply some additional information. The black BMW, with Corinne inside, had driven some distance northwards on the M1, but had subsequently been identified heading back south sometime later. All trace was then lost until it turned up as a burned-out wreck.

'It could have gone as far north as Luton or Milton Keynes, but one or two witness observations might have it located as heading towards the Chilterns at one point. We can't be sure, though. We have a number of search teams in that area just in case.'

'Okay, thanks. Listen, I've been trying to put together a picture of Corinne and what she was like. You'll have spoken to her work colleagues and her neighbours. So, tell me, what did they think of her?'

'Why are you doing this? It isn't in your remit, surely?'

'Paul, don't you think I know that? I'm treading on eggshells here. I've talked to a couple of people who met her, way back in the past. She was calm, understanding, empathic. Is that what you've discovered?'

The pause was slightly longer than normal. 'Yes, broadly. She was very controlled, always rather guarded. Most people appeared to think a lot of her.'

'Do I hear a *but* coming?'

'Not really. A few people said it was difficult to get below the surface.'

'Did anyone say that she had a temper or showed intolerance?'

'Well, yes. One or two people who happened to run into her unexpectedly, but they were a bit vague about it.'

'That fits in with what I've been told. Someone speculated that if she ever let her guard down, she could have made enemies. I can give you my contact's details if you want. He suggested that might provide a motive for her kidnapping.'

'You don't really think that, do you?'

She laughed. 'No. Not really. Maybe something else, but not kidnapping. Let's face it, it's got to be linked to the rest of the case.'

* * *

Later in the evening, Sophie was relaxing in the lounge, her head against Martin's shoulder and somewhat unsuccessfully trying not to nod off in front of a TV drama. The trill of her mobile phone made her jump.

'Hello, Paul.'

'She's turned up. Corinne Lanston. Dirty, confused, bedraggled and injured. Apparently, she's been wandering about for hours in the Chilterns woodland after managing to escape this afternoon.'

'Where is she now?'

'In hospital, under sedation. Her injuries are only superficial, though the medics don't think she's had much to eat for days. Steve hopes to be able to talk to her tomorrow or Sunday. She could be discharged in a couple of days if the tests are positive, so we'll try to get her in for a full debrief next week, maybe Monday or Tuesday. Do you want to be there as an observer?'

'Don't I just.'

CHAPTER 29: WORRIED POLITICIANS

Saturday morning

Barry had spent several days following up possible links with the murders in Normandy. He'd stayed in touch with the local police there and had received a number of reports from Natalie Bouchet, his counterpart in the French police. CCTV footage had recorded a large dark blue BMW with UK plates driving onto the ferry from Portsmouth to Cherbourg on the previous Saturday night, but the occupants had remained largely out of sight while on the ferry. Natalie told him that several witnesses had noticed a similar vehicle in the area of the murders on the Sunday evening, with what looked to be a man and woman inside. They were both wearing brimmed hats, scarves and sunglasses, so it was difficult to obtain any precise details about them. Maybe middle-aged? Maybe she had fair hair? It was impossible to be sure on either count. They didn't seem to have returned on the same ferry route, not yet anyway. No vehicle with the same plates had shown up on the ferry's booking system.

Natalie wondered if they could have returned via a different route as a precaution, so she and Barry had checked the other ferry service, via Le Havre. Sure enough, there was a record for the vehicle, and the CCTV images showed the same couple as on the outward journey to Cherbourg.

The names, of course, had been false. The vehicle had been hired from a Portsmouth agency, and the name used was Charmaine Cookson. A dead end, possibly. But the shadowy figures each had a driving license and passport. Were they false, and if so, how had they managed that? The hire vehicle in question had been taken in for close examination, but it held no useable forensic traces. These people knew what they were doing.

Even so, Barry was moderately pleased. Several days of intense activity had paid off, at least in one respect. He felt that the investigation was yielding small but significant results, and they were beginning to gain an understanding of how these people operated. He looked at his watch. About now Gwen, his partner, should be interviewing Peter Zelinski with her boss. Maybe more would come out of it. Zelinski was the most senior person left from the secret security unit, although that might change given the latest news about Corinne Lanston's escape. Surely that would result in some useful information?

* * *

Gwen was unimpressed by Zelinski's continued distant, almost uncooperative manner, although he had clearly been shaken by the report of his boss's abduction and asked for news of her.

'She's been found,' Jack Dunning said. 'So far, all we know is that she managed to escape from her captors yesterday afternoon. She's currently in hospital but doesn't seem to have any serious injuries. We'll learn more in a few days.'

Zelinski gave a sigh of relief and visibly relaxed. It was almost as if a great weight had been lifted from his shoulders, which probably reflected reality. Gwen wondered if they might now get more out of him, but it quickly became apparent that the opposite was the case.

'Corinne might be better placed to answer that,' became the stock answer to any question about the personnel and decisions made inside the security unit.

'We think your house had an intruder a couple of nights ago,' Jack said.

Zelinski stiffened. 'What?'

'One of your neighbours reported seeing a flickering light in your back room, as if someone with a torch was inside. The police were called but nothing seemed amiss. There were no signs of a break-in, but the neighbour was adamant that he'd seen it.' Jack consulted his notebook. 'A Mr Cassidy? Could that be right?'

Zelinski nodded, frowning. 'That would be right. The window in the back room looks out onto the garden, but it has a small side window, facing across the drive to his house. But why would anyone be there?'

Jack was exasperated. 'Get real, Peter. Hasn't it clicked with you yet? This is a ruthless group of people we're dealing with here. They're tidying up the loose ends and eliminating anyone who might finger them. It's a good job we insisted on moving you out. I'll go so far as to say you may well owe your life to us. Come on. You must know something.'

'But I don't, that's the thing. I don't really know any of the details about the smuggling operation. That was Corinne and Louise. I'm an operations person, dealing with the practical side of things.'

Gwen almost held her breath. This was the first time he'd opened up about the roles within the unit.

'Could you elaborate?' Jack asked.

'Corinne's ferociously well organised. She kept an eye on everything and ran the lot, but it was almost getting to be too much for her. Louise was meant to just deal with the administration but started doing more in-depth work. She was struggling.'

'Why was she moved into that safe house? Come on, Peter. We need to know.'

'She received a death threat, a text message from a mobile that we couldn't identify. It said she'd regret it if she talked. Then she got knocked about by someone as she arrived home one night. It was very suspicious but there was no clue as to who it was or why it happened. Corinne was worried and decided to play safe. That's why she moved her.'

At last they were getting to the bottom of Louise's back story.

'But they still found her, didn't they? How could that have happened?'

Zelinski looked bemused, almost panic-stricken. 'I don't know. I just don't know. Don't you think I've asked myself that a thousand times?'

'What about the first victim, Robert Bunting? Were you overseeing him?'

'Not really. I think Louise had taken him on.'

* * *

Sophie was in London, in Whitehall. To be more precise, she was in the office of the Junior Immigration Minister, Ken Burke, along with Paul Baker and Steve Lamb. Also present was the minister's Parliamentary Private Secretary, Yauvani Anand. Sophie was present at the invitation of Paul, the AC, who wanted her insight into the Dorset crimes.

'Mad' Ken Burke cut an imposing figure on TV but was less so in the flesh. He had heavy jowls, a blotchy complexion, thinning hair and he wheezed, sounding slightly asthmatic. His clothes were crumpled. A man well past his prime, Sophie thought, living on past rabble-rousing successes.

'I must offer my congratulations, Assistant Commissioner, on finding Corinne alive.' He spoke in a theatrical growl. That explains a lot, Sophie thought — a Churchill complex. Too many second-rate politicians thought, mistakenly, that emulating the great man was an easy route to success. He rumbled on. 'I was beginning to think time was running out, but I should never have doubted you and your people.'

'Thank you. But I'm not sure that our efforts had much to do with it. She managed to escape by her own efforts. She's a resourceful woman.'

'Yes, she is. Which is why she's in the position she is.'

'I'm still not sure of the setup of this security unit of yours, nor its *raison d'être*, Minister. Would you care to enlighten us?'

'Well, ah, I'm not sure it's necessary, not now Corinne's safe.' Burke was beginning to bluster.

'Oh, but it is. We have three murders to clear up in the West Country, which is why Detective Superintendent Allen is here. Plus, two murders across the Channel in Normandy, in which she's liaising with the French police. Add to that Corinne's abduction, several break-ins and the tragic deaths of those poor people on the boat last week. To put it bluntly, Minister, we at New Scotland Yard need to know what's going on.'

Ken Burke was watching the AC through narrowed eyes. The silence that followed his words was broken by the silky tones of his PPS. As always, Yauvani Anand looked immaculate. A maroon wraparound dress showed off her figure to perfection and matched the colour of her shoes exactly. Her black hair shone and her skin glowed.

'Shall I explain, Minister?' she said, not waiting for his reply. 'It was thought that we needed a small intelligence unit of our own, with the specific task of monitoring the activity of the gangs who smuggle migrants into the country illegally. Highly focussed on that one task and reporting directly to the minister and me.'

Sophie couldn't help but interrupt. 'But you're a PPS, Ms Anand. You have no direct political responsibility, surely. Or has that code changed? Am I being naıve?'

'No, of course you're not. You are technically correct, but this is such a serious crisis that I'm happy to help the minister in any way I can. It is not actually outside the PPS's remit.' Yauvani's tone was smooth. 'You were on the beach with your chief constable last Saturday, weren't you?'

Sophie sensed a challenge. 'That's right. I'm the SIO for the murders and the migrant deaths.'

'But not for Corinne's abduction,' was the terse reply.

'No, you're right. That's here, with Paul and the Met. But I'm also present today on behalf of Hampshire CID, who are looking into Louise Bennett's murder. We're working jointly.'

Sophie really didn't want to become embroiled in the female equivalent of a pissing contest, but she wasn't willing to accept being relegated to a mere observer, not after coming all the way from Dorset to attend this meeting. Anyway, she had a certain amount of admiration for Yauvani, even if she didn't share her political views. The daughter of a poor Asian family, she was hard-working and ambitious, refused to kowtow to the strict gender roles that many from her own community insisted upon, and she was a role model for young women from poor backgrounds wherever they might be. She was bright and forward-looking but could be abrasive. She was clearly destined for higher things within her party and was tipped for promotion at the next ministerial reshuffle. No, she wasn't a person to be underestimated or to upset without good reason.

'I'm only interested in solving these murders. That's my job,' Sophie went on, still looking at Yauvani. 'I have to get under the skin of the people involved, the victims, the perpetrators and those who are connected to them. I think the two murders in Dorset might revolve around Louise Bennett, who worked for your unit during the last two years or so. I am aware that I could wait until the middle of next week to get answers from Corinne herself, but that could be five days away, which is a long time in an inquiry as pressing as this. Things are changing by the day, even by the hour, so anything you can tell us about the operation of this security unit and the personnel within it would be very helpful.'

'There has to be a mole,' Paul added. 'Someone has been giving information to the traffickers and they've been acting on the tip-offs. Ruthlessly. So, let me get this right. The plan was to establish contact with gang members who were perceived as weak links, then to entice them to break ranks and slip away. They'd be given a new identity and a safe location in exchange for inside information. Is that right, Minister?'

'Exactly. And it was working so well. We had our first trafficker across here. In Weymouth, I believe. Then it all seemed to go wrong.'

'Whose idea was it?'

'The three of us, I think,' Ken Burke said. He was beginning to look worried.

'You must understand, it didn't happen at any one particular time,' Yauvani added. 'The idea evolved. We massaged it into a workable plan and Corinne's job at that point was to put it into practice.'

Sophie frowned in concentration. 'So, Corinne wasn't just appointed to run the unit, she was involved at the planning stage? Or even earlier, at its inception?'

'Yes.'

'Can I take it one stage further? Was it, if truth be told, Corinne's plan in the first place? Please think back to those initial discussions.'

Burke was showing signs of confusion. Clearly, he couldn't remember. Either that or he could see the political benefit of shifting the responsibility for the recent fiasco onto someone else, and was weighing up the pros and cons. He was saved from the need to decide by his PPS, who broke in once again.

'Corinne and I were out for a meal together a few years ago, after a Commons debate on the refugee crisis. We were wondering if the scenes in the Mediterranean would ever be repeated in the Channel. It seemed to me at the time to be idle talk over slightly too much wine. I think Corinne saw the future more clearly than I and made the initial suggestion.'

Sophie was genuinely puzzled. 'You knew Corinne before the unit was set up? Well enough to be out for a meal together?'

'Oh, yes. We were at the same university. We've been friends since those days.'

'Was she working in the department at that time?'

Yauvani shook her head. 'Not directly. She was heading up a think tank looking into the politics of migration. She was the ideal person to bring in and head up the unit.'

Sophie sat back and left Paul to ask the rest of the questions. There was just too much to think about.

CHAPTER 30: HOSPITAL DISCHARGE

It was strange to be saying a last goodbye to this place. Kamal looked around the ward that his mother had occupied for the past few days, since being transferred from intensive care. He and Arshi had visited every day, brought in either by their aunt and uncle or by Rose and George, the police sergeant and her partner. Back in Iran, he'd always been scared of the police and other authority figures. They seemed to wield an arbitrary power, ignoring wrongdoing committed by their own family and friends but tough on other people's minor misdemeanours. Until they fell out of favour themselves, that was, and then their whole family might be punished. But these two, Rose and George, seemed just like anyone else. They were here today, come to check that all went well during the discharge.

Their mother had lost weight during her stay in hospital. She'd never been a big woman, but now she looked even thinner than usual. Though she managed to smile when she saw them, her eyes were still sad. She was dressed, sitting in a small waiting room, bags at her feet. It took little more than ten minutes to complete the paperwork and then they were ready to leave. Several of the nurses and doctors came out to say goodbye and wish them luck. Kamal was pleased that his mother was joining them in his aunt and uncle's home, but still he watched everybody and listened to what they said. Most people at home in Iran could be just like this, helpful and friendly. But they were still wary, nervous even. You just never knew. He picked up his mum's small bag.

'It's really good, their home,' he said to her as they moved towards the door. 'Me and Arshi have been out in the town where they live. There's a beach, and the sea. It's nice, Mum. We like it.'

Roya squeezed his hand. She looked close to tears.

* * *

The grown-ups were in the kitchen, discussing the kind of questions that might be asked during the asylum process.

'We came through several other countries on our way here,' Roya was saying. 'I've been told they view that as a mistake and that the immigration officials will argue that we should have sought asylum in the first country we reached. But we all speak English. Zaan studied here. We have you here, close family. It seemed the best place for us. And if it works out, I can get legal status and get a job. I'll pay my taxes and contribute to the country. Why should that be a problem?'

'Because the whole attitude towards asylum seekers and immigrants in Britain has changed in recent years,' Soraya's mother, Jenny, said. 'It's the same in other parts of Europe. There's a new mood and people no longer trust outsiders. They treat you differently now. More and more immigrants are being turned away. The government says the country is full up and can't take any more. But when you look below the surface of those words you find that the reality is something else. If you have good qualifications, it's easier to get permission to settle. That should help you. But out on the streets, there's another feeling. Some narrow-minded British people are happy to let white people come in from Australia or America. It's only people of colour or from lower status countries who they want to keep out. Even white people from Poland get insults thrown at them. I think it was always there, but those people were afraid to let their feelings be known. Now they feel able to let their prejudices show. It isn't nice.'

'But we'll be alive, Jenny,' Roya said, leaning forward, 'which we wouldn't be if we'd stayed in Iran. Those revolutionary guards were working their way through a list and we were on it. There were spies everywhere. We didn't know who to trust. Our neighbours were betrayed by someone from their own family. How could they do that? Send their own cousins to a camp where they'd probably end up dead? And those poor children? There may be unpleasantness here, but I can live with that if it means Kamal and Arshi have a future.' She paused. 'I'll need to get in touch with that professor. She said that her charity would help once I got out of hospital. I still don't know whether I should accept help from those police officers. Back home, we'd never expect to get that from anyone in authority. I'm sure some of them meant well, but we never knew who to trust. It was awful, Saman. It's all so different since you were there. There is fear and deprivation in every town and village. We couldn't go back now, not without Zaan.' She sobbed. 'What will I do?'

Rose stood up to leave. 'You must go through the asylum process, Roya,' she said. 'And the sooner the better. I'll help where I can but do contact that charity. Her name was Alice Linklater. One of my bosses knows her, I think. Do it today. We'll be back in touch soon. Some of those photos of Kamal's are likely to be used as evidence once we catch the traffickers. And we may need to ask you a few more questions about what you remember.' She glanced out of the window. 'I'd better go and drag my partner off. He's having way too much fun.'

The children were out in the back garden, kicking a football about with George. They shrieked as Rose ran across the lawn and booted the ball, only to see it fly off over the fence, into the neighbouring garden.

'You've got to go and get it back, Rose. That's the rule,' Arshi said. 'But I'll come with you.'

Rose took her hand. 'Why do these things always happen to me?' she complained loudly.

CHAPTER 31: DEBRIEF

Monday morning

Sophie was in an observation room watching Corinne's debrief, along with Paul Baker and several other officers from the Met. Steve Lamb was conducting the interview in a small, comfortably furnished office. The three of them were all in soft chairs set around a low table, with a pot of coffee and a plate of biscuits in front of them. The third person present was Marie Friesmann, a behavioural psychologist employed by the Met for exactly these kinds of debriefs, involving people freed from hostage situations or kidnappings. She'd become an expert in such meetings, although she'd warned Paul that she didn't expect to say much on this occasion. Realistically, she was only present because of the strict protocol for a debrief such as this. Corinne seemed very calm and matter of fact.

She was exactly as people had described her — rather taller than average, with pale ginger hair and freckled skin. She was smartly dressed in a black fitted jacket, cream silk blouse and black slim-fit trousers. She was wearing shiny black two-inch court shoes. Sophie wondered if her hair might be coloured, although it was difficult to be sure from the screen display. It might be difficult to be sure even up close. A woman so well kept would surely be able to pay for the best of hair treatments. Her manner was correspondingly immaculate — cool and collected.

Steve began by stating how pleased they all were that she'd managed to escape from her captors, and that the police were doing all they could to apprehend her abductors. They'd identified the small remote cottage where she'd been held and were carrying out a thorough and detailed search of the premises. No obvious clues had been left though, which was why this detailed debrief had proved necessary. He then asked her to take him through the events on the evening of her abduction. She took a sip of coffee and began. She had a slightly deep, almost husky voice and spoke in an economical, almost emotionless way.

'I was in the kitchen tidying up my supper things and stacking the dishwasher when the intercom from the main door rang. It was a young man's voice saying he had a delivery of flowers for me. He knew my name. I told him I was on the first floor and asked him to bring them up. A minute or so later, my doorbell rang, and I opened it after checking through the eye hole. I had the security chain across, but the gap was too narrow to get the bouquet through, so I was forced to close the door, disengage the chain and reopen it. Then he pushed it hard and it swung into me, hitting me with some force.

'He came through shoulder first, dropped the flowers and punched me hard in the face, and I staggered back, cannoning off the wall behind me. I'd hit my head hard, and I nearly passed out. He dragged me through to the lounge and told me to stay still and keep silent, otherwise he'd kill me. I wasn't in a fit state to resist anyway. I was dizzy from the punch and hitting my head. I think it must have caught the edge of the mirror on the wall. I could feel blood. I tried to move but felt nauseous and was worried that I'd pass out.

'He came back from the bedroom, stuffing something into his pockets, then grabbed me by the wrist and hauled me back into the hall. He grabbed a coat from the rack, threw it at me and told me to put it on. While I was trying to get into it, he opened the door and peered outside. Then he grabbed my arm and pulled me to the lift. It was still on my floor, so we got down to the entrance lobby very quickly. I kept hoping that someone else would be around, but no one was. It was late at night and many of my neighbours are elderly. He was pushing something into my ribs. I think it was a knife.

'It was all I could do to stay upright. I was still feeling very sick and dizzy. He had a car outside and he opened it and pushed me in, saying that if I did anything stupid, I'd suffer — well, something like that. I was too dizzy to remember exactly. While I was still thinking about what I could do, he was already in the driving seat, so it was too late to do anything. He tied my wrists before driving off, so I couldn't try to escape.'

She stopped, took several sips of coffee and closed her eyes. Sophie was impressed. Corinne had recounted that evening's events in a clear and concise manner, despite the emotional toll it must be taking.

'Are you okay to continue?' Marie asked.

Corinne's eyes opened and she nodded. 'Yes, of course.' She finished her coffee.

'Can you remember much about the car journey?' Steve asked.

'Not really. I felt as if I was inhabiting my own bad dream. I was still sick and dizzy. I know we ended up on the M1, heading north. Beyond that, I can't say much. We came off the motorway at some point and I think we drove west, but I can't be sure. The roads got increasingly narrow. I don't know how long I was in the car. It just seemed to go on and on.'

She refilled her coffee cup and swallowed another mouthful.

'I must have dozed off because the next thing I knew, we'd stopped. It was still dark. The man got out and opened my door. He dragged me from the car, gripping my arm with such force that I couldn't think clearly. He pushed me through a low door into an old building. He didn't switch on any lights. He shoved me into a room, slammed the door behind me and locked it.'

Another sip of coffee.

'The room was in complete darkness. I felt around the wall near the door and found a light switch. I was surprised when a light came on. I was in that room for the next week. He only came back twice, after gaps of about two or three days. I wasn't tied up and the room had enough food in it to keep me alive. There was a small en-suite, so I had a toilet and a wash basin.'

'What kind of food?' Steve asked.

'Nothing the first night. But the next morning he unlocked the door and threw in some packets — biscuits, some cheese slices, a packet of dried apricots. Even some cake. I didn't starve. I don't think they had planned to keep me a prisoner there. If that had been the case, I'd have expected to find food, and maybe some clothes. But there was nothing like that.'

'What about the furniture and fittings?'

'There was a bed and a chair. That was it. There were two towels in the en-suite, and a tablet of soap. Oh, and a plastic tumbler that I drank from. The bedroom had a plug-in convection heater and that was useful. Not only to keep the room warm, but it meant I could rinse my clothes and drape them on the chair to dry overnight. The bed had a duvet, so I was warm enough during the night. It was very basic, but I could stay clean and keep myself alive.'

'Anything else about the room?'

'There was a window, but it had outside shutters that were closed. Even so, light came in during the daytime. I could see that the window faced south by the sunlight that came through the cracks in the shutters.'

Corinne paused and lowered her head. Sophie wondered if she was becoming distressed. Marie leaned across, squeezed her hand and asked her if she needed a break, but Corinne said she wanted this over as quickly as possible.

Steve raised his eyes enquiringly. Corinne nodded.

'You said you thought your captor called twice,' he said.

'Yes. I think it was the Monday and Wednesday. He was only there for a minute or two though, just long enough to throw a bag of food in. I don't think he stayed in the house. Each time, I heard the outside door shut soon afterwards and the sound of a car driving away. I tried to speak to him, but he ignored me. I didn't even see him. The door was only open long enough for him to shove the food in.'

'What did you spend your time doing?' Steve asked.

The question seemed to annoy her. 'What do you think? I explored every inch of the room. I sat thinking, planning, looking for a way out. There was a book on a shelf by the bed. Some cheap thriller. I read it and re-read it. What else was there for me to do? I'll probably hate that book forever.'

'How did you escape in the end?' Steve asked.

'I realised that the window latch was slightly insecure. It was fastened in place by a little grub screw. I kept working on it. Then, on Friday morning, I decided to break the plastic tumbler and try to do something with the shards. I managed to scrape one piece down to fit the screw and undid it. I could open the window a little until it caught against the shutter. I put the chair against the window, climbed onto it, sat on the sill and kicked through the gap at the shutter. It wasn't as secure as I expected, and I had it open within ten minutes. They were the longest ten minutes of my life. I kept imagining I heard a car approaching. Once I got outside, I just kept heading south, avoiding the roads. I followed a footpath through the woods and across some farmland. I got to a village with a small post office, so I went in. I think you know the rest.' She paused. 'I was lucky in a way. I had access to food, water, a decent bed, a toilet and a wash basin. I could keep myself clean and nourished, even though the food was just dry — nothing cooked. It could have been a lot worse.'

* * *

Sophie walked slowly out of the observation room with Paul Baker. Outside, she dawdled, taking her time to move along the corridor. She couldn't have said precisely why, but she wanted to see Corinne Lanston in the flesh. They were entering a more open-plan area, with a row of seats next to a water cooler, when a door opened and the trio from the debrief appeared.

There was Steve, strolling towards Paul Baker, starting to relax after the tension of the past hour. Marie came next, hanging back so that Corinne wasn't left alone. Corinne advanced slowly, replacing a pen inside her shoulder bag. She looked around her, watchful, and her eyes met Sophie's. Sophie gave her a brief smile and Corinne smiled back. The smile didn't reach her eyes, which were distrustful, cautious. Was she still suffering the effects of a week in solitary imprisonment, when she must have had doubts as to whether she'd ever escape alive?

'Are you still okay with going to the cottage tomorrow?' Paul asked. 'We can delay it if you prefer. But it'd be very useful to see the place. You didn't get a look at the rest of the house, did you?'

'It'll be fine,' she said, as controlled as she'd been during the debrief. 'Then maybe I can start to forget it. It's not easy.'

Sophie slipped out of the room. She'd already arranged with Paul Baker to be included on the next day's visit. It was even more important now.

CHAPTER 32: FOOD — AND THEN DRINK

Monday evening

'So, Mum, tell me all about why you're in London. I miss getting the gossip.' Hannah Allen was sipping her wine. They were in Hannah's favourite restaurant, a family-owned Italian eatery near Russell Square in Bloomsbury. Hannah was Sophie and Martin's elder daughter, a newly qualified actor, fresh out of drama college and already getting positive reviews for her occasional roles on the stage, which varied from light comedy to Shakespearean drama. Like Sophie, she was slim, average in height and blonde. Unusually for her, she was wearing jeans and a T-shirt. Her mother was also in jeans, with a thin, wool jumper in pale blue.

'It's all linked to the migrant smuggling operation. I can't give you any details though. To be honest, it's all over the place. We keep thinking we might have it nailed down, then something pops up somewhere else that throws a completely different light on it.'

'Right up your street, then?'

'You always were a shrewd one, Hannah. Anyway, I had an unexpected day at New Scotland Yard and there's a follow-up session tomorrow. It made sense to stay over, even if it does mean kipping down in your spare room. Lucky that Jess has moved out.'

'We're all reaching that age, Mum. It's a mid-twenties thing, I expect. You know, making big decisions about commitments. Jess and Magnus are talking about getting hitched. The skittles are starting to fall, one by one.'

Sophie looked her elder daughter in the eye. 'You make it sound like a prison sentence. Settling down can be fun, Hannah — if the time's right.'

'Jade messaged me to say you were in Oxford last week.'

'That's right, I was there on Wednesday, again linked to the case. We met up for lunch. It's partly the reason I wanted to see you tonight. You see, she discovered something about me by sheer chance.'

Sophie paused and took a gulp of wine. This was going to be hard. She told herself to grit her teeth and just get on with it.

'We were chatting during lunch on Wednesday and she asked me a totally unexpected question. I couldn't control my reaction, and she guessed. It's just that when I was there as a student, before I met your dad, I had a brief fling with another woman, a close friend. I thought it only right to tell you as well, Hannah, what with Jade knowing.'

Hannah's reaction was unexpected.

'Phew. That's a relief. It makes me feel better.'

Sophie couldn't help but smile. 'Not you as well?'

Hannah looked at her apprehensively. 'Rather more times than you'd want to know about, Mum. It worries me because I really love Russell and want to be with him. I wish life was a bit simpler. Does it alter anything between us?'

Sophie reached across and laid her hand on Hannah's. 'Of course not. This is us, you and me, Hannah. If I wasn't your mum, I'd be your big sister. I've always hoped that you and Jade both feel that you can tell me anything.'

'Well, that's true, up to a point. How's Jade getting on with George, do you think? He's really nice. If it wasn't for the fact he's going out with Jade, I might have made a move on him myself.'

Sophie laughed. 'You never fail to cheer me up, Hannah, whenever I manage to see you, which isn't often enough. Anyway, they're besotted with each other. I sometimes spot George at work, wearing this dreamy look on his face. Not recently though, since she's been away at Oxford.'

'I'm spending a few days with her later this month. She's only been there a couple of weeks and she claims she's already sussed out the good places to eat. And drink too, I expect. Have the pubs changed much since you and Dad were there?'

Sophie shook her head. 'We only went to one and that was a quick visit for lunch. She didn't drag me round on a pub crawl. I couldn't cope anyway, not at my age.'

'Don't kid me, Mum. I know you and your beer. Good job you've got Dad to rein you in. Where are you off to tomorrow?'

'I'm not totally sure. It's probably up the M1 somewhere, then off towards the Chilterns. I'm there as a sort of observer, the Met is taking the lead. They're taking a kidnap victim back to where she was held for a week. It's all a bit peculiar if you ask me.'

They stopped talking as their food arrived.

'We could do a mini pub-crawl of our own, Mum, once we've finished here. There are two great pubs across the road, down Cosmo Passage. Then we could get a cab back to the flat. What do you reckon?'

'You're a bad influence, young lady.' Sophie took a mouthful of her spaghetti. 'But I could be persuaded.'

It would take her mind off tomorrow's expedition. Up the haunted highway, through the gloomy woodland, then across the spooky glen to the evil gingerbread house. Or should that be the other way around? Sophie sighed. Maybe she'd already had too much alcohol. But only maybe.

CHAPTER 33: THE COTTAGE

Tuesday morning

The vehicle convoy pulled up outside a secluded cottage, set back slightly from the narrow lane. There was a gravelled parking area beside the road, already containing two police cars, so the newly arrived vehicles were forced to use the verge. The building stood beyond a grey stone wall. It looked deserted and somewhat neglected. Only the crime-scene tapes fluttering in the breeze added a splash of colour. Sophie had travelled in the second car, along with Paul Baker and the driver, a woman officer from his staff. Corinne Lanston, Steve Lamb and two other Met officers were in front, followed by a minivan containing a number of police security personnel, including several armed officers.

Sophie climbed out of the car and looked around her. It was exactly as Corinne had described, a single storey stone cottage, the only one in a narrow lane, which meandered away towards open farmland. Sophie noted the old wooden windows. It looked as though the scrawny rambling roses had climbed up the walls at some time in the recent past, but these now looked tattered and neglected, as did the rest of the narrow, weed-infested front garden. A decrepit wooden gate lay half across the entrance. One hard shove and it would probably topple over.

A faded wooden shutter, covering one of the narrow front windows, was hanging from a single hinge. It was split, long splinters protruding in several places, evidence of having been kicked from the inside. Several uniformed police officers were standing guard at the small porch, one with a gun that he held with the barrel pointed at the ground. Birds sang and the tree branches swayed gently in the light breeze. It was a beautiful setting, yet it seemed full of menace.

Sophie attached herself to the rear of the group as it made its way into the cottage. Corinne accompanied the lead officer inside, followed by Steve Lamb and Paul Baker. She didn't say much, apart from a few brief comments. They entered a narrow hallway, dark and forbidding, lit only by the daylight entering through the small glass panes in the door behind them. Sophie glanced at a couple of letters that lay opened on a small shelf near the front door — circulars and a bill. The small group turned immediately left into the room that had served as Corinne's prison for a week. It was exactly as she had described, bare, with the minimum of furnishings. The walls were painted a faded cream colour. The bare boards of the floor had evidently been varnished at some time in the past but were now worn and grey.

There they saw the small cubicle with toilet and basin that had allowed Corinne to keep herself clean, and thereby maintain some measure of dignity. Sophie was last to peer in. There were still two rolls of toilet paper sitting on the cistern. The toilet bowl itself looked moderately clean, as did the wash basin, with its single tablet of soap sitting behind one of the taps.

'Have forensics finished?' Sophie whispered to Paul.

'Yes,' he replied. 'They've had three days. They've got everything they need.'

She flushed the toilet, listening for a second or two as the cistern filled. She ran the hot tap. The water was tepid.

'That was what it was like. No hot water,' Corinne said to her as she emerged.

Sophie smiled. 'Not ideal, but at least you had running water to use and to drink. You must have been thankful for that.'

'Yes. It could have been so much worse.'

They went back out into the hallway, and then explored the rest of the cottage. Corinne looked as curious as the rest of the group. She'd told them that she'd never had an opportunity to see the rest of the building, its small, dark rooms, the slight smell of mildew and damp in the rear kitchen and lounge — two rooms that must have received little direct sunlight. A narrow stairway at the end of the hall led upstairs to two bedrooms, tucked under the eaves of the cottage, each with a dormer window. The main bathroom was also upstairs.

Sophie slipped away from the group, made her way downstairs and out into the front garden. It must be around here somewhere. She glanced around the paving slabs that led the few steps to the rickety gate, then the gravel path that ran along the front of the building. No sign. She walked out into the lane, looking left and right. Nothing obvious, but there was a pile of freshly blown leaves and other detritus piled up against the wall at one point. She kicked the rubbish away to reveal a mains water point, the location of the stopcock. She extracted a pen from her bag and used it to lift the cover. There was the water meter she was expecting. She took a note of the reading, closed the lid and made her way back into the cottage. The top letter on the shelf was a water bill. It should have been addressed to the cottage owner by name, but instead bore the irritatingly bland greeting, *To the Registered Proprietor*. Sophie scanned the details, then looked up as the rest of the group started to descend the stairs. Corinne was looking at her intently, so Sophie smiled once more. This time it was not reciprocated.

Corinne then led the group across the lane and onto a narrow footpath that vanished into a copse of trees some twenty yards further on. This was the track she'd followed four days previously, heading across some farmland towards a small village about a mile away. As the group followed the path, heading south for the most part, Sophie sidled up to Paul Baker.

'This is a complete pack of lies, Paul. It's utter tosh, from beginning to end.'

* * *

The group arrived at the village green, opposite the local store and post office. Sophie glanced at her watch. Almost twenty minutes. Corinne had told them that she'd half-run and half-walked, covering the distance in less than fifteen. As she was speaking, the shop-owner came out and told them how shocked she'd been the previous week when a bruised, dazed and injured woman had suddenly staggered into her shop.

'It scared me, I can tell you.' She smiled at Corinne. 'I'm so glad you've recovered so quickly.' She turned to Paul Baker, his uniform identifying him as a senior police officer. 'I kept her safe in a back room until the first police car arrived and tried my best to look after her. She was distraught but calmed down a bit after she'd had a cup of tea and a bun. It's terrible that these things happen. What's the world coming to?'

The cars arrived and the various members of the group climbed in, ready to head back to London. Paul, Steve and Sophie lingered at the roadside.

'This is surreal,' Sophie said. 'It's pantomime, pure and simple.'

'Okay, I take your point about the water use. Could there be another explanation?' Paul asked.

Sophie shrugged. 'I can't think of one. She was there for more than a week. She would have flushed the loo, what, ten times a day? Each flush uses about seven litres. That's about six hundred litres. Then she told us she washed every day and washed her clothes twice. That must be another fifty litres at least. But that meter showed no significant change from what was on the bill, recorded several weeks earlier. It should have shown almost another cubic metre, surely? It doesn't add up, Paul.'

'How did you calculate that? I'm not disputing your total, Sophie, although it will have to be checked.'

Sophie chuckled. 'It's what being married to a maths teacher does to you. Martin does conversion calculations for fun. Well, he calls it fun. I call it extremely sad. He did that one recently when we changed over to a water meter, now that Jade's no longer with us. She loved her baths and now she's not at home, we're using far less water. And while we're talking of washing, there's another thing. Think about the tablet of soap. To me it looked as though it had hardly been used, yet the fragrant Ms Lanston claimed to have washed every day and used it several times to launder her underwear and blouse. She's having us on. It wasn't just the abduction that was staged. So was this supposed incarceration. The real question is, why? What's her game?'

'We can do pretty much anything we want to keep tabs on her, because of the national security angle,' Paul said. 'But she's got powerful friends. We can't afford to get it wrong.'

'I'll keep away from now on. She spotted me outside the cottage, when I was looking for the water meter. Luckily it wouldn't have been visible behind the front wall, but she must have wondered what I was doing out there. Don't underestimate her, Paul. She's very devious and very clever. And we face a real problem. If she wasn't here last week, under lock and key in that cottage, where was she? And how much did she manage to learn about our investigations?'

CHAPTER 34: OCCASION TO SWEAR

'We've been bloody lucky,' Dave Nash said. 'It was almost too faint to see anything, but we think one of the dyes in the ink stuck harder to the paper than the others. Given the right treatment, this shows up.'

Barry, Rae and Tommy were all at the forensic labs, looking at a screen showing a small shop receipt with several lines of characters faintly visible.

'I can't make anything out,' Barry said.

'Neither could we at first,' Dave said. 'But we are nothing if not painstaking.' He ignored the sound of mock coughing and choking coming from the two senior detectives and moved to the next slide. This was much clearer.

'This is enhanced further,' he added.

'Tyndall's Chandlers,' Tommy said. 'And is that a Southampton address? That's where old Andy Coates said Dorry O'Brian had moved to.' He leaned forward and peered at the screen.

Dave continued. 'As far as we can tell, it's the receipt for some clothes, a dark blue tracksuit and a set of waterproof outers. Does that tie in with what you expected?'

Rae nodded enthusiastically. 'Oh, yes. That's exactly what the people on the boat said the crewman was wearing. It's why we thought those tracksuit trousers might be his. They were found close to the coast path. What else can you tell us?'

'It's what you thought. They'd been immersed in seawater. The grit and bits of seaweed were exactly right for the bit of shoreline the boat washed up on.'

'No DNA though?' Barry asked.

Dave shook his head. 'Nothing so far. I've got someone still looking, but don't hold your breath.'

'I think Tommy and I need to pay a visit to that chandlery,' Rae added.

* * *

The chandlers were an integral part of a relatively new quayside development on the River Itchen, just to the east of Southampton city centre, well away from the main docks in the west. Rae parked facing out over the sparkling water, dotted with boats and yachts. The whole of the Solent waterside was a mass of marinas, quays and docks, interspersed with nature reserves and country parks.

Tyndall's Chandlers was a new building that looked across a brick-paved walkway to the water's edge. Spacious as a small warehouse, it seemed to sell everything that a boating person could ever want, and more. Rae asked Tommy to take the lead. He needed the experience to boost his confidence, which was still woefully lacking. He identified himself to a member of staff and asked to see the manager.

John Duke was a tanned, roguish-looking man in his late fifties, short and stocky.

'We're trying to find some details about a purchase that was made a few weeks ago,' Tommy explained. 'We've got the receipt although it got wet, so it's badly faded.' He produced a copy of the enhanced image and handed it to John. 'It's for some waterproof clothing and a tracksuit. Can you help us?'

John took the sheet and studied it carefully. 'Fairly late on a Tuesday afternoon,' he said. 'And the till operator was Naomi. You're in luck, she's in today. I'll find her for you.'

He went over to a young woman on a stepladder, tidying boxes on a high shelf. She took the paper and studied it.

'Yeah, I remember this one. He was a tall, thin bloke with really piercing eyes. He made me kinda nervous. He paid in cash, which is unusual these days.'

Tommy frowned. 'Oh. You sure? We thought it was a bearded man. Irish accent?'

'Oh, yeah. Of course. The one I described was the guy who paid. He made me a bit nervous. The other guy was the one the clothes were for. I think he had a bit of a squint. Would that be right?'

'That's the one.' Tommy looked relieved.

'You didn't happen to pick up on any names by any chance, did you?' Rae asked. 'Did they talk to each other at all?'

Naomi thought hard. 'I think one was Phil. The Irish guy, the one with the squint, said something like, "that's the least you can do, Phil, buy me some half-decent clothes." I can remember the guy who paid, Phil, looking annoyed. I'd never seen them before, and they haven't been back since. Are they in trouble or something?'

'We don't know. That's why we're trying to trace them. Did you see them get into a car or van after they left?'

She shook her head. 'No, sorry. You're lucky I remember that much. It's usually too busy for any customers to stick in my mind. They did, mainly because they were such an odd pair.'

The detectives thanked the two staff and left.

'Phil, eh,' Rae murmured. 'Well, it's added a name, at least. And we know that the clothes did belong to that boatman. We're getting somewhere, Tommy. Slowly but surely.'

* * *

On the way back to the incident room in Weymouth, Rae decided to pay a quick visit to Charmaine Biggs. Maybe she'd remembered something else about either the woman who'd threatened her with a knife as a teenager, or the young man at the centre of the adolescent love tussle. She rang the doorbell twice but there was no answer. Rae started to walk around the side of the house, stopping when a woman called out to her from the neighbouring garden. She'd been clearing dead flowers from a bed. She asked Rae who she was.

'I'm a police officer,' Rae said and showed her warrant card.

'I don't think you'll find them in, not for a few days at least,' the woman said.

'Why's that?'

'They both left the day before yesterday. They had bags with them. I asked if they were off on holiday and Charmaine said yes. A surprise break was what she said. She was a bit vague about how long they'd be gone.'

'Did she say where they were going?'

'I expect it was on one of their sailing holidays. They keep a yacht down in the harbour. If the weather looks good, they often sail to places along the south coast. They even get as far as the Channel Islands and France.'

Rae was starting to feel worried. 'What kind of car do they have?'

'A big thing. You know, one of those huge German tanks. Well, that's what my husband calls them.'

'A BMW?'

'That's it. A big dark blue monstrosity.'

'And you are?'

'Maureen Callaghan. I'm sixty-three, fit and a vegetarian,' she said proudly.

'Thanks. Maureen, what's Charmaine's husband's name?'

'Philip. He manages a used car dealership in town. We always get our cars through him because he says he can get us any make of car we want at a good price. But he specialises in used BMWs.'

Rae beckoned to Tommy and they made their way back to the car. She rarely swore, but now she was doing so repeatedly under her breath, driving fast back to the incident room. The boss wasn't going to be happy.

The bosses weren't happy, either of them. Barry sat with his head in his hands for several moments and Sophie, just arrived back from London, went over to the window and stood staring out. She took a deep breath and turned back to face Rae, who was pale by now.

'How did we miss it?' she asked.

'You mean, ma'am, how did *I* miss it? It was me that interviewed her. And I still can't believe it. She had me totally fooled.' She paused. Sighed. 'I don't know what to say. Do you want my resignation?'

Sophie realised that Rae was being serious. 'Absolutely not. It really isn't that bad, Rae. Anyway, I've never had cause to doubt your judgement.'

'Up to now,' Rae added despondently.

* * *

Sophie's request for a search warrant produced one of the speediest responses she'd ever had. Within two hours, a search and forensic team arrived at the Biggs's house in Poole. Maureen Callaghan was at the door within a few seconds of their arrival. She quickly spotted Rae.

'Don't bash it down. I've got keys, Sergeant. I keep a set for Charmaine, and she does the same for me. It's a lot safer than hiding them under a flowerpot.'

Sophie glanced anxiously at Barry as he took the proffered set of keys and unlocked the door.

'We'll be careful, Mrs Callaghan,' Rae said. She still felt sick.

The house, a three-bedroomed semi, was clear of anything that might be deemed suspicious. There were no laptops with suspect data, no weapons secreted in dark cupboards or hidden under floorboards, no unusual planning documents in locked cabinets. Even the garden shed contained only garden tools and the garage an old bicycle, an unused puncture repair kit and various bits of boating paraphernalia. The only suspect items in the house were a set of walking maps, with some sections of the Dorset coast path marked in blue ink. These were on a shelf next to a pair of binoculars.

Apart from the maps, the only other item that the police removed from Charmaine's house was an old cardboard box, found in a far corner of the loft. It looked as though it had been sealed many years before. They opened it only to find childhood mementos, items that might mean something to a teenage girl. At first Rae was tempted to leave it in place. It was hardly likely to contain anything relevant to the current inquiry, surely? The sticky tape sealing the box was aged and brittle, and the dust on the surface indicated that the box had lain undisturbed for many years. A forensic technician gave the box a quick scan and agreed with Rae about its age.

Rae began to relax. Had she been right after all? Her hopes were dashed somewhat by Barry's comment.

'If you were on a sailing trip, wouldn't you take binoculars with you?'

Sophie looked at him and frowned again. 'If you were up to no good, would you leave a set of keys with a neighbour? And how do we know that set of binoculars is the only pair they have? Rae, you and Tommy go and visit her employers. I think you reported that she claimed to work as a magazine editor. Talk to her boss. Get her history of absences and time off. Barry, you do the same for the husband. And I'll analyse the pen marks on these coastal maps to see if they correspond to possible landing spots. You can go through the box tomorrow morning, back in the incident room, Rae. If we have made a complete mess of this, we need to get on top of it quickly. I'm still not convinced though. I need to do some thinking. We all do.'

* * *

Dinner was over. It was a strange feeling, just the two of them in the house, night after night. With Jade gone, there was none of the chatter that normally filled the place. It only took a few minutes to clear the table and stack the dishwasher, then they often had the rest of the evening to themselves. Martin always had work from school, but he tried to get it completed before eating. They relaxed on the couch, Sophie leaning on Martin's shoulder.

'Nearly forgot,' she said and jumped to her feet. 'I've got some maps I need your help with. They're walking maps of the coast path, all the way along to Lyme Regis, and they've got pen marks on them in some places. Could you have a look at them and see if you can spot a pattern? You probably know the path as well as anyone.'

Martin looked at each of the four maps carefully. 'Most of the marks seem to be at small beaches,' he said. 'I can't really see anything else that links them. Seatown, West Bay, Burton, Charmouth. But right along here, Studland is marked with a double line. It's a much bigger beach, of course.'

'They could all be places where a boat could land, I suppose,' Sophie said. 'That's the only thought I had.'

'Well, there is something else, if you want to hear it.'

Sophie sat up, suddenly alert. 'What?'

'Umm, they're all places where you can sunbathe with your kit off, if you're careful. Except Studland of course, where you're totally free to take your clothes off without a problem whenever you feel like it.'

He started to slide to one side but was too late to avoid the elbow that jabbed him hard in the ribs.

'You,' Sophie hissed. 'You total pest. Here I am, needing some help with something really serious, and all you can think of is topless sunbathing. And before you ask, the answer's no.'

'What, not even at Studland in the official nudist section?' He looked horrified. 'We don't have Jade to contend with anymore. You mean, even if I offered to make the picnic?'

Sophie hesitated. 'Will you make that really tasty egg and mushroom flan?'

'Of course, if you so desire.'

'And the temperature has to be more than twenty-two, and the wind mustn't be coming off the sea.'

'If you say so.'

'Maybe. That's as far as I'm willing to commit myself.'

'That's good enough for me, sweetheart. And I still think I'm right about the maps.'

CHAPTER 35: NOWHERE TO HIDE

Wednesday morning

Rae hadn't slept well. She rose early and arrived at the incident room long before anyone else. The box was waiting on her desk. She slipped on a pair of latex gloves, opened it, and started to lift the contents out, listing each item carefully on a sheet of paper. There was a small jewellery box containing an assortment of rings, necklaces, bangles and earrings, most of them badly tarnished. A set of Russian nesting dolls that were scratched and faded. Some cards for a fifteenth birthday, all to Charmaine, and all containing the kind of messages that teenage girls wrote to each other. Three Valentine cards, one of them with a slightly dubious message inside that you wouldn't want a parent to see. Four unopened miniature bottles of vodka that looked as if they might have been stolen from a hotel room. And finally, down at the bottom, several diaries. Yes. These were what Rae was looking for.

She lifted the diaries out and placed them carefully on the desk. Charmaine had written something every day, often several paragraphs in length. Was there one for the year she was sixteen? It looked as though Rae was in luck. She opened it and started to read. She reached March before there was a mention of something that might prove useful. The name Phil was mentioned, a dishy boy with fair hair and blue eyes. Apparently, despite the fact that he was tall and a bit lanky, the teenage Charmaine had drooled over him, and wondered what it would be like to snog him. She worried about whether her breasts were big enough to attract his attention. The entry went on to wonder if some bra padding might increase her chances.

Several other entries carried on in broadly the same vein, until he asked her out on a date. The writing became wildly romantic for a few days, although the tête-à-tête itself must have seemed a bit of a let-down to the hopeful Charmaine. She commented that the young Phil seemed slightly distant and a little nervous. And then, a few days later, had come the terrifying encounter with the unknown young woman wielding a knife. She'd obviously been waiting outside Charmaine's school, and had followed her to a quiet spot, under a brick wall. Rae read of Charmaine's sheer terror at feeling the knife pricking her throat, and cold, calm, calculating eyes boring into her. *I'll use this on you, pretty Charmaine Cookson. I'll cut your eyes out and slit your throat.* The words had their effect. The diary entry went on to say that she'd decided not to see Phil again. She never found out what the girl's name was. She had fair hair and blue eyes. She was well dressed and had a neat hairstyle. She was evil.

Rae sat back and closed her eyes. It still made sense. She still felt that she'd been right to believe Charmaine, so how had this mess happened? Was the Phil mentioned in the diary entry the same Philip she was now married to? Was that even of any importance?

She looked up to see Barry coming into the office.

'Morning, boss. I've got something interesting here. That box from the loft yesterday. It had some diaries from when Charmaine was a teenager, and there's an entry for that episode she told me about. Do you want to see?'

Barry looked over her shoulder. 'How did you get on at her employer's place?'

'They all say she's one of the nicest and most reliable people they know. They're a publishing stable, producing magazines that cover a range of interests. She's been there for nearly twelve years, employed on a sailing magazine and working her way up to becoming editor. It's what I thought originally, boss. She can't be some kind of deranged killer. It doesn't add up. What about the husband?'

He shrugged. 'Same as you. The people there looked at me as if I was mad when I let slip what we were investigating. He's widely liked and well respected.' He looked at the clock. 'It's only seven thirty. Have you been in long?'

'About an hour. Too much on my mind. But I feel better now, with what you've said and what was in this diary. We still need to find them, though.'

'Did anyone know where they're headed on this yachting trip?' he asked.

Rae shook her head. 'No. Apparently, they follow the weather. And with it being fine like this, they could be anywhere. Do you want a look at this?' She pushed the opened journal across so that he could read it properly. 'I still wonder if there's a lead in there somewhere.'

'Well, this other girl must have been local, surely. But it happened, what, twenty or more years ago? We've got to be realistic, Rae, and concentrate our efforts on whatever's likely to give us workable leads. Ameera will be in later. She's completed the analysis of that tower-dump she talked about, so it'll be interesting to see if anything's come of it. And Gwen sent a message for you. She wonders if some of the properties that were being used as safe houses were let to migrants.'

Rae looked up at him, interested. 'She probably told you we've decided to do a bit of checking up on them, but I haven't had much time yet. We only speculated that they were being used by people the security unit were questioning. You mean someone was making a lot of money out of them?'

He ran his fingers through his hair. 'That's what she was thinking. She's found there are more than you both thought and the one she checked up on in Portsmouth had recently had a large family staying there. If there were enough of these properties, they could be clearing a quarter of a million each year, maybe more. And all in cash.'

Rae thought hard. 'Do you realise the implications of what you're saying, boss? It could be a lot more tangled than we thought. And if it's really that murky, who exactly are the good guys and who're the bad? Sometimes I'm glad I'm only a DS. We could be treading on some important toes here.'

* * *

Sophie arrived a few minutes later, almost colliding with Ameera, who was carrying a bulky folder.

'That looks ominous.'

Ameera laughed. 'It's amazing how many calls go through each mobile tower on any given day. Imagine if it was the city of London rather than just central Dorchester. That would be really worrying.'

They arrived at Rae's desk, where she and Barry were still talking.

'So how many calls are we talking about in total?' Sophie asked.

'Tens of thousands. That's why the folder is so big. It's not as daunting as it looks, though, I've already done some narrowing down. We can ignore all calls to or from a land-line. Same for calls going via another mast because we know both numbers were in the hospital area. We can also narrow it down to the hospital's immediate neighbourhood, because the mast is close by. Signal strength can play a part, you see.'

'Just give us the lowdown, Ameera. You're keeping us in suspense. Have you identified the call we're looking for?'

Ameera grinned, something Sophie hadn't really seen before. She was usually so intense. Maybe a bit more gentle teasing might be called for. 'Yes. At nine twenty in the morning. A brief phone exchange between two mobile numbers that looked to be both in the area immediately around or inside the hospital. It only lasted thirty seconds.'

'And the numbers?'

Ameera shook her head. 'Not registered to anyone. They were both burner phones.'

'We can't listen in to the conversation?'

'Well, it's possible that GCHQ in Cheltenham might be able to help. You'd know more about that than me. And would it be worth it? From what you've said, it was just a warning from someone outside to someone inside that they ought to get out. Isn't that right?'

'Yes. That call might have saved a life, and all thanks to Rose Simons. If she hadn't been so alert, the inside person, whoever he or she was, might have got to the ward. And God knows what could have happened then,' Sophie said. 'It was our woman, we're sure of it. She turned round when she got that call and hurried out. We got that much from the CCTV images. Thanks, Ameera. This is really useful.'

They waited until Ameera had left before starting the early morning briefing.

Barry told them of the Hampshire team's suppositions. Sophie was so concerned at the implications that she left them and went to her office to call both Matt Silver at county headquarters and Paul Baker in London. Maybe the most worrying aspect was that it slotted in so well with the way her own thoughts were going. Corinne Lanston clearly had her own secret agenda, quite separate from the one she was officially presenting to her political bosses and to the Met's investigating team. What exactly was she up to? And were Charmaine Biggs and her husband somehow involved?

'This all needs more thought,' Sophie said when she returned. 'Let's leave it aside for the moment. We ought to review what we've gleaned from interviewing all the people on that boat. Maybe there's something we missed at the time.'

The statements were spread in small piles across the tabletop, each corresponding to a family group. Added recently was an extra set, statements from several witnesses on the Normandy coast, gathered by the French police.

Some of the statements were rather confused but on the whole, there was a remarkable level of consistency.

* * *

Tommy arrived half an hour later, having spent the early part of the day at the hospital, complete with measuring tape and notebook. He'd planned which measurements he needed to take and had checked them with Rae the previous day. At his desk, he called up some stills taken from the CCTV recording of the dark-haired woman in the hospital corridor and started the, for him, slow job of calculating some details about her. Once he'd finished, Rae came across to take a look at the figures.

'Five foot six,' he said.

'You've done a good job there, Tommy. Can you do a bit more? Try for her leg length as well, then her shoulder width. It shouldn't take long now you've got her height.'

'Okay. But are we certain she's the person we're looking for? She's brunette and all the other images and descriptions talk about someone who's fair or blonde.'

'Except for the murder of Louise in Southampton. The killer had dark hair, but we think she was wearing a wig. Ask yourself why.'

'She might have been recognised?'

'Or caught on CCTV. And whoever it was would realise there's CCTV at the hospital and she'd be recorded. There's some CCTV footage from the hostel in Southampton, so you can do that next. Gwen has sent measurements of the wall height, just like you took, and some initial data has arrived from the French police at Cherbourg.'

When he'd finished, Rae checked the figures, made some comparisons and took their conclusions through to Sophie and Barry.

'We think it could be the same woman, ma'am,' Tommy reported. 'Same height, same hip-to-foot measurement, same shoulder width as far as I can tell. The hair looks similar too.'

'Every action leaves a trace,' Sophie said with a gleam in her eye. 'The phone call warning prevented her from going any further, but we still got useful information from her visit to the hospital. That's what the thugs don't realise. Given enough resources and time, we'll always find them. In the end, there's nowhere to hide. Leave those calculations, will you?'

She waited until Tommy and Rae had left her office, and then turned to Barry. 'Okay. Now comes the interesting part. Can you keep your eye on that door and stop anyone coming in? Let's do a comparison.' She extracted a sheet of paper from her desk drawer which had a different set of figures. Attached to it was a full-length photograph of Charmaine Biggs, copied from a portrait that had been on display in her lounge.

When they had finished, Sophie asked, 'When are the Biggs couple due back from their holiday?'

'According to their workplaces, they've taken a week off, but they always wait to see what the weather forecast has in store before heading to any particular destination.'

Sophie looked at her watch. 'Can you take charge for the rest of the day, Barry? I'm getting the next train to London for a review with the Met people. They're growing edgy. I wonder if they've uncovered something else?'

CHAPTER 36: BEYOND OUR KEN

Wednesday midday

An offhand remark that Rae had made as she drove her to the station set Sophie wondering.

'I wonder why that woman was visiting the hospital. What did she hope to achieve? Would they really gain that much from following the coach? They could easily find where it was headed by other means. The asylum camps aren't exactly hidden away, are they? Did they think someone in that group might finger them somehow?'

Now on a fast train to London, Sophie began to wonder if they'd missed something. They had the photos of the Normandy beach scene from Kamal's camera, though if it came to a court case, few of his shots would provide a clear and positive identification. The beach rendezvous had taken place at dusk, after all. They had several shots from other cameras and phones, but those were of even poorer quality. Of course, the gang members wouldn't know whether any of the photos were useable or not, which might give them a motive to trace some of the people on the boat, just as a precaution. But Sophie wasn't convinced that it was a strong enough reason to risk a visit to the hospital at a time when security was bound to be tight. And the man and woman involved were half-expecting problems. The speed with which they'd aborted their plan — whatever that was — showed that. No, they must have been worried about something.

Sophie opened her laptop and once again brought up the photo Kamal had taken of the group in angry discussion on the beach, the man with the sticking plaster on his nose clearly visible among them. This was the only photo in which the woman appeared, at a distance, leaning against a tree, watching. She was right at the edge of the photo and only half of her was visible. Who or what was she watching? It wasn't the group of men, arguing about money or life vests. Could she be looking directly at the camera, even at that distance? Was it possible that she'd spotted Kamal taking his pictures and had remembered? More importantly, if they got measurements of that tree from the French police, could they calculate the woman's height?

She had just sent an email to Henri Dutoit in Cherbourg when her mobile phone rang. She glanced at the caller display.

'Hello, Paul.'

She listened, her eyes growing wide.

'The train's about halfway there, so I'll be with you in an hour or so,' she said. 'Can you get a car over to Waterloo to meet me? It would save a bit of time.'

She ended the call and turned back to her laptop, hammering out an email, marked 'top priority' and 'confidential,' to Barry and Jack Dunning in Hampshire.

Ken Burke, the Junior Immigration Minister, has gone missing. His wife lives in their constituency home in Yorkshire and was unable to contact him at his London flat this morning. Neither could Yauvani Anand. His mobile's not being answered. The local squad got into his flat and found no evidence of him arriving home last night. According to the cleaner, his bed looked as though it hadn't been slept in. He was last seen heading away from Whitehall in a taxi, late yesterday evening. They're trying to trace the taxi driver now.

* * *

Yauvani Anand was frustrated and angry. As far as the public, the press and the party were concerned, she and Ken Burke were as one, united in their political stance, centred as it was on maintaining strong homeland security and keeping immigration levels low. In reality, she despised him. He was a revolting individual, and she really didn't know how much longer she could stomach being his PPS. It wasn't just that he was having an affair, it was that he was also deceiving his mistress — whoever she was — by carrying on with a string of tarts. Maybe the shadowy mistress figure knew what he was like and conveniently turned a blind eye. One thing was for certain, Burke's wife was unlikely to be aware of what her husband got up to in the capital. She was a stiff, cold, matronly figure with a condescending manner and an air of entitled superiority — a racist snob, in other words. Yauvani often wondered which of them she disliked most, Ken or his wife.

This time Ken had gone too far. Yauvani had always managed to contact him before when he'd been late in for work. He had a secret mobile phone whose number he had given her several years before, along with an instruction to only call it in an emergency. But this morning he wasn't even answering that one. Where was the man? They were due to hold an important lunchtime meeting with a delegation from the Greek embassy, and they hadn't had their usual pre-meeting brief with their advisors. He'd get fired if this kind of behaviour went on, regardless of how convenient it was for the present prime minister to have someone like 'Mad' Ken Burke holding this particular hot potato of a job.

In the end, she contacted the government security chief to report that the minister seemed to be completely out of contact, not answering any number she'd tried. He told her to leave it with him, saying he was sure the minister would quickly be found once the security staff got moving. His manner was, as usual, patronising. Yauvani wondered how he'd ever got himself appointed. He was as oily as a squeezed olive and not a great deal more insightful. He promised to phone her back with an update, but an hour passed during which she heard nothing, so she decided to bite the bullet and phone Paul Baker at the Met. At least he'd get something done.

He called her back within the hour. Burke had been seen by one of his officers during the previous evening. The minister had got out of a taxi outside Corinne Lanston's home and entered the building. An hour later he'd left. It was raining hard and his coat collar was turned up and his usual trilby hat was pulled down over his forehead. He'd hurried to a taxi that was waiting outside.

Yauvani was perplexed. This couldn't be right. Surely, it wasn't possible that her old friend was the secret woman in Burke's life? How could her taste in men have sunk so low? Corinne had standards or, leastways, that's what Yauvani had always believed. God, the thought of it! Fastidious Corinne having sex with that lump of lard. It was hard to stomach.

She phoned Corinne's numbers, both landline and mobile, but to no avail. This was worrying. Corinne had only just escaped from a week-long incarceration in a cold, dank cottage in the back of beyond. What if she'd come to further harm? Yauvani got straight back on the phone to Paul Baker. He seemed to know what he was doing, which made a pleasant change from the seemingly inept security people employed by the department itself. None of them appeared to have a clue.

* * *

The hastily arranged meeting took place in Yauvani's office. Present were the two Met officers, Sophie and Yauvani herself.

'When was the last time you saw the minister?' Steve Lamb asked Yauvani.

'Late yesterday afternoon,' she replied. 'I tidied everything away as usual, then popped my head into his office to say goodbye when I left. There were no debates in the House that either of us needed to attend, so we'd decided to get away at a reasonable time for once. I went home. I assumed he was planning to do the same.'

'As we've already told you, he took a taxi from here to Corinne's flat, stayed there for about an hour, and then left. We have someone watching her flat for security reasons, and the minister's arrival and departure were logged,' Steve said.

'That's another thing. She isn't answering her phone. I'm getting worried about her.'

'She must be okay,' Steve said. 'Apart from the minister, no one else arrived or left.'

Sophie was also worried. 'I wonder if we should get across there. This is far too strange for my liking.'

'I agree,' Yauvani said. 'It would set part of my mind to rest at least. I have a key to her flat, in case of emergencies.'

They drew up outside Corinne's apartment block within fifteen minutes and used Yauvani's key to get in. They took the lift to the first-floor apartment and Yauvani unlocked the door.

'Corinne?' she called.

There was no answer. The lobby had been cleaned since Sophie had last visited just after Corinne's abduction, as had the lounge. Sophie was uneasy. She glanced at Steve Lamb and saw that he too was frowning.

'Best if you stay here,' he told Yauvani and Paul Baker.

He and Sophie walked slowly through the flat, checking each of the rooms, one after the other. The master bedroom was at the end of the hall, the heavy drapes across the window still closed, leaving the room in darkness. Someone was lying in the bed, covered with a white quilt, head resting on a pillow.

Ken Burke lay staring at the ceiling, lifeless, his mouth open, his face a greyish white and his lips blue.

'A heart attack?' Sophie said. 'What do you think?'

'Looks like it. But let's not be hasty. You know as well as me that these things can be staged.'

Turning away, she noticed the small, neatly folded pile of clothes on a chair, along with his suit jacket hanging on the back. His shoes, trousers, overcoat and trademark trilby hat were nowhere to be seen.

* * *

It was early afternoon before the distraught Yauvani Anand was able to speak coherently. She sat with the detectives in a small but comfortable meeting room at New Scotland Yard. The Metropolitan Police Commissioner herself had spent five minutes with them before departing for an emergency meeting at Downing Street accompanied by Paul Baker.

'Corinne's the key to this, Yauvani,' Sophie said. 'You need to tell us everything you know about her, and all your suspicions. Please be honest with us. That's the only way we'll get to the bottom of what's been going on.'

Yauvani took a sip of water. 'I always knew he was having an affair with someone, but I never for a moment thought it could be Corinne.'

'Maybe he wasn't. Maybe he called on her for a different reason,' Steve said.

'No, you're wrong. It all makes sense now.' She looked across at the two detectives and grimaced. 'He was a disgusting pig, you know. Everyone thinks we were close but on a personal level I despised him. I always have. Bottom line, he was a petty racist who had no morals whatsoever. But in politics we have to pretend to get along with all kinds in order for the system to function, so that's what I did.'

'What about Ms Lanston? You told us before that you've been friendly with her since you were at university together,' Sophie said.

Yauvani looked as if she'd aged a decade in a single day. 'Yes. We shared a flat. But I knew her before that. We went to the same school. I can't comprehend this. I thought I knew her, possibly better than anyone else.'

Sophie frowned. 'Where did you both go to school?'

Yauvani tugged at the hem of her skirt. 'A boarding school in Surrey — Egremont Manor. It's in Epsom. We both arrived when we were fourteen and were made to feel like outsiders for a while by the rest of the girls in our year, so we naturally paired up together and remained good friends until we were in our mid-teens. We drifted apart in the sixth form because we did different subjects at A level. I did sciences and she did history, Latin and English. We both ended up going to UCL, so we got together again and shared a flat for a year.'

'What was Corinne like at school?' Sophie asked.

'Hard-working. Like me, I suppose. And she was rather lonely. Her mother died when she was young and her father was a diplomat, based abroad. He remarried and didn't want much to do with her, so she was at a bit of a loss during the holidays. Although there may have been a wilder side to her, but only out of school.'

'You'll need to explain,' Sophie said.

'The school owned a small outward-bound centre in Dorset, near Lyme Regis.'

Sophie felt a shiver run down her spine. Was this it, the link she'd been looking for? She waited.

'Each class spent a week or two there every year. We were meant to be totally involved in the activities of the centre, but Corinne managed to slip out late in the evenings and met up with a couple of local teenagers. I always thought it was pretty innocent — at first anyway.'

'At first?' Sophie repeated.

'Well, it was difficult to know exactly what was going on. You see, we all went home for the holidays, but Corinne and a few others spent some of that time down in Dorset. I heard rumours, but I didn't really believe them.'

'I need to know, Yauvani. You're aware that I'm investigating some strange events in that area. I realise the importance of maintaining loyalty to close friends, but this could be important.'

Yauvani glanced nervously at Steve Lamb. 'When we started back in September, some of the other girls gossiped about what Corinne'd got up to with some of the local boys. Apparently, there was one boy in particular that she was keen on. As I said, I didn't believe them at first, but the next time we went as a class, she took me with her one evening when she slipped out. I suppose I was feeling adventurous. Anyway, this group of local teenagers was hanging around outside the fence and we went for a walk through the woods. Nothing much happened. They only snogged, but she kept glancing at me. I got the feeling that they might have gone a lot further if I hadn't been there.' She was looking pensive.

'Can you remember his name?'

'No. But one of the other girls might. Sally Abercrombie was a year older than us, so we didn't mix much at school, but she went to the holiday camps with Corinne. I think it was her who spread the gossip when term started again. They fell out over it and Corinne nearly got expelled for fighting.'

Sophie became aware of Steve Lamb listening with renewed concentration. Had the name Sally Abercrombie meant something to him?

'And Corinne was there at the centre most summers? What, from July through to early September?' she asked.

'Well for some of the time. She was meant to be a volunteer worker, helping out around the place. In the summer break they ran courses for local disadvantaged youngsters. Corinne was keen on sailing and helped to train some of the local teenagers. I think that's when she might have met this boy. The alternative was to visit an ageing great aunt who lived in the Midlands.'

'Do you know if she ever became close to her father? After he retired perhaps?'

Yauvani shook her head. 'No. I don't think he came back to Britain for long. I think he may have died soon after returning from abroad, but I can't be sure.'

'Where did they live?'

'I think it was Hampshire somewhere.'

Sophie thought for a while. 'Yauvani, does the name Charmaine mean anything to you? Charmaine Cookson?'

'No, I don't think so. Look, what do you think happened last night?'

Steve answered. 'We don't know for sure. But one explanation is that Mr Burke arrived at the flat because of some arrangement they'd made. Our observer was keeping an eye on the place from a car across the road and spotted him arriving. He's adamant that someone closely resembling Mr Burke left an hour later. But it was raining heavily so visibility was poor, and the taxi was waiting right outside the door. It looks as though the person he saw could well have been Ms Lanston wearing his trousers, shoes, coat and hat. From that point on,' he shrugged, 'we're still investigating.'

Sophie stood up. 'I've got to go. I'm concerned about the safety of a group of migrants back in Dorset. There's something going on that hasn't completely played out yet.'

'That name you mentioned,' Yauvani said. 'Charmaine? It's familiar somehow, but from a long time ago. I'll need to think about it.'

'Please let me know the moment you remember. It's very important. I have someone with that name back in Dorset, and she might be at risk,' Sophie said.

The three of them left the meeting room. Yauvani went on ahead, phone in hand, calling for a taxi.

Sophie turned to Steve. 'Well? Are you going to tell me about this Sally?'

He smiled. 'Yeah, of course. It was a bit of a shock to hear her name. She's my sister-in-law, as a matter of fact. She runs a therapy business not a million miles away from here. She's sort of new age, if you get my meaning. I've always got on well with her, but my wife is a bit less enamoured of her approach to life. It's a bit too freewheeling for her. Shall we visit for a quick word?'

* * *

Steve took Sophie to a tiny shop in a neat mews off a side street near Victoria Station. Sally Abercrombie sold perfumes, herbal skin products, candles and ethnic clothing, and also took bookings for massage therapies and 'mystic analysis' sessions, according to the sign outside the door.

'What's mystic analysis?' Sophie asked as she and Steve ducked inside the low door.

'Haven't a clue,' he replied. 'I asked her once but couldn't really follow her explanation. Something about hidden dimensions and soul travel, I think.' He shrugged.

As they closed the door, a head popped up from behind the counter. The woman who bounded out to give Steve a hug and a kiss wasn't the earth mother type that Sophie expected. She wore a tight leopard print top that showed off an ample cleavage and skinny jeans. Her fair hair was pulled back into a tight bun, which suited her open, cheerful face.

'Well, look who the cat's brought in,' she said, laughing. 'Who's this, a new lover-girl?'

'Sadly not,' Steve replied. 'We're here on a case. This is Superintendent Sophie Allen from Dorset. We don't have much time, Sally, so I'll get straight to the point. Do you remember Corinne Lanston from your school days?'

Sally stood back in surprise. 'Whoa. Her. I shouldn't be surprised really, should I? She's been in the press recently, what with her disappearing and then reappearing. Yeah, I remember her. Did well, didn't she, considering what a nasty piece of work she was.'

'What do you mean?' he asked.

'Completely two-faced, a goody two shoes at school, and an utter slut out of it.'

'You ended up in some kind of altercation with her, is that right?' Steve asked.

'Well, you could say that. It was more like a fight, a really nasty one too. I'd had a few before, with other girls, but she was something else. I ended up needing stitches. The school was going to expel her but, to be fair, it was me yacking about her behaviour that probably started it. The school brokered some kind of deal with our parents, and it all got hushed up. Bad publicity, you see. Private schools are terrified of it.'

'Can you tell us about the background to it, Sally?' Sophie said. 'We understand that something happened at the school's outward-bound centre in Dorset.'

Sally's eyes widened. She raised her eyebrows. 'Do you want the pretty version the school got, or the full uncensored story? That one comes with a health warning, by the way.'

Steve sighed dramatically. 'That's the one, Sally, sad to say.'

'I was afraid of that. I'll need to close up for a while, so we're not disturbed, and put the kettle on. Let's find some seats.'

Once they were seated, mugs in hand, Sally began.

'Every year each class spent a week at the centre. It could be a bit boring and I liked boys, so in the evenings me and three others from my class used to sneak out for an hour or so for a bit of snogging and the like. Some of the local lads used to hang around at the back, where there was a bit of rickety fencing that we could climb over. That was during our usual class visits to the centre. Then one summer my parents went abroad, and they had to find something to keep me occupied here. So, I went back to the centre for a few weeks. We were meant to be helping to run events for local disadvantaged youngsters. That's when I met Corinne. She was in the year below me, so we'd never really run into each other before, but at the centre we both helped out with the sailing group. She was really good at it. We got chatting and I found out that she too used to escape over the same bit of loose fencing. We arranged to go out together one evening. I didn't know what I was letting myself in for. I'm not sure I would have gone if I had.'

Sally took a sip of tea and said nothing for a while. 'Well, we slipped through the fence and made our way to the footpath, where two boys were waiting. Corinne took charge right away. *Phil's mine*, she said. *Roger's for you. You can do what you want with him*. Phil was good looking, whereas Roger had grubby marks on his face, a tear in his shirt and he leered at me. I didn't fancy him at all. We left the path and went into some woods. We snogged for a bit, though it was no fun kissing Roger — he had bad breath. Then things got heavy really quickly. Corinne led Phil to a grassy area that was in sunlight, and then she stripped off. I was a bit shocked. I think I must have stood with my mouth open, wondering what was going on. There was me thinking I was all sophisticated and knowing, yet really I knew nothing, as I was about to find out.'

She took another sip of tea. 'She helped Phil take his clothes off, then crouched down and sucked him off. I'd never seen a real hard-on, not in the flesh, as it were, and I'd never even imagined such a thing as oral sex. I'd seen diagrams of normal sex in biology lessons, and I'd felt something when I'd snogged a couple of boys, but nothing remotely like that. Then they were at it, on the grass, with her on top. I remember coming out of a sort of trance when Roger tried to paw at my breasts. I shoved him away and ran back to the centre.' She took another gulp of tea and stared at the floor.

'Are you okay?' Steve asked.

'Yeah, of course,' she replied, and shook her head. 'I was just so naive back then.'

'Did Corinne say anything about it afterwards?' Sophie asked.

'I tried to stay away from her. It had come as a shock to me and I needed time to process what I'd seen. But she sought me out, pushed me up against a wall and threatened to harm me if I told anybody. We stayed away from each other for the rest of our time there.'

Sophie was on edge. 'What exactly did she threaten?'

'I can't remember. I know I was scared. I really wasn't going to tell anyone but back at school in September, someone asked how my Dorset break had gone. I suddenly started crying. I couldn't stop myself. I suppose it was all the pent-up emotion. I told her a bit of what had happened, which was enough for the gossip to start. Corinne came looking for me, and that's when the fight started. I've stayed well clear of her ever since.'

* * *

Sophie was on the train back to Dorset when her mobile phone rang. It was Yauvani.

‘I told you about the local teenagers when we were in Dorset, at the school’s outward-bound centre.’

‘Yes, I remember.’

‘Well, I think one of the girls was Charmaine. And I think her surname could have been Cookson.’

‘That’s very helpful. So that means the two of them knew each other.’

‘Yes, I suppose so. But this Charmaine, there was talk that she got involved with what was going on. I can’t remember all of it. It was so long ago.’

‘Okay, Ms Anand. I’d appreciate it if you kept trying to remember. Let me know, please, if anything else occurs to you.’

‘Sure. And call me Yauvani. Ms Anand sounds a bit too formal. My close friends call me YoYo.’

She closed the call. Sophie sat looking out of the window, thinking. There had been more to this relationship than Charmaine Biggs had admitted. Would it be worth ploughing through the rest of her diaries? None of this solved the immediate problem, though. Where was Corinne now and what was she up to? And why hadn’t the Biggs couple turned up yet? They’d notified every police force along the south coast, along with the Channel Islands and Cherbourg in France. They hadn’t heard a word. She called Rae with a long list of instructions for her and Tommy. Every single item relating to the backgrounds of both Corinne Lanston and Charmaine Biggs was to be researched and logged — family histories, educational backgrounds. Hobbies, interests, holiday breaks, finances. Something, somewhere, would yield the one snippet of information they needed to slot the pieces of the puzzle into place.

CHAPTER 37: CHARMAINE

Thursday morning

Charmaine Cookson frowned, took off her reading glasses and laid them on a table beside her chair. The newspapers always seemed full of bad news and tragic stories these days, but she could usually wave them aside with a flick of her wrist. What were they to her? Tales of tragic events in distant places, bad things that happened to people she'd never met and probably wouldn't want to. Uncouth people who drank too much, shouted too much and had the morals of sewer rats. They probably got what they deserved.

Nevertheless, the article she'd just read was deeply troubling. It seemed to involve Corinne and some immigration scandal she'd got herself mixed up in. That girl had always been trouble, from the moment she'd first set eyes on her. Sullen, self-centred, devious. And far too clever. Charmaine still yearned for the days when girls of good stock were tutored at home, learning about those things deemed important for well brought up ladies to know. Poetry, music, art, embroidery. Latin, Greek history. How to oversee a large household, along with the staff that kept it ticking over. But what had they taught in that so-called school that Neil had sent her to? Science and mathematics. Equality. Really! Politics and all the other tedious 'social' subjects that seemed to be all the rage in modern society. Even sex education. In lesson time too.

She sat back and closed her eyes. Why had she ever married that toad of a man, Neil Lanston? It was the biggest mistake of her life. What a blessing when he died of some strange tropical disease, probably picked up from some harlot in a Middle Eastern brothel. The only good thing that had come out of their marriage was the money she'd inherited. Six long years of indulging him and his squalid fantasies had paid off. She, Charmaine, might have had the breeding but he had the money. And, in her opinion, he'd left far too much of it to Corinne. If Charmaine had got her way, that spoiled brat would have inherited nothing but a few worthless Lanston family heirlooms. The money would have all come to her and she wouldn't be stuck in a second-rate residential home like this.

The newspaper had slipped to the floor and she couldn't reach it from where she sat. Luckily one of the servants was just passing, helping another elderly, sickly resident to a seat. Charmaine tried to attract his attention, but he was looking the other way.

'Pick it up,' she barked angrily, pointing to the dropped item. 'I say there, pick it up for me.'

The staff member came across and deposited the newspaper on her table. 'A little courtesy wouldn't go amiss, Charmaine. We're not servants, you know.' He smiled at her, his teeth very white in that dark face.

She curled her lip. Who did he think he was, talking to her like that? She was about to say exactly what she thought but restrained herself at the last moment. *They* had all the power now. Not just here, in this residential home, but in society at large. The great unwashed. The common muck with their piercings, tattoos, unacceptable hair colours and the ridiculous clothes they insisted on wearing. She counted for nothing, even though her money was helping to pay the wages of every staff member in the place. She'd been warned several times to rein in her tongue. What did that mean? That she couldn't speak her mind? Ridiculous. But she'd noticed how her portion size at dinner was smaller after one of her altercations with the staff. Not that she wanted big helpings of the muck they served, but she expected to receive what was hers by right, even if she couldn't eat it all.

'Thank you,' she said, through gritted teeth.

'You're very welcome, Charmaine,' he said with another broad smile.

That was another thing. Why were they always so cheerful? They had no right to be. Obedience, that's what was needed. Not smiles.

'Someone's coming to see you later this morning, from Dorset police. What have you been up to, Charmaine? Have you been naughty again and not told us?'

'Don't be ridiculous,' she snapped. 'What did this person say?'

'No explanation.' He shrugged. 'We're all agog in the office.'

She opened the newspaper and pretended to read until he went away.

* * *

A staff member showed Rae into a small private sitting room, where she was introduced to a small, wizened woman sitting in an armchair by the window, gazing out across the garden. There wasn't much colour left in the flower beds, just a few late-flowering roses and struggling dahlias that hadn't yet been cut down.

Rae held out her hand, which the elderly resident ignored. The manager had advised her that Miss Cookson was one of their more 'difficult' residents, but no further explanation had been offered. Rae sensed herself being scrutinised closely as she sat down.

'I'm grateful that you could see me, Miss Cookson. We're in the middle of an important investigation and it's possible you may be able to help. I'm Detective Sergeant Rae Gregson.'

Charmaine merely looked at her.

'I need to ask you if you have ever known someone called Corinne Lanston.'

Charmaine nodded slightly. Was that wariness in her eyes?

'Is that a yes? It would be helpful if you could give clear, definitive answers to my questions, please.'

'Yes.'

'Would you mind explaining the context?' Rae was picking her words carefully. She had the feeling that Corinne was not a welcome topic.

'She was my step-daughter.'

Rae was puzzled. 'She *was* your step-daughter? I don't fully understand why you said *was*.'

Charmaine gave an exasperated and dramatic sigh. 'If you must be so pedantic, then she *is* my step-daughter. But I haven't seen her for many years.'

Rae hadn't expected to hear this. She'd only come to Basingstoke because Sophie had decided to follow up on the Hampshire lead provided by Yauvani Anand. Rae had remembered that one of the Charmaine Cooksons she had discovered weeks before was a resident in a Basingstoke care home. Neither of them had thought there was much chance of discovering a link. But now this. It needed careful handling.

'I take it you don't get on with her?'

Charmaine curled her lip. 'That, Detective Sergeant, is something of an understatement. I'm sure it didn't take much *detecting* on your part to pick up on it.' Charmaine sipped at a glass of water that had been left on the table. 'Lazy devils. I asked for a slice of lemon in it.'

'Did she feel the same way about you?'

'Hah,' Charmaine snapped. 'She certainly did, and more so. She never failed to stick the proverbial dagger in my ribs at every possible opportunity and then twist it. She was devious and nasty. Her behaviour was utterly loathsome. We didn't know what to do with her, so we sent her away to boarding school. I'm glad to say that after that, I don't think I ever saw her again. We went abroad for some years because of her father's occupation. He worked for the diplomatic service.'

'You say "her father" rather than "my husband." Why's that?'

Charmaine fixed her with a piercing glare. 'Observant little thing, aren't you? On second thoughts, maybe not so little. What are you, about five nine? Five ten? That's part of the problem. Women aren't *delicate* anymore. She wasn't. She hurtled around our house like a demented goat.'

'That's as may be, but you haven't answered my question.'

Charmaine sighed. 'Because he turned out to be almost as loathsome as the girl. Maybe more so. I was at my wits' end. But he very conveniently died, and I could wave a permanent goodbye to them both.'

'And you changed your name back to Cookson?'

She curled her lip. 'Yes, right away. I could then try to forget about that whole disastrous marriage.'

'Has Corinne ever tried to get in touch with you?'

'Thankfully not. If I thought that was likely to happen, I'd ask for an extra lock on my door. And maybe an armed guard outside it.'

Rae glanced at the newspaper lying open on the table. There on the page was the photo of Corinne.

'But you're reading about her in the press. You know that she's gone missing again, for the second time in a few weeks.'

Charmaine snorted. 'She won't be up to any good, you mark my words. And if by some peculiar chance someone has abducted her, they'll most likely regret it within a few hours and will want to do away with her. I probably would.'

Rae decided to change tack. 'As far as we're aware, she never married.'

Charmaine glared at her. 'Are you telling me or asking me? I'll assume the latter. No, she never married. Well, not as far as I'm aware. Who would want to marry someone like her? She always has to be in control and make it obvious. We all do, but women need to go about it with a measure of subtlety. Aim for the long-term gain even if it means short-term loss. Be gently manipulative.'

'And you're not aware that she's ever had children?'

Charmaine almost exploded with contempt. 'What? And go through the perils of pregnancy? Never.'

Rae was beginning to grow angry. What a nasty individual. 'But you've not had children of your own, have you?'

'No, but that's because I can't, not because I wouldn't. It's very different, as you should know.' She paused. '*Do* you know?'

'I am painfully aware of my inability to bear children,' Rae admitted, 'but my partner and I are happy to consider adoption.'

'Well, I never would. Bring up some other woman's brat? You must be joking.'

Rae scanned her notes. Had she missed anything? 'One last question. Have you any idea where Corinne might be? Did she have any favourite places?'

'Why would I know? I have had no contact with her for twenty years. She always liked Dorset. But then the school informed us of the grubby things she got up to down there. Maybe she's gone back, like a rat to a sewer.' She sneered.

Rae recognised that the comment was deliberate, aimed at her. What an unpleasant, vicious woman Charmaine Cookson was. Just the type that would make you happy to drag their name through the mud, given half a chance. She stood up and left.

* * *

Phil drew up in the car park of the residential home and switched off the engine. His fellow occupant was about to open the car door but spotted a figure she vaguely recognised descending the front steps. It was one of those detectives from Dorset. What was she doing here? She put a hand on Phil's arm before he could open his door.

'Wait.'

They watched the detective make her way to a parked vehicle and drive away.

'I need to think. They must be further ahead than I thought they'd be. Scrap this. Let's get away. We'll have to come up with a plan B.'

'You're the boss, Charmaine,' Phil said. 'Anyway, I told you this might be a mistake. It could have been dangerous and messy.'

She turned on him. 'I do the thinking, Phil. Not you. Not now, not ever. Just remember that. God, I hate these other bloody Charmaines. Two bits of scum, that's what they are.' She paused, looking unseeing around the car park. 'I've made a decision, Phil. It's time to tie up all the loose ends and cash in. Everything's ready for us in the Caribbean and the weather looks to be set fair for the crossing. Are you okay with that?'

'It's what we always planned, isn't it?'

* * *

Rae Gregson had joined Dorset's Violent Crime Unit three years earlier, a recruit with a mixed-up private life and deep-rooted insecurities. Her new work environment had provided her with exactly the stability she had needed. Her personality and self-confidence had blossomed, and she'd repaid the confidence her bosses, Sophie Allen and Barry Marsh, had shown in her by constantly striving to improve her skills as a detective. She observed carefully and thought deeply, and it was no different now, as she walked out of the main entrance of the care home. As she descended the steps to the car park, she noted immediately the large, dark-coloured BMW parked in a deserted area at the far end. She stopped to extract her sunglasses from her shoulder bag and used those few seconds to take another look. Dark tinted windows. Possibly two shadowy figures inside. Rae went to her own car, got in, started the engine and drove out into the tree-lined avenue, but after a hundred yards she turned back into the entrance driveway and pulled up by the side of a large delivery van. Hidden by the van, she had a clear view of the BMW through the bushes, just as it started to move away. She followed at a safe distance.

The BMW threaded through the busy roads on the southern edge of Basingstoke, heading towards the main junction with the M3. As it waited to filter onto the motorway, Rae took the opportunity to edge closer. She'd been right. There looked to be two people in the vehicle, a man driving and a fair-haired woman in the passenger seat.

The lights changed and the vehicle accelerated away onto the westbound lane of the M3, heading towards . . . where, exactly? Dorset? Rae decided to follow. She radioed back to the incident room, asking Tommy to trace the vehicle's registration and inform Barry. All went well until they reached a junction just west of Basingstoke. The left lane led due west towards Salisbury and Exeter. The BMW, however, had opted for one of the lanes on the right, as if the driver intended to remain on the M3, heading south-west, past Winchester and Southampton towards south Dorset — and maybe Weymouth? That would make sense. Rae edged closer. But she lost them when an elderly lady in a small car realised that she was in the wrong lane and pulled across in front of Rae who was forced to brake and move into the fast lane to avoid a collision. At the very last second, the BMW veered left into the inside lane and took the spur leading to the A303. It was too late for Rae to follow. She cursed loudly. She was stuck on the M3 for another twelve miles until the next junction at Winchester.

Her radio crackled into life and she heard Tommy's voice.

'It's a hire car,' he reported. 'From a company called Oak Hire, a small business in Kingston upon Thames.'

'Get onto the local Hampshire and Wiltshire traffic cops, Tommy, and be quick about it. They're on the A303 heading west. We need to pick them up again before they get too far.' But it might already be too late. Someone who was being cautious was likely to move off the dual carriageway as soon as possible and take one of the many alternative routes to the West Country.

CHAPTER 38: PAST PORTLAND

Thursday afternoon

Sophie couldn't quite believe what she was hearing. Her phone to her ear, she listened carefully, asked a few questions, and then sat thinking. She went to find Barry and Tommy.

'Not what I expected to hear,' she said. 'The initial post-mortem results on Ken Burke show he died from a massive heart attack. There's no indication of foul play. Not yet anyway.'

Barry sat back in his seat and scratched his head. 'But in that case, why didn't she report it? Wait. I can guess. When, or if, she turns up, she'll claim that he was as right as rain when she left.'

Sophie nodded. 'That's exactly what the Met team think.'

She made herself a cup of tea and stood by the window, sipping slowly and musing over the complexities of what they'd recently discovered. What had Corinne been doing since she left her apartment? Nothing innocent, that was for sure. She wouldn't have gone to the extraordinary lengths of sneaking out of her apartment block in Ken Burke's clothes, under cover of darkness, merely to visit a secret lover. No, she'd been out in the car, probably with her accomplice. What was his name? Phil? Was this morning's visit to the old folks' home part of tying up loose ends?

A dreadful thought struck her. She pulled her phone out of her pocket and called Paul Baker.

'Paul, would Corinne have had access to the reports on the boat crossing that went wrong? And if yes, would that have included the fact that we managed to get some photos from the boy with the camera?'

'Hang on a minute.'

Sophie waited, tapping impatiently on the windowsill.

'It's possible,' Paul said eventually. 'She called into her office late on Tuesday to catch up on some reports. For some reason, her name was on the distribution list for the summary report into the boat tragedy and its aftermath. I think the report contained a reference to a family group that had suffered a tragic loss, but also that their evidence would be of use in any court case and would strengthen their claim for asylum.'

'Oh Christ.'

'They weren't named, though, Sophie.'

'I don't think they'd have to be. Their names would probably be on other documentation she'd have. And she doesn't know that the photos aren't particularly good.'

She swallowed the rest of her tea and hurried over to Barry and Tommy. 'We need to move. Fast. It's the usual dilemma. A danger and an opportunity, both tangled up together.'

They drove to the Moradi family's house on the western fringes of Weymouth. It was at the end of a cul-de-sac and backed onto the town's sports ground. Sophie looked at it in despair, shaking her head.

'Just look at it, Barry. It's completely open ground at the back and round this side. We could never guarantee their safety here.'

The two detectives took a walk along the footpath that led beside the property and surveyed the open field in front of them. A second footpath ran along the back of the houses, separated from them by slightly ramshackle garden fences.

'Those two kids have only just started school,' Barry said. 'They're not going to be happy at the prospect of moving yet again.'

'Maybe not, but we can't leave them here, none of them. I don't know what these killers have on their minds, and what they might do to anyone they find here. If we're lucky we'll find somewhere else in the town and the youngsters can still go to school, but under close watch. We'd better get onto it and move them as soon as we can. Let's go and talk to the family.'

* * *

The dark-coloured taxi drew to a halt at the side of the road. The driver cut the engine. In the silence that followed, an owl hooted. A ragged cluster of dark clouds moved across the moon. The doors opened, and two black-clad figures slid out, made for the trees and disappeared into the shadows beneath. They waited for about ten minutes, watching the area at the rear of the sports field, and then moved slowly along the tree line.

'What do you think?' the man whispered.

The woman frowned. 'I don't like it. It was the same when I came by earlier. You'd expect a house with kids in to show some signs of activity in the late afternoon or early evening, but there was none. I think they've shifted everyone out and laid a trap for us. I hate this. I hate finding that someone is a step ahead of me. Let's get down to the boat. We'll slip away tonight while it's still dark.'

They made their way back to the vehicle and climbed in.

'Was it that important anyway, Charmaine?'

She frowned. 'I don't like loose ends, Phil. You know that. Anyway, there'll be plenty of time later for me to fly back for a quick visit and get it all tidied up. The cops can't keep them hidden forever. The money transfers have gone through, so we're all set.'

The man started the engine and drove slowly away. 'Caribbean, here we come.'

* * *

In the coldest, darkest, loneliest time of the night a sleek blue oceangoing yacht slipped out from the marina. A fresh breeze blew streams of cloud in from the west, but they didn't presage rain. Not yet, anyway. The boat made its steady way across Portland Harbour and through the southernmost of the gaps in the long breakwater, beneath the looming mass of the Isle of Portland, moving rapidly towards Portland Bill. Having rounded the famous landmark, now little more than a gigantic block of ghostly pale stone towering above them in the darkness, the boat was out in the huge expanse of Lyme Bay with a long fifty-mile gap of open sea to the next landmark at Start Point in Devon. By then they should be safe. They put a sail up.

Turning to his partner, Phil noticed that her eyelids were beginning to droop. 'I'm okay here. Why don't you get some sleep? The last few days have been tough for you. It'll be a couple of hours before we round Start Point and I can wake you then.'

She gave him a tired smile and nodded. 'A few hours' sleep would be heaven,' she murmured.

Out on deck, Phil settled into his seat. The weather was perfect. A gentle, southerly breeze meant that the boat was making good progress. Once past Start Point, they could move further out into the Channel, sail beyond the Scillies and head past Fastnet, south of Ireland. He and Charmaine had sailed in the Fastnet race a couple of times, so they knew the ropes. This journey had been long in the planning. It was time to bring this business to a close and enjoy the fruits. A luxury life in the Caribbean for as long as they wanted it — a spacious villa with a glorious view across sun-drenched sand to an azure sea. All those years ago as teenagers, they had dreamt of such a life, spending their adulthood yachting from a tropical island or lazing on some deserted beach. He kept those dreams in his mind while their yacht made its way steadily across Lyme Bay. Even the sails were dark blue, designed to reduce the chances of being spotted at night. Charmaine had thought of everything. He was in awe of her. He always had been.

An hour later he caught the first sound, a distant buzzing. He decided to move closer to the coast, and then wake Charmaine. Instantly alert, she hastened up on deck.

'You were right,' she said. 'It's a helicopter.' She listened intently. 'Can you hear something else? A deeper note? I think they've got boats out as well.' She looked at the chart. 'It's a toss-up. We could keep going and hope they miss us, or we can put in somewhere for a couple of days. On balance, it's too chancy to stay out here, not with that helicopter and the clear sky. They'll pick up our wake. Let's slip quietly into Lyme and lay low for a day or two. It doesn't change the plan, Phil. Trust me.'

CHAPTER 39: OUTWARD BOUND

Thursday night

Barry and Rae, along with two firearms officers, waited in the Moradi house into the early hours. No one approached the building.

'Maybe we got it wrong, boss,' Rae said.

Barry shook his head. 'I don't think we did. I'm wondering if they guessed. Remember that movement under the trees just after midnight? It could have been them, and they decided it was too risky. Check again with Tommy, will you? He may have spotted something.'

Tommy was in a car parked by the side of the nearby main road, watching for vehicles.

'Still no BMWs, boss,' he said in reply to Rae's question. 'A handful of other cars and a couple of vans, but nothing suspicious.'

'Did anything pass you and then reappear a few minutes later?'

Rae heard the rustle of paper, presumably Tommy turning the pages of his notebook. 'A taxi, just after midnight.'

'You think it dropped someone off and then came back empty?'

There was a silence for a few moments. 'I can't be sure it was empty when it came back, boss. It was a local cab. I know the driver. Shall I give him a buzz?'

Rae and Barry waited for several minutes until, finally, Tommy came back with the explanation.

'His cab's been stolen. He didn't realise until just now when he looked out onto the street.'

Rae relayed the information to her boss. 'It was a pretty old Ford. Let's face it, they're not the most difficult of cars to steal, are they?'

Barry sighed loudly. 'I'll put out an alert for it. Not that there's much chance of spotting it round here. It must have been taken a good three hours ago, maybe more.'

In fact, Barry was wrong. The abandoned taxi was spotted within fifteen minutes of the alert being raised. It was found on the quayside at Portland marina, near to an empty yacht berth. It looked as though the birds had flown. On hearing the news, Sophie quickly organised a search helicopter and several boats. The problem was, where would their quarry be heading? East towards the Isle of Wight or the Solent, to hide among the thousands of boats that were based there? Or across the Channel to France? Possibly the Channel Islands, which were close to the Cherbourg peninsula but had the advantage of much less red tape for British passport holders. They were forced to wait until the manager of the marina arrived for more information. Barry almost pushed him into his office, desperate to see the records. He switched in his computer and opened the database. There it was — Lady Charmaine.

The manager pointed to the log. 'It doesn't have a permanent berth here. It was booked in for two months but spent a couple of weeks away in one of the local yards getting a refit and makeover. I think the home marina is along the coast at Lyme Regis.'

'Could you tell me the name of the owner?' Barry asked.

The manager shook his head. 'No record of that. It was booked in by a Philip Watson. He was the one who paid the bills. It's due to be with us for another week.'

Rae was puzzled. Lady Charmaine. Where had she heard that name before? She went back outside and wandered along the quayside, trying to clear her mind of thoughts of her soft, comfortable bed. The boats' rigging tapped in the light breeze. Then it came to her. She hurried back in.

'Jason Lamb,' she said. 'The lad who found the body on the train. He works in a boatyard. He told me that he'd just finished painting a boat dark blue. Its name was Lady Charmaine. He said it was being fitted out for a trip to the Caribbean.'

'So, they're heading west,' Sophie said. 'Let's get moving. They can't have got far.'

* * *

Despite the boats and helicopters crisscrossing the fifty-mile-wide bay, Lady Charmaine was nowhere to be found. Where had they got to? The team of detectives gathered round a map of the south west.

'Let's take a different approach,' Sophie was saying. 'What if it's us out in that yacht, and we hear the boats and helicopters. We know what they're out there for — to find us. What would we do?'

Barry replied. 'One of two things. Either keep going or put in somewhere and lie low until the dust settles. If they were still out there on the water, surely one of the teams would have spotted the boat by now? I know it's been painted dark blue and its sails are dark, but wouldn't they have seen its wake on a night as clear as this?' He looked at the map. 'Lyme Regis is halfway along the bay. Didn't the marina manager say the boat came from Lyme?'

Sophie thought for a few moments. 'Let's leave the teams out searching, just in case. We'll grab a few hours' sleep and head down to Lyme tomorrow morning. I'll get the search teams primed and ready. Sunrise is at seven thirty, so let's be there by then. If I remember rightly, the main mooring area is in the harbour, though a few boats are drawn up on Monmouth Beach. Have I got that right, Barry?'

'I think so. If they have beached the boat, it's a bad move on their part. They'd have to drag it back into the water. The marina would be a better bet. They can just push off like they did at Portland.'

'Okay, everyone. See you in six hours.'

* * *

In Lyme Regis they came across yachts with all kinds of entertaining names, but no Lady Charmaine. At mid-morning Sophie called the team together for a rethink.

'Maybe they went further along the coast, ma'am,' Rae suggested. 'They have a wide choice further west — Axmouth, Sidmouth, even as far west as the River Exe.'

'Please, no,' Barry said, 'not upriver towards Exeter. It'd be a nightmare.'

Sophie shook her head. 'They wouldn't do that. They might get trapped. Going up a river means they'd have to return the same way, and they'd know we'd be watching. Remember, she's a canny operator.' She looked up from the map she'd been examining. 'I think they're here. They must be if their plan is to head for the Caribbean. What about dark blue boats of any name? Does anyone remember seeing one that looked newly painted?'

Stu Blackman was on the search team. He pointed to one of the rows of boats. 'There's one at the end of that row. Lovely-looking boat. No one on board, though.'

Sophie looked at Greg Buller, the snatch squad commander. 'You're a sailor, Greg. Let's go and have a look.'

The yacht in question was tied up at the very end of one of the timber walkways. The name Kitty stood out in white paint on the stern. Greg bent down, touched the white lettering and sniffed his fingers.

'Fresh paint,' he said. 'It's still tacky. If you look closely, you can see a few spots where the previous name has been painted over. This is the one.'

'What made you so sure it would be here?' Barry asked.

Sophie smiled at him. 'Remember me telling you about an outward-bound centre linked to a school she went to? It's just up the river valley, a couple of miles inland from here. Ever since the school closed it down some years ago it's been derelict. It was small and a bit lacking in the basics, apparently, so no other school wanted to share in the costs of upkeep. Shame, really.' She looked across the marina to the assembled search team, still on the main quayside. 'Let's go get them.'

* * *

Sophie's description of the centre as derelict was spot on. The place looked tired and run down. Greg put his binoculars down and returned to the new command point, in a lay-by further back along the narrow lane.

'No obvious signs of occupancy,' he said. 'But there wouldn't be any, would there? The lock on one of the smaller huts isn't sitting right, so it might have been forced. As far as I could see, the padlock on the larger hut was still in place. I should be able to use the parabolic from where I was back there and listen for any sounds.'

Wearing their safety vests, Barry and Sophie followed Greg as he made his way quietly through the bushes.

'They might be sleeping,' Barry whispered. 'They must have been up most of the night.'

'Someone's moving round inside. I can hear boards creaking.' Greg continued to listen. 'Voices. A woman and a man, I think.'

'We should move in,' Sophie said. 'They probably still have a gun, so we need to be cautious. I don't think a sudden raid would be a good idea, in case they panic, so let's just drive in and show them what they're up against. We'll put people round the back in case they try to do a runner. Does that sound okay?'

They returned to the command point to organise the teams. Greg's deputy in the snatch squad, along with Rae, Stu and Tommy, made their way to the back of the premises, while a small convoy of vehicles moved into the open area in front of the hut and spread out. Greg took up a loud hailer.

'Armed police. We have the premises surrounded. Come out with your hands in the air.'

Two faces could be seen peering out of a window, then moving away again. Listening in on the parabolic device, Sophie could make out the sound of a heated discussion. Finally, the door opened, and two figures appeared. Greg directed a couple of his squad members to go and handcuff them.

Sophie stepped forward. 'Hello again, Corinne. I have to hand it to you, it looks like you nearly made it.'

Corinne stared coolly at her. 'It was the water meter at the cottage, wasn't it? I wondered what you were up to out there.'

Sophie shook her head. 'Not entirely. If you must know, I'd already guessed but didn't have the evidence. In a way, a major crime is a bit like an explosion. There are all kinds of little consequences, like bits of shrapnel flying from a bomb. Even someone as thorough as you couldn't possibly tidy them all up. And anyway, some just can't be hidden. Like your own birth record — Corinne Charmaine Lanston. You may have dropped your middle name in all your employment and academic records, but it's still there in the register. And even if you'd managed to somehow remove that, we'd have spotted that your grandmother's name was Charmaine, and we'd have chased up a couple of teenage friends who would have remembered you using the name when it was in your interest to do so. And then there's the name of your boat. We found that too. No, we'd have got you in the end.' She nodded to Greg. 'Take them away.'

* * *

'It's possible Ken Burke's heart attack may have been precipitated in some way,' Paul Baker was saying. There was a short silence. She could hear him breathing down the line. 'When did you first wonder about Corinne's involvement, Sophie? Was it that business of the water meter at the cottage?'

'Possibly.'

She didn't elaborate. What would he think? That she was bragging? The possibility had always been there, right from when her team, her great team, had spotted what was amiss at Bunting's house, that it was only a place of temporary refuge. Then, gradually, as each new piece of information had emerged, her suspicion had grown. It had culminated in Corinne's strange debrief at New Scotland Yard, when they had finally met face-to-face. No words had been exchanged but that glance had said it all. Everything that followed was merely confirmation, particularly the previous day's hurried phone call from Charmaine Biggs, finally responding to the messages Sophie's team had been sending. She and her husband had reached Gibraltar after being out of contact for days while they sailed from the Canary Islands. At first, she'd been furious that her house had been searched in her absence, but her anger had soon subsided when she'd realised who had been behind the tragic deaths.

'She might have been in the group that taught me to sail as a teenager,' Charmaine had said. 'I was going to tell you when we got back. That could be why there was something familiar about her when she threatened me. My God, to think this has all happened more than twenty years later. But why?'

There was no answer. Could there ever be an explanation for what lay in the dark recesses of some people's minds? How long had Corinne been planning this operation? Had the seed been planted all those years ago when she'd first discussed the possibility of a special security unit with Yauvani Anand? It was quite something to set up a criminal operation in which she was both the senior investigator and the chief perpetrator. Of course, the fact that Corinne's British bank accounts now held more than four million pounds would have helped settle any internal conflict she might have had. Did she also have accounts elsewhere? Time, along with a great deal of forensic accounting, would tell.

Sophie waited until Rae and Tommy had left. Barry was about to follow when she stopped him and gave him a hug. 'Give my love to Gwen.'

He glanced at his watch and looked up at the lightening eastern sky.

'Like ships in the night,' he said. 'We share the same house but this whole week we've hardly exchanged more than the occasional word. Is that the basis for a good relationship?'

She smiled. 'Come on, Barry, remember what you said to me last week. You know you love your job. And Gwen does too. You're two of a kind.'

CHAPTER 40: CAFÉ AND PUB CRAWL

Saturday afternoon, later in the month

Rose was in her favourite Weymouth café, tucking into a cream bun.

'This place is great,' she said. 'George and I come in here sometimes at the end of a shift. It does the best ham, egg and chips in town.'

The children giggled as she tried to use her tongue to fish for a large dollop of cream that decorated her chin. Her teenage son, Nick, handed her a serviette.

'Do it properly, Mum.'

Rose poked her tongue out at him and grinned. After struggling to bring up a rebellious young boy as a single parent, a corner had been turned in their relationship. Was it due to that hospital visit when he had become aware of the trauma suffered by migrants battling to reach safety? Whatever the reason, her previously self-centred offspring was beginning to show more awareness of other people and their struggles. And not a moment too soon, as far as she was concerned.

'I'd better not eat anything else,' she said. 'Tony and I are going out for a curry tonight. I wouldn't want to spoil my appetite. Are we still on, Tony?'

Her partner nodded. 'Yep. Chicken Madras for me. Can't be bettered.'

Rose rolled her eyes. 'He's just so boring. He has that every single time.'

'You must all come round to ours soon,' Roya said, 'and I'll cook you an Iranian meal. You'll love it. Kebabs and lamb casserole with pomegranate. Arsi makes lovely ice cream.'

'That would be lovely, Roya. I'll make sure George is free as well.'

'Where is George?' Kamal asked.

'He's in Oxford, visiting his girlfriend, though whether he's enjoying it is another matter. The rest of her family are there too.'

'Didn't you want to go?' Arshi said.

'What, and leave you to visit this café by yourselves? Not on your nelly.' She squeezed Arshi's hand.

* * *

There were eleven of them, all crammed around a large table in the Turf Tavern in Oxford. Sophie and Martin, Jade and George, Hannah and her boyfriend Russell, Rae and her partner Craig, Barry with Gwen, and even Tommy Carter, looking as bemused as ever. Martin had somehow managed to find a good group deal at one of the Oxford city centre hotels. It meant that, for once, a weekend in one of the most expensive tourist hotspots in the country was actually affordable.

They had started in the Kings Arms, on the corner of Holywell Street and Parks Road. The idea was to move from there to the Turf, then head to the White Horse on Broad Street before making their way down to the High to visit the Chequers. Jade had calculated that a rest would be needed at that point before an early evening meal at her parents' favourite eatery, the Thai restaurant in Wheatsheaf Yard, followed by a visit to the theatre later in the evening. A late-night visit to the Eagle and Child, and maybe the Lamb and Flag, was also a possibility. As is usual on a pub crawl, things didn't go according to plan.

'I don't know whether I can manage this.' Sophie leaned back in her seat and groaned. She surveyed the table in front of her, now cluttered with empty glasses and plates. 'That ham sandwich was lovely, and the second beer was just great. But I think I just want to go to sleep now.'

'Mum, show some backbone, for goodness sake,' Jade said. 'There's time for you to have a snooze back at your hotel later, before we head out for the evening. I thought it would be Dad who'd cave in first, not you.'

Martin looked hard at his younger daughter. 'And what made you think I'd cave in first? Why pick on me? What have I ever done to offend you? Please tell.'

Jade spluttered into her beer. 'What? Dad, don't make out you don't know. You've teased me mercilessly for years, along with regularly reducing me to a useless heap of giggles with your constant tickling.' She suddenly realised the mistake she'd made in mentioning tickling, as her father made a lunge towards her. 'Help! George, do something!'

'More than my life's worth,' George replied. 'That's my boss's husband you're asking me to lay into. Not a hope!' He picked up his glass and moved to a safer position.

Jade finally managed to push her father away. 'Why don't you tickle Hannah for once, nuisance?'

Hannah laughed. 'While I can still speak, I have something to tell you all. I've been offered a part in a TV drama series. I went for the audition last week and they contacted me yesterday. It's only a minor part, mind, and I get killed in the third episode, but it's a start.'

Chaos ensued as everyone stood to congratulate Hannah, fighting to give her a hug or a kiss.

'You lot are just far too *dramatic*,' she said, moving aside before Martin could slide his outstretched fingers into her armpit. Hannah glanced at her mother, ensconced in her corner seat, her eyes closing.

'Please God, don't let her sn—'

On cue, Sophie let out a loud snore.

THE END

ACKNOWLEDGMENTS

I'd like to thank all of the staff at Joffe Books for their continued help and support. In particular, Anne Derges has done her usual great job of editing my rambling text. The enthusiasm of Emma Grundy Haigh, the Managing Editor, has been infectious. Also, to my fellow authors at Joffe for being so companionable, particularly Helen Durrant, Janice Frost, Charlie Gallagher, Joy Ellis and Anne Penketh.

GLOSSARY

A and E: accident and emergency unit in a hospital.

Bug: slang for an infectious disease.

Home Office: a ministerial department in the UK government, responsible for immigration, security and law and order.

Jurisprudence: the theoretical study of law.

Outward-Bound Centres: residential centres in rural areas where teenagers can experience outdoor life, hiking, boating and ecology.

PPS: Parliamentary Private Secretary. An MP who functions as the eyes and ears of a government minister. Often seen as the first stepping stone to a future ministerial career.

Pub crawl: a British tradition. Visiting a sequence of pubs, with a drink (usually a beer) in each.

Skiving off: unofficial absenteeism.

Semi: short for semi-detached house, one that is joined to another by a shared wall.

Special Branch: an arm of the UK police service that deals with terrorism.

Terrace: a form of housing in which a row of attached dwellings share side walls. Called townhouses in the States.

UK Police Ranks (in descending order of seniority)
Chief Constable (or Commissioner in London's Metropolitan Police force)
Deputy CC (Deputy Commissioner in London)
Assistant CC (Assistant Commissioner in London)
Chief Superintendent

Superintendent
Chief Inspector
Inspector
Sergeant
Constable

Detectives hold the same ranks but with a prefix before the name (Detective Constable, Detective Sergeant, etc.) There is sometimes career movement back and forth between detectives and uniformed ranks.

THE JOFFE BOOKS STORY

We began in 2014 when Jasper agreed to publish his mum's much-rejected romance novel and it became a bestseller.

Since then we've grown into the largest independent publisher in the UK. We're extremely proud to publish some of the very best writers in the world, including Joy Ellis, Faith Martin, Caro Ramsay, Helen Forrester, Simon Brett and Robert Goddard. Everyone at Joffe Books loves reading and we never forget that it all begins with the magic of an author telling a story.

We are proud to publish talented first-time authors, as well as established writers whose books we love introducing to a new generation of readers.

We won Trade Publisher of the Year at the Independent Publishing Awards in 2023 and Best Publisher Award in 2024 at the People's Book Prize. We have been shortlisted for Independent Publisher of the Year at the British Book Awards for the last five years, and were shortlisted for the Diversity and Inclusivity Award at the 2022 Independent Publishing Awards. In 2023 we were shortlisted for Publisher of the Year at the RNA Industry Awards, and in 2024 we were shortlisted at the CWA Daggers for the Best Crime and Mystery Publisher.

We built this company with your help, and we love to hear from you, so please email us about absolutely anything bookish at feedback@joffebooks.com.

If you want to receive free books every Friday and hear about all our new releases, join our mailing list: www.joffebooks.com/free-books

And when you tell your friends about us, just remember: it's pronounced Joffe as in coffee or toffee!